I0822789

BURIED BENEATH

A Fiona Sullivan Series: Book One

By

Patricia Ann Williams

ACKNOWLEDGEMENT

I am grateful to members of my writing group—Bea Lewis, Carren Strock, Bunny Shulman, and Lea Becker—for their comments, suggestions, and support. I would also like to thank Sandra Pressman for her editorial assistance.

DEDICATION

I dedicate this book to my recently deceased husband, Chuck, whose encouragement, support, and devotedness enabled me to write this novel.

ALSO BY PATRICIA ANN WILLIAMS

The Two Weddings of Zhao Ping

E-Vengeance

The Garret on Boulevard Voltaire

Chapter 1

Cambridge, Massachusetts, October 2000

"Don't run alone," Alan had warned Ciara when he phoned to say he had to study and couldn't join her. "It's not safe to jog this late by yourself." But headstrong as she was, Ciara ignored his advice. Besides, she was angry. This was the second day in a row that Alan had bailed on their nightly run.

Turning right out of the dorm, Ciara took her usual route. She passed the Mugar Library, where Alan was holed up with his textbooks, and headed toward the BU bridge. A rusting, graffiti-streaked structure by day, its steel trusses appeared lacelike under a forgiving harvest moon. Once across the span, she headed east toward the Longfellow Bridge, where she would traverse the Charles River again to return to the dorm. Total distance: roughly 4 miles.

Jogging along the Cambridge side of the Charles River, she moved at a steady pace, her auburn ponytail swinging behind her. The silver heart-shaped locket on her neck bounced with each stride. She never took it off—Alan had given it to her on the anniversary of their first date.

The crisp autumn air refreshed her as she ran, and despite the nearby traffic, the river's gentle murmur prevailed over city noises. Approaching the MIT boathouse, she listened instinctively for footsteps behind her. Nothing. The path ahead lay deserted.

She checked her watch: 11:10 p.m.—too late for most joggers. Above, thick clouds gathered, cloaking the moon and veiling the path in shadow. The trail that had always felt familiar suddenly appeared ominous.

***

The man waited patiently in a copse of sycamore trees just beyond the MIT boathouse. The setup couldn't have been more perfect. From his car, he had watched Ciara leave the dorm and begin her run alone—just as she had the day before. He'd been watching her for two weeks now, waiting for just the right moment.

He smiled, rubbing his hands together. No joggers on the path tonight. No strollers at this late hour. They would be completely alone. A metal garbage can stood at the entrance to the thicket where he hid. *Another bit of luck,* he thought. He had removed the large black trash bag from the can and placed it in the middle of the jogging path. Ciara seemed too considerate to leave it there for someone to trip over. He was counting on her to pick it up and toss it into the garbage can—right next to where he waited. That's when he would make his move.

"There she is," he murmured, heart pounding as Ciara approached. She stopped abruptly in front of the trash bag, hands on her hips, scanning the area—probably hoping to spot the slob who had left it there. With a sigh, she picked it up, glanced around once more, then slung it over her shoulder and headed toward the only garbage can in sight.

As she neared the thicket, the path darkened. She hesitated, shuddered, then quickly pulled the lid off the garbage can and dropped the bag inside. Ciara wiped her hands on her jacket and turned around. A man in a ski mask stood before her, his cold, dark eyes locked onto hers. She jumped back, mouth open to scream—but a gloved hand clamped over it. His arm wrapped around her neck. Gasping for breath, she drove her foot backward, slamming it into his shins.

Her attacker cried out. But her moment of triumph was short-lived as he once again grabbed her in a chokehold and dragged her into the thicket. His lips brushed her ear. "You're a feisty one."

Twisting her head from side to side, Ciara freed her mouth from his grasp. She screamed for help. Once again, her assailant clamped his hand over her lips, but this time, it was rougher. He pulled a knife from his pocket and held the cold steel blade against her neck.

"Yell again and I'll slit your throat."

He removed his hand from her mouth. Ciara trembled; her skin translucent under a blanket of sweat. He pushed her back against the trunk of a tree hidden from the path.

"I know you so well, Ciara," he mumbled. "I knew you wouldn't leave the garbage bag on the trail." His eyes twinkled behind the mask.

"Please don't hurt me," Ciara said, lips trembling.

Holding the knife in one hand, he slipped the other under Ciara's T-shirt and fondled her breasts. He breathed heavily as his gloved hand encircled her nipples. She struggled as he slipped his fingers inside her jogging shorts.

In desperation, she spat into one of the eyeholes of the mask and pushed her attacker away. Caught off guard, he stumbled backward but quickly regained his balance. "So, Ciara, you want to play," he said, brandishing the knife and shifting back and forth in front of her to block her escape.

In a final attempt to flee, Ciara sprinted toward the jogging path. He caught her by the ponytail, yanking her backward and sending her sprawling to the ground. With a cold shake of his head, he pressed the blade to her throat. "Such a pity you couldn't be more cooperative," he muttered, his voice devoid of remorse.

He carried her limp body back into a clearing among the trees, undressed her, and placed her on a blue blanket that he had put there earlier. Eyes aglow, genitals throbbing, he pulled a camera from his jacket pocket. He took a picture of Ciara's lifeless form, blood dribbling from her mouth.

As he pulled off his jeans, a smile crossed his lips. "Not breathing, not moving, completely still—just the way I like it." He lowered himself onto her body. "You can't push me away any longer, my beautiful angel."

***

The morning sun ascended over Cambridge, its reflection in the river not yet splintered by the oars of the crew teams. At the MIT boathouse, a group of young men clad in thermal shirts, sport shorts, and sculling gloves came upon a grisly sight—a coed clad only in a Boston University T-shirt lying on the ground, her throat slashed, her clothes neatly folded beside her. The heart-shaped locket was no longer around her neck.

Chapter 2

Boston, May 2004

He sat alone in the last row of the packed courtroom, eyes scanning the headline in the *Boston Globe*: *"Verdict Expected in the Cambridge Slasher Trial."*

Cambridge Slasher. He held his head high, chin lifted, proud of the nickname the paper had bestowed on him. But now, someone else was staking claim to that title.

For the past three weeks, he had attended every court session of the trial, watching another person being tried for the crimes he had committed. The jury had been deliberating since mid-morning. Soon, they would return with a verdict, and Henry Winfield would be brought back to hear his fate.

He pitied Henry. Such a wasted-looking fellow. The ravages of heavy drinking and being homeless had taken their toll. No amount of grooming by the defense team could erase the roadmap of broken capillaries across his cheeks, the dull look in his eyes, the red, bulbous nose. He couldn't have asked for a better stand-in if he had gone to central casting. Henry was perfect. Large enough to overpower his alleged victims and addled enough to plausibly commit brutal acts in a drunken haze. And then the fool had confessed—not only to the murder in Riverbend Park where he was found asleep a few feet from the dead woman, her blood all over his clothes—but to five other killings as well.

He turned to the sports section, pretending to read, though his real interest was in the hushed conversation between two reporters in front of him.

"Rumor has it the jury has already decided. Christ, it hasn't even been three hours."

"The guy confessed to the crimes. What more do they need?" the other replied.

"But it's obvious he doesn't know what he's doing. The guy's a nut case."

"His lawyers do seem legally challenged."

The reporter gestured with a nod of his head to the two attorneys at the defense table. They wore dark polyester suits and couldn't have been more than in their early thirties. The one on the end had a baby face. He looked too young to shave, much less have a law degree.

"You're right. Weakest defense I've ever seen."

"Bet the cops are celebrating—six closed cases in one go."

"Maybe the jury didn't buy the prosecutor's story. After all, the evidence presented was mostly circumstantial."

"Care to make a bet on whether they find him guilty?"

The reporter shook his head. "No. You couldn't give me high enough odds."

Seated before the reporters were the friends and relatives of the six victims. They waited, biding their time. One woman knitted, and a few wearing earphones listened to music. Others chatted or read. Some paced up and down the aisles, occasionally leaving the room to make a phone call or to visit the restroom. The families had brought photos—snapshots of the girlfriend, sister, or daughter they had lost. For three long weeks, they had sat through testimonies and cross-examinations, absorbing every painful detail. Now they waited to hear the one word that would help assuage their grief—guilty.

A young woman rose from her seat in the front row and, accompanied by her father, moved toward the aisle. As they made their way to the courtroom doors, she nodded and smiled to familiar faces. Transfixed, the man with the *Boston Globe* studied the pair. Just before they reached his row, the woman turned toward him and, for a moment, met his gaze. For a fleeting second, their eyes locked. His heart thundered.

He nudged the lady beside him. "Would you mind watching my seat?"

She nodded and shifted her legs to let him pass. He stood, left the newspaper on the bench, and edged his way down the row. Slipping into the aisle, he walked directly behind the young woman and her father. His eyes fixed on her—the sway of her hips, the elegant curve of her neck, the long crimson hair held loosely by a barrette with a few loose strands feathered against her back.

He knew her name: Fiona Sullivan. He had done a double-take when he had first seen her in the courtroom three weeks ago. She was the mirror image of one of the women he had killed—a red-haired, green-eyed beauty with finely chiseled features. He never forgot the faces of his angels.

By eavesdropping on corridor conversations, he'd learned Fiona was the sister of his first victim. Like him, she and her parents had attended the trial every day. He was grateful for her presence. Watching her made the long hours in court bearable. He often fantasized about an encounter with her—one that echoed the night he had spent with her sister. Outside in the hallway, he moved closer to where Fiona and her father were chatting.

"What's the matter, Fiona?" her father asked.

"Something about this guy Winfield bothers me. He's a drunk and a drifter, but he doesn't strike me as a serial killer."

"Then why would he confess?"

"Who knows? Guilt for something he once did. The attention he's getting."

"I don't think even this guy is crazy enough to exchange life without parole for fifteen minutes of fame."

Fiona pushed back a strand of hair from her face. "I can't explain why, but I'm sure Henry Winfield did not kill Ciara."

Her father sighed. "Please, don't tell your mother that. If Winfield is convicted, she'll have closure. If he isn't…"

The shuffle of feet around him drowned out the rest of the conversation. Spectators were filing back into the courtroom as the clerk announced the session would resume. The man's gaze followed Fiona as she disappeared into the crowd.

He returned to his seat. A hush fell over the courtroom. Black robe billowing, the judge entered and took his place at the bench. One by one, the jurors filed in, their faces giving no indication of their decision. All eyes turned to the side door as deputies escorted the defendant into the courtroom.

Henry Winfield appeared in an orange jumpsuit, ankle chains rattling with each step, his hands cuffed behind him. He shuffled toward the defense table, the metallic clank of his restraints echoing against the wooden floor. At the table, a deputy removed the shackles and cuffed him to his chair. He sat between his attorneys, head bowed, shoulders slumped.

"Has the jury reached a verdict?" the judge asked.

"Yes, we have, your Honor," the foreman replied.

The clerk took the slip of paper from the foreman and handed it to the judge.

"Will the defendant please rise?"

Winfield rose slowly, his head bowed as if he already knew their decision. He stood motionless, his face blank, as the word *guilty* rang out across the courtroom.

Reporters sprang to their feet, cell phones in hand, rushing to alert their editors. Cries of relief and grief erupted from the gallery. Some embraced, their faces lit with joy; others wept silently.

In the front row, Fiona Sullivan folded her arms and slowly shook her head. In the last row, the man with the *Globe* smirked, lifted his eyes upwards, and made the sign of the cross.

Chapter 3

Belmont, a Boston suburb, November 2010

Sheltered from the snow, he waited in the doorway of an apartment building, a quarter of a block from the bus stop. White flakes fell steadily, muffling the sounds of the cars and buses as they crawled past him down Trapelo Road.

Adjusting his backpack, he checked his watch. Six o'clock. Five more minutes until the bus arrives. A sudden gust of wind made him shiver. He pulled the dark scarf over his nose and chin and yanked the woolen cap down on his forehead until only his cold, steely eyes were visible.

After watching Henry Winfield get sentenced to six consecutive life terms with no possibility of parole, he had decided to stop his "activities." The Lord in His infinite wisdom had spared him. No one was looking for him. No one suspected that he was the Cambridge Slasher. He had been given a second chance. Whenever he felt the urge, he would attend mass to remind himself of the Lord's beneficence.

But then two weeks ago, he picked up a crazy broad in a bar. Back in her apartment, his old problem returned—he couldn't get it up. The bitch laughed at him, reached into her nightstand, pulled out a dildo, and started masturbating in front of him. Fortunately for her, he left. If he had stayed, that would have been her final climax. But impulse killing was not his thing. He was smarter than that. Everything he did was carefully planned.

He had noticed the girl he was waiting for in McDonald's on Saturday before last and followed her home. Obsessed, he took off from work and tailed her. After eight days, he knew her routine.

During the week, she took the 8:22 AM bus from Belmont into Boston and returned at 6:05 in the evening. She walked from the bus stop to her apartment five blocks away—always alone.

He checked his watch again—6:08. The bus was late. Then, without warning, it appeared: a wide white-and-yellow cab that towered over the surrounding cars. Its brakes screeched as it came to a halt. Only one passenger stepped off.

A young woman stood at the corner, struggling to open her umbrella against the wind. His eyes lit up. His pulse quickened.

She turned down the side street. The farther she moved from the lights and traffic, the deeper she sank into his world. Bent against the storm, she held the umbrella like a shield, snow slicing sideways across her path. Strands of flaxen hair spilled from beneath her charcoal hat, trailing down the back of her coat. She walked quickly. He would have to move faster.

He slipped from the shadows, silent and deliberate.

The first two blocks were quiet—houses tucked behind fences, smoke curling from chimneys like lazy ghosts. Just days after Thanksgiving, Christmas lights already twinkled from porches and yards.

He kept his distance. But even if she noticed him, she wouldn't be alarmed. She knew him. Over the last week, he had approached her twice, walking in the opposite direction. The first time, he nodded as she passed. She replied, "Good morning," her large blue eyes meeting his. The second time, she was singing along with her iPod, her voice as sweet and pure as an angel's. She smiled self-consciously when she saw him. He relished these intimate moments with his women. He didn't like to kill strangers.

He picked up his pace. They were almost to the third block where the houses gave way to a cemetery concealed from the road by a tall, thick hedge. He snuck inside the graveyard through a break in the dense bushes. Snow accumulated from recent storms slowed his steps. Would she get away?

Anxiously, he peered through another gap in the hedge. But the young woman hadn't gone far—she was forced to tread carefully along the slick sidewalk. He shook his head. Whatever possessed her to wear high-heeled boots in this weather?

Moving as swiftly as the snow allowed, he caught up to her on the far side of the hedge. She must have sensed him. The crunch of her boots in the snow halted. He froze, holding his breath. When her footsteps resumed, he slipped past her, gliding silently ahead.

About a hundred feet farther, he paused at another opening in the hedge. She was still navigating the icy path, now about half a block behind.

He scanned the area. The road was empty. The nearest streetlight stood far off in the distance. If this attack followed the same pattern as the others, suspicion might shift away from Henry Winfield. This time, the Slasher wouldn't strike in Cambridge. He'd hunt in other cities near Boston. He wouldn't leave the bodies to be found—he'd bury them. And he wouldn't stab his victims anymore. He'd strangle them. He had replaced the knife with a garrote. Three nights ago, he had crafted the device himself, winding white synthetic cord through and around two thick, five-inch sticks. He reached into his backpack and pulled it out. He was ready.

The wind surged, whipping up miniature funnels of snow that danced across the graveyard. Overhead, the moon slipped behind a veil of murky clouds. The young woman approached the opening in the hedge—unaware he was waiting.

With his prey directly in front of him, he lunged from the bushes.

She froze, eyes wide with terror. Her scream pierced the night—a futile cry on this deserted street. Instinctively, she thrust her open umbrella between them, but a swift blow from his fist sent it spinning into the snow.

Headlights flickered several blocks away, forcing him to act faster. Slipping behind his victim, he wrapped one arm around her neck, the other around her waist, and dragged her through the opening in the bushes into the cemetery. Crouching low, concealed from the road, he clamped a hand over her mouth until the car passed. Then he shoved her face forward onto the ground, placed his knee on her back, and slid the garrote around her neck. He crossed the cord behind her and pulled on the dowels.

She thrashed violently. Desperate fingers clawed at the cord. Her mouth gaped, searching for air. He flipped her over, yanking harder on the cord. Her face flushed crimson. The whites of her eyes burst with red veins. Her body went limp. He checked her pulse. Nothing.

Scooping the woman into his arms, he carried her across the snow-covered ground.

Chapter 4

Earlier that day, he had checked out the cemetery. He had seen workers with a backhoe struggling to dig a grave in the frozen earth. Hidden behind a grove of white pine trees, he watched them excavate the hole. When they finished, they covered the opening with a tarp in preparation for a burial the following day.

At the fresh gravesite, he undid the edge of the tarp and slid his angel's body inside. He pulled out a rope ladder, two stakes, and a hammer from his backpack. The wind that whipped through barren tree branches muffled the sound of his pounding. The ladder secured, he tossed it over the edge of the open grave, dropped in the backpack, climbed in, and repositioned the tarp over the gravesite. Once inside the grave, he frowned. Not much room. It was only about eight feet long and two and a half feet wide.

He took out a flashlight from the bag and turned it on the victim. A purple mark, about an eighth of an inch, ringed her neck where the garrote had been. The ground was cold and damp. He didn't want his angel to be uncomfortable. Grabbing a blanket from his backpack, he spread it out and gently moved the body on top, face up. He took off his gloves and pushed back the strands of hair that fell across her forehead. *So beautiful, so pure*, he thought, as he studied her face. Pulling out a cell phone from the backpack, he snapped a photo of his victim.

He always took a picture of his angels before they became intimate. During his years of inactivity, he would look at those earlier pictures to remind him of his women.

He knelt beside his newest victim, took off her boots, and set them upright, one next to the other. He pulled down her stockings, careful not to snag them. Sliding down her black bikini panties, he thrilled at the voyage of his hands along her silken legs. He grabbed a towel from the backpack to clean her body. Finally, he pulled down his jeans. He thought about using a condom but decided against it. No one would ever find the corpse.

Positioning himself on top of her, he inhaled her essence. She wore an intoxicating floral perfume. A wave of ecstasy coursed through his body. He felt his penis harden. There would be no disappointments tonight.

***

The wind howled above the tarp, rousing him from sleep. He blinked, disoriented, and took a moment to remember where he was. Then, with sudden urgency, he stood and pulled on his jeans. There was work to be done.

From his backpack, he pulled out and unfolded a soldier's foxhole shovel. He moved his angel to one side of the open grave and began to dig. Fortunately, the gravediggers had already broken through the frost line. Dripping in sweat, it took him less than an hour to add another two feet to the depth of the center of the grave.

He returned to the woman and illuminated her with a flashlight, examining her jewelry—the imitation diamond studs, the knockoff Rolex, the silver-plated bracelet. He always took a keepsake from his angels, a token of their final night together. With care, he removed the bracelet from her wrist, wrapped it in tissue, and tucked it into his backpack.

Then he rolled her body into the center of the hole he had dug. Rummaging through her purse, he found her cell phone and turned it off. He placed it beside her, along with her clothes and the garrote. Finally, he began to shovel the mound of earth over the woman, covering her completely.

Minutes later, he put his tools away and used the ladder to climb out of the grave. Once above ground, he shone the flashlight into the hole. There was no trace of the body, nor any hint of what had transpired. Satisfied, he pulled up the ladder, filled in the stake holes, secured the tarp, and left the cemetery.

The following afternoon, he returned to the gravesite dressed in a black suit, coat, and hat. He stood among the mourners as the priest gave a final benediction over the coffin. When the ceremony ended, he lingered, watching as the workers lowered the casket into the earth—into the same grave where his angel now rested, sealed away for all eternity.

Chapter 5

A knock at the door drew Chief Paul Mahoney's attention from the paperwork on his desk. "Come in," he said.

Fiona Sullivan stepped into the office. With her long auburn hair and flawless skin, she looked younger than her twenty-eight years. "You wanted to see me, Chief?"

"Yeah," Mahoney said, leaning back in his chair. "I'm assigning you and Rick to the missing woman case. Not much to go on. The last person to see her was a bus driver, who said she was a regular on his route. The day before yesterday, she got off as usual at Cushing Square. Her boss filed a missing person report when she didn't show up for work the next day. We checked her apartment—no sign that she ever made it home."

He pulled a file from his drawer and slid it across the desk. "Here's everything we've got."

"Thanks," Fiona said, picking up the folder. "I'll get right on it."

Mahoney watched her leave. She had surprised him. When he'd met her two years ago, he thought she'd quit after her first assignment. With her sweet face and slender build, she looked more like a beauty queen than a cop. Plus, she had a degree from Brown University. College grads from Ivy League schools were a rarity on the force. But Fiona had proved him wrong. She was sharp, relentless—and one of his best detectives. If anyone could find out what happened to the missing woman, it was her.

***

That afternoon, Fiona and her partner of two years, Rick Garfinkel, sat at their desks in the Belmont Police station. At 6'4",

Rick was one of the tallest men on the force. He didn't walk so much as lumber. His size intimidated most people, but not Fiona. She thought of him as a gentle giant. What he lacked in grace, he made up for with uncanny eye-hand coordination. After high school, he'd told Fiona he'd wrestled with a choice: accept an offer to play semi-pro baseball or join the force. Twenty years into his career with the Belmont P.D., he claimed he had no regrets.

They flipped through the report on the missing woman. Her name was Maureen Doyle. A native of Lowell, Massachusetts, she worked as a financial analyst for Randolph Investments, a securities firm in downtown Boston. Police had searched the area from the bus stop to her apartment but had found no trace of the woman. It was as if Ms. Doyle had just disappeared into thin air.

Fiona studied a photo of the young woman, then turned to Rick.

"Don't say it," he said, holding up his hands.

Fiona frowned. "You don't know what I was going to say."

Rick smirked. "After two years working with you, I know exactly what you were going to say."

"Alright, smart guy. What was it?"

"She fits the profile of the Cambridge Slasher's victims. And you're about to remind me that Henry Winfield may—or may not—be our guy."

Fiona grinned and shook her head. "Guilty. Am I really that predictable?"

"You are when it comes to your sister's killer," Rick said, then paused, regret flickering across his face. "Sorry. I shouldn't have brought that up."

He leaned back and gestured to the file. "But seriously, nothing about this case matches Winfield's M.O. His victims didn't vanish—they were found within hours, brutally murdered. It's been two days since Maureen Doyle went missing, and there's no body, no evidence. For all we know, she could've taken off on a trip and just didn't tell anyone."

Fiona nodded slowly, though doubt lingered in her eyes. "I hope you're right."

Chapter 6

At the end of the day, Rick dropped Fiona off at her home in Watertown. She lived on the second floor of a white vinyl two-story walk-up, not far from Cushing Square— the dividing line between upscale Belmont and blue-collar Watertown.

Fiona liked her apartment. Her rent was low enough that she didn't need a roommate, and the four-room unit was larger than anything she could afford in Boston's trendier neighborhoods. There were nice touches—a window seat in the living room perfect for reading, recessed wall niches for photos and knick-knacks, and a working fireplace. So what if the hardwood floors needed refinishing? So what if it had taken her three days to scrub the grease and grime from the oven when she moved in? It was worth it.

As she climbed the stairs to her unit, she heard her dog barking. The rich aroma of marinara sauce drifted into the stairwell, courtesy of her downstairs neighbor. Her Italian landlady was likely making pasta again. Occasionally, she and her husband invited Fiona to join them for dinner, but judging by the number of cars parked out front, they had other guests tonight.

The minute Fiona opened her door, Jasmine leapt up, her paws nearly reaching Fiona's shoulders. She was a solid black lab mix. Her square face suggested some pit bull in her blood, but her temperament was pure Labrador—gentle, affectionate, and loyal. Still, when provoked or sensing danger, Jasmine could flip into full-on guard dog mode.

"Okay, okay," Fiona laughed, ruffling the dog's ears. "I know you're ready for a walk. Just let me get out of my uniform."

As Fiona walked towards the bedroom, Jasmine trotted behind her. The dog's tail moved back and forth, slapping furniture and anything else in its way. With the force of a baseball bat, it hit a small table, knocking it over along with the framed photo perched on top.

"Jasmine," Fiona said, hands on her hips. She picked up the framed photo of Ciara. Fortunately, it wasn't broken. She missed her sister. Since joining the police force, she had made a few friends. Most of the girls she did things with accused her of never getting out of detective mode. Instead of talking, she grilled them.

A year ago, she'd dated someone for a few months who seemed genuinely interested. But like the others before him, he eventually walked away. He couldn't handle the constant stream of questions, the relentless probing.

Fiona set the table upright, repositioned the photo, and went into the bedroom to change. Ever cautious, she slipped a 9mm. Beretta into her pocket. Once Jasmine's leash was clipped on and the front door swung open, the dog bolted down the steps, nearly toppling Fiona in the process. Outside, the dog squatted by the nearest bush, adding a yellow topping to the black streaked snow.

"We'll walk to the 7-Eleven. I need milk and dog food." Jasmine wagged her tail and tugged eagerly at the leash.

It was one of those cold, crisp Massachusetts evenings that Fiona loved. She inhaled deeply, letting the sharp air fill her lungs. The holidays were approaching. Gaudy displays of multicolored lights and inflatable Santas cluttered front yards. She preferred the homes adorned with only a Christmas wreath on the front door and a single candle in each of the front windows. That kind of simplicity felt more in tune with the true spirit of the season.

Although it was pricier than chain supermarkets like Shaw's, Fiona did most of her shopping at the local 7-Eleven. The Nguyens, a hardworking Vietnamese family, ran the store. As a regular, Fiona often found a muffin or a handful of dog treats tucked into her bag—small gestures that made the extra cost worth it.

As they approached the store, Jasmine halted abruptly. A low growl rumbled in her throat. *Odd*, Fiona thought, glancing at the entrance. *Why would the front door be partially open on such a bitterly cold night?*

Inching forward, she peered through the plate-glass window. Her chest tightened. A man in a ski mask towered over Mr. Nguyen, who crouched behind the register, visibly shaken. The man's right arm was bent at the elbow, and though Fiona couldn't see the weapon, she had no doubt he was armed.

She glanced around the store. A male customer lay prone on the floor in one of the aisles, his head turned sideways, eyes watching the activities at the register. He didn't appear to be hurt.

Fiona reached into her pocket for her cell. She needed backup. Her phone wasn't there. Of all nights to forget it. She cursed under her breath, then slipped her hand into her jacket, drew her Beretta, and cautiously advanced toward the entrance.

Inside, the owner had opened the cash register and was stuffing bills into a plastic bag. "Hurry up," the gunman barked, waving his pistol. "I haven't all day." Mr. Nguyen's hands trembled, and perspiration dripped from his forehead.

Unnoticed by the gunman, Fiona and Jasmine slipped through the front door. She tiptoed toward the register. Spotting Fiona, Mr. Nguyen's head shot up, a hopeful look on his face. Alerted by his victim's change of expression, the gunman spun around.

"Police. Don't move," Fiona said, brandishing her pistol. At the same time, she released her grip on Jasmine's leash. The dog lunged forward, teeth bared. Surprised, the thief stumbled backwards against the counter. Fiona grabbed the man's right arm. The gun flew from his hand and slid across the floor. He twisted free, shoved Jasmine aside, and bolted for the door.

Jasmine was faster. She sprang forward and clamped her jaws around his ankle, dragging him down. He hit the floor hard, face-first. Fiona stepped over him, gun trained on his back. "Don't move," she said sharply. Then, to Mr. Nguyen: "Call 911."

Minutes later, a squad car, lights swirling, sirens blaring, stopped in front of the store. Two officers jumped out and rushed inside the market, their pistols drawn. Fiona stood next to the thief lying on the ground, her gun pointed toward him. Uttering a series of low growls, Jasmine remained by her side, ears flat against her head.

"Watertown PD," one officer yelled. "Drop the gun and call off the dog."

"Hey, Lou," said the second officer, lowering his weapon. "She's one of us. She's with the Belmont PD." He grinned. "Hi, Fiona. Nice work."

Meanwhile, Fiona had pulled out her ID. "Detective Sullivan," she said, holding it up for the first cop.

Lou swaggered over to examine it. "Looks like you've got this handled. Wouldn't have guessed someone your size could take down a guy like this."

Fiona rolled her eyes. Lou's partner chuckled and shook his head. "Fiona's the one who nailed those bank robbers last year—

you remember, the ones that slipped through our fingers? She's one of Belmont's finest."

"Detective Sullivan was incredible," the male customer seconded. "That guy never stood a chance."

Face scarlet from the compliments, Fiona turned to Lou. "Handcuff the guy already. I'm getting tired of holding this gun." She pointed to the weapon on the floor. "You'll want to bag his pistol. No one touched it. Only his prints should be on it."

Lou asked his partner to get an evidence bag from the patrol car. Off to the side, the customer watched with a grin. As the officer turned away, he gave Fiona an enthusiastic two thumbs-up.

Chapter 7

Mud from passing cars splattered across the windshield as Detective Garfinkel made his way to Watertown. It was the day after the 7-Eleven incident, and the weather had turned unseasonably warm. Spear-shaped icicles dropped from eaves like falling daggers. Branches lost their crystalline covers. Melting snow mixed with grime coated the undersides of vehicles.

Rick pulled up to Fiona's house and honked the horn. A few minutes later, she appeared in the doorway and bounded down the steps—then stopped short. Rick stood by the patrol car's passenger side, holding the door open like a valet.

Fiona raised an eyebrow as she slid into the seat. "What's this all about?"

Rick shut the door and lumbered around to the driver's side. "I'm riding with a celebrity today."

She gave him a sideways glance. "What are you talking about?"

"You're in the morning *Globe*."

"Seriously?"

"Page seven. Paper is on the back seat."

Fiona twisted around, grabbed the newspaper, and turned to page seven.

"The guy made you out to be a real hero," Rick said.

"What guy?"

"The one from the 7-Eleven. Claims you saved his life."

Fiona smirked. “I don’t know about that. He was kind of cute, though.” She buckled her seatbelt and continued reading as Rick pulled away from the curb. “His name’s Mickey Foley. Lives in Back Bay.”

She put down the paper and turned to Rick. “I wonder what he was doing in this part of town?”

Rick shrugged. “Beats me.”

“Mind if I keep the article? I’d like to send it to my parents.”

“Sure. That’s why I bought the paper.”

Glancing out the window, Fiona noticed they weren’t headed in the direction of the station. “By the way, where are we going?”

“The chief wants us to check out a burglary on Christian Way. The House was hit last night while the owner was at his father’s funeral.”

“That’s strange, Fiona said. “This is the third time this month that a burglary occurred in a house where the occupants were attending a funeral.”

Rick nodded grimly. “What do you expect? The family of the deceased puts an announcement in the paper giving the date and time they won’t be home. It’s like an open invitation to burglars.”

Rick turned onto Christian Way. “This is my least favorite area of town.”

“Why is that?” Fiona asked.

“It’s a tight-knit community,” Rick said. “Most of these two-family homes have been in the same families for generations. A son or daughter lives upstairs with their own family while the parents stay in the unit below. When the parents pass, the kids move downstairs, and their grown children take over the top floor."

Fiona raised an eyebrow. "What's wrong with that?"

Rick sighed. "Everybody knows everybody. The kids all went to grade school and high school together. They go to church together. They party together. It's like one big extended family. And they sure protect their own. If someone breaks the law, no one on the street will rat them out."

Fiona looked down the block of similarly built houses that differed only in the landscaping and the color they were painted. From behind lace curtains and drawn shades, faces peered out at them. A man throwing salt on the sidewalk and a woman walking her dog stopped and stared at the patrol car.

The car pulled up in front of a light green clapboard two-family. Fiona and Rick unbuckled their seatbelts, stepped out of the car, and walked up to the front door. Rick rang the bell. A heavyset middle-aged woman answered, dressed in a flowered housedress partially covered by a cardigan duster. White ankle socks and worn bedroom slippers completed the look. She squinted through the glass storm door.

"Angela Wysocki?" Rick asked.

"Who wants to know?"

"I'm Detective Garfinkel," he said, flashing his badge. "And this is my partner, Detective Sullivan."

After glancing at their IDs, she opened the door and let them in. "Just a minute." She waddled down the hall, bedroom slippers flopping against the hardwood floor. She opened the door to the basement and called down. "Hey, Denny, c'mon up. The cops are here."

A few seconds passed with no response. The woman raised her voice. “Denny! Are you deaf? The cops are here!”

A gruff voice bellowed, “Hold your horses, woman. I’m coming.”

Fiona heard the clump of heavy boots on the stairs as Denny made his way up.

Without waiting for her husband, Angela returned to Rick and Fiona and ushered them into the living room. An elderly woman sat in a Barcalounger, dressed in a black dress with her gray hair pulled into a tight knot. Wire-rimmed glasses were perched on her nose as she watched *The Price Is Right* with laser focus.

Angela gestured to the couch by the window. “Have a seat.”

Denny—a large red-faced man with a beer belly—entered from the hall. “Thanks for coming,” he said. “This is my mother, Sonja Wysocki.”

“Sorry for your loss, ma’am,” Rick said. She ignored him, her eyes glued to the TV.

Denny turned to Angela. “Take Mom to her room so the detectives and I can talk.”

Angela shot him a look, but turned off the TV, much to the chagrin of her mother-in-law. “Calm down, Sonja,” she muttered. You can finish watching when the cops leave.”

Once his mother and wife had left the room, Denny sank into the Barcalounger with a sigh. Rick took out his notepad.

“When did the burglary happen?” he asked.

“Last night,” Denny replied. “We were at my father’s funeral.”

“Was anyone upstairs at the time?”

"No. My son and his family live up there, but they came with us."

Rick glanced up from his notes. "I thought the TVs were taken during the break-in?"

Denny squirmed uncomfortably and ran his fingers through thinning hair. "Yeah, they were. But my mom was so upset about missing her shows, we went out and bought her a new one, the same model as the one that was stolen. Honestly, I think she missed the TV more than she misses my dad."

"Was there an obit in the paper?" Fiona asked.

Denny nodded. "Yeah."

"Did it give the date and time of the funeral?"

"Of course. Standard stuff."

Rick scribbled something down. "There's been a string of similar break-ins lately. We've sent around fliers advising families to leave someone at home or hire someone to stay during the funeral."

Denny stuck out his lower lip and shook his head. "Don't remember seeing one."

Fiona leaned forward. "How'd they get in?"

"They broke a window in the back door."

Rick closed the notepad and slipped it into his pocket. "You said you had a list of the stolen items?"

"I needed it for the insurance company," Denny replied. "I'll grab you a copy."

"You wouldn't happen to have the serial numbers for the larger items—like the TV?" Fiona asked.

Denny shook his head emphatically. "No. I never write those down."

"Any chance you kept the original receipts?"

"Nope," he said as he hurried out of the room. "I'll get the list."

When Denny returned, Rick and Fiona asked a few more questions, checked the area where the thieves had entered, dusted for fingerprints, and left. Walking back to the car, Rick questioned Fiona. "Our victim got pretty jumpy when you started asking him about serial numbers and receipts. You think this could've been staged? Maybe he's angling for an insurance payout?"

Fiona shrugged, "Could be."

"I'll flag it for the insurance company," Rick said. "Let them know we've got doubts."

Chapter 8

Fiona had just opened the patrol car door and was sliding into the seat when she heard someone call her name. She turned and spotted a man sprinting from the house next door. It was the guy from the 7-Eleven robbery. And he was even better looking than she remembered. He looked to be early thirties, tall and trim with dark hair and a ruddy complexion.

"What a coincidence," he said, slightly out of breath. "I was just at my dad's, telling him about what happened last night."

Rick, who was about to start the car, got out and walked over to where Fiona and the young man were standing.

"This is my partner, Detective Rick Garfinkel," Fiona said as the two men shook hands.

"Hi. I'm Mickey Foley."

He turned to the porch where another fellow stood watching. At Mickey's signal, the man walked briskly across the lawn. "Joe Foley, Mickey's father," he said, extending his hand.

Joe's handshake was firm. Like his son, he was dressed in a dark parka, jeans, and boots. His thick hair—mostly dark, though graying at the temples—framed a ruggedly handsome face.

"Fiona's the one who saved my life," Mickey said.

Joe looked at her warmly. "So, you're the young lady—and even prettier than my son said.

Fiona could feel herself blush.

"And I'm Rick Garfinkel," Rick said, extending his hand. "Fiona's partner."

"Glad to meet you," Joe said, shaking Rick's hand. "I guess you're here about the break-in next door. What's this world coming to when you can't even attend a funeral without someone robbing your house?"

Rick sighed. "We sent mailings asking families to arrange for someone to stay in their home while they were at the service. Unfortunately, people tend to ignore these requests."

Joe winced. "I didn't mean to suggest the police were at fault…"

"No offense taken," Rick interrupted. The two men continued to talk about the boldness of the thieves and how the neighborhood was changing. Meanwhile, Mickey smiled at Fiona, who shifted uneasily from one foot to the other.

"Dad," Mickey said, turning to Joe. "Why don't we invite the detectives to your Christmas party on Saturday?"

Joe nodded. "Good idea. We're just having the family, a few friends, and neighbors over. Nothing fancy. It's a chance to exchange greetings before holiday chaos takes over."

"Thanks, but I'll have to pass," Rick said.

"Fiona?" Mickey asked with a hopeful look in his eyes.

She hesitated, then offered a polite smile. "I don't think I'll be able to, but thanks for the invitation."

Mickey searched in the pocket of his parka. "If you change your mind," he said. "Call me. Here's my card."

Fiona looked at the card, studying it for a moment.

Mickey Foley

Assistant Vice President

State Street Bank

His contact information was listed at the bottom—both work and cell phone numbers.

The detectives said their goodbyes and climbed into the patrol car. As Rick pulled away from the curb, he glanced at Fiona. "He seems like a nice guy. Why not go to the party?"

Fiona shrugged. "He does seem nice, but I don't like mixing my professional and personal lives."

Rick raised an eyebrow.

"If the 7-Eleven perp doesn't plead guilty, Mickey Foley could be asked to testify," she explained. "It wouldn't be smart to party with a potential witness."

"You're right."

Fiona tilted her head, a hint of a smile playing on her lips. "But if the perp pleads out... I'll think about it."

Chapter 9

After leaving Christian Way, the detectives headed down Trapelo Road toward the police station. As they neared a busy intersection, Fiona peered out the patrol car window. “We’re close to Cushing Square, where Maureen Doyle was last seen. Why don’t we retrace her route from the bus stop to her house?”

Rick shook his head. “Our guys already did that. They came up empty.”

“But that was days ago, before the snow melted. Something could’ve been buried.”

Rick pulled into the parking lot of Smiley’s Restaurant. “Fine. It’s easier to say yes than to argue with a mule. We’ll leave the car here and grab lunch after.”

Fiona narrowed her eyes. “Did you just call me a mule?”

“Kidding,” he said with a wink. “But you’re almost as stubborn as one.”

Feigning anger, Fiona followed him as they walked the block to the bus stop where Maureen Doyle had last been seen. They moved slowly, studying the sidewalk and the shrubbery lining her route home. Fiona checked both sides of the hedge bordering the cemetery, her boots squishing in the mud left by the melting snow.

Three-quarters of the way down the street, on the cemetery side of the hedge, Fiona stopped and crouched. “I found something.”

Rick ducked through a gap in the hedge and knelt beside her. “What is it?”

“Looks like a button.”

Rick snapped a picture of the spot. Fiona pulled a pair of rubber gloves from her pocket, slipped them on, and reached beneath the bush. Her fingers closed around something half-buried in the mud.

"A large black button," she said, holding it up. "Probably from a coat or jacket." She dropped it into a plastic evidence bag. "There's still black thread in the hole—looks like it was torn off. If someone dragged Maureen through the hedge, and there was a struggle, this could have popped off."

"I think you're onto something. Let's see if we can find any other evidence in the area."

Fiona squinted into the noonday sun. Rivulets of melted snow snaked through the cemetery. She carefully separated the leafless twigs near where she found the button, while Rick examined the opposite side of the hedge.

Something caught her eye in the undergrowth. She leaned in and gently lifted what appeared to be a thread from a branch. She placed it in her palm and summoned Rick.

"What's this, Hawk Eyes?" he asked, peering at the filament.

"Not sure. Could be from the victim's clothes—or maybe her kidnapper's."

"We'll have the lab take a look. Anything else?"

Fiona gave the area one last sweep. "Nope. I think we covered it."

"Then let's head over to Smiley's for lunch. I'm starving."

"Somebody's hungry," she teased.

"Jeanne has me on this crazy diet," Rick grumbled. "The only time I get a real meal is when I'm out of the house."

"I'll tell her if you order fries."

"Don't you dare."

Fiona shot him a mischievous *I've got something on you* look, then carefully bagged the fiber. After sealing the bag, she stood up, brushed herself off, and joined Rick as they headed toward the restaurant.

"If we can link these to Maureen Doyle," Rick said, his tone shifting. "This might not be a missing person case anymore—it could be a homicide."

Chapter 10

Mickey Foley pulled his Prius up to the curb where Fiona stood waiting in front of her house. The 7-Eleven perp had pleaded out in hopes of a lighter sentence. After mulling it over, Fiona had called Mickey. He did seem nice—and besides, it wasn't really a date, even though he had offered to pick her up.

Fiona opened the car door and slid into the front seat. "There was no place to park, or I would have gotten out and held the door open for you," Mickey said.

Ah, a gentleman, Fiona thought. "Will your whole family be at the party?"

"Pretty much. And so it's not too overwhelming, I figured I'd give you a rundown on my siblings and their families during the drive over."

"Should I take notes?"

Mickey grinned. "Absolutely. There'll be a quiz. If you don't pass…"

"Yes?" Fiona asked.

"…no eggnog for you."

She smiled. "Harsh."

"First up, the star of the family, Julia."

Fiona widened her eyes in mock surprise. "What. It's not you?"

"I'm a close second. But Julia's got it all—looks, brains, the whole package. She has an MBA from Harvard and a really good job at Issacs and Holms, the investing firm. Just a heads-up—she might try to rope you into investing in whatever product her company's pushing."

Mickey suddenly braked as a cyclist swerved into the street ahead of them.

"Whoa—sorry," he said. "That guy's nuts. Look, he's not even wearing a helmet."

"Should I give him a ticket?" Fiona asked.

"Nope. Tonight, you're off-duty."

"Fine by me. So, after Julia, who's next?"

"Ann. She's married to Haim. She's a stay-at-home mom, and they've got a seven-year-old daughter named Rebecca. Total sweetheart."

"Will Rebecca be at the party?"

Mickey shook his head. "Not sure. It's mostly an adult thing."

He continued, "That's it for my sisters. I've also got two brothers—Ed and Owen. Ed's a die-hard Celtics fan. He could probably give you a play-by-play of every game they've had this season. He's married to Mary and they've got two kids. Owen, my other brother, might show up… might not. He's kind of a loner."

Mickey turned a corner and slowed as they approached his father's house. "So, let's see if you get the eggnog. Sisters' names?"

Fiona hesitated. "Julia and…"

"Starts with an 'A'," Mickey teased.

"Oh, right—Ann," Fiona said.

"And my brothers?"

"Ed and…I'm blanking."

"Owen," Mickey prompted.

Fiona sighed. "So, I guess that means no eggnog for me."

"You only missed one," Mickey said with a grin. "And since it's the season of giving, I'll be generous. You get a C. You passed."

"I just hope the eggnog's worth it."

Chapter 11

"There's quite a crowd," Fiona said, glancing at the cars in the driveway and in front of the house.

"Most of the people are family, friends of my dad, or neighbors," Mickey replied.

Fiona pointed. "Who rides a motorcycle?"

"What motorcycle?"

"The one behind the Ford."

Mickey moved to where he could see the bike. "Oh, that's my brother Owen's. I guess he decided to come after all."

The slate-gray two-family home loomed above the barren branches of an oak tree set between the sidewalk and the curb. Its sprawling roots had already raised part of the pavement, inviting a lawsuit. Twin chimneys flanked the gabled roof, one of them exhaling a thin stream of smoke into the night sky.

As Fiona and Mickey approached the house, a cloud drifted across the crescent moon, dimming its glow. However, multicolored Christmas lights on the bushes and porch illuminated the walkway. In the center of the yard, a brightly lit Rudolph pulling a sleigh offered a cheerful welcome.

"Will any other members of your family be here?" Fiona asked.

"Possibly Granny Rose—my dad's mother. She's in assisted living, but we bring her here for the holidays. She's a little out of it, but harmless."

Mickey opened the glass storm door that was partially ajar. Behind it, the front door stood wide open. Once inside, Fiona realized why. Between the roaring fire in the hearth and the tightly packed front room, the heat was stifling.

The layout was typical of the two-family homes built in the 1940s. The small front room served mostly as a cozy spot for after-dinner drinks by the fireplace. Tonight, however, most of the guests had gravitated toward the much larger dining room, chatting in small clusters around a table overflowing with holiday food and drinks.

Joe Foley greeted the couple warmly. “So glad you could make it. Fiona, come here—I’ll introduce you.”

Mickey helped Fiona out of her coat. Joe whistled his approval. “You look absolutely lovely tonight.” Fiona lowered her eyes, flustered.

While Mickey hung up her coat, Joe took Fiona by the arm and began ushering her from group to group. “This is Fiona,” he would announce to a cluster of guests, “the lovely lass who interrupted the robbery at the 7-Eleven and saved Mickey’s life.”

With each round of “Wow!” and “Tell us about it,” Fiona felt increasingly on edge. She wasn’t used to the spotlight and scanned the room anxiously for Mickey. Just as Joe was leading her to another group, a large man in a Boston Celtics sweatshirt stepped in front of them. His eyes lingered on Fiona.

“And who’s this young lady?” he asked, ogling her.

Joe placed a protective hand on Fiona’s shoulder. “It’s your brother’s guest, Fiona Sullivan.” He turned to Fiona. “This is my eldest son, Ed.”

A large clammy hand grasped Fiona’s. “Well, honey, if you ever get tired of my little brother, look me up. We Foleys like to keep things in the family,” Ed said with a wink.

Joe's jaw clenched. "Fiona's with the Belmont P.D. She's the detective who saved your brother's life."

"A cop?" Ed blinked, withdrawing his hand. "You sure fooled me."

He staggered off, and Joe turned to Fiona with a sigh. "Sorry. I think my son's had a bit too much to drink."

Fiona felt a wave of relief as she spotted Mickey approaching with two glasses of eggnog. Joe excused himself, and she and Mickey stood silently for a moment, sipping their drinks.

Fiona only half-listened as Mickey pointed out some of the guests—a high school friend, his old baseball coach, his father's next-door neighbors, the victims of the burglary. Angela Wysocki had traded in her housedress for dark slacks and a festive red and green Christmas sweater adorned with tiny bells. She jingled with each movement she made.

Fiona cringed as she saw Ed weaving toward her with a woman in tow. His flushed face was a puffier version of Joe's, and his gait was unsteady. He stopped abruptly in front of Fiona and Mickey and shoved the woman forward.

"Meet the gal who saved my baby brother," he slurred. "This is my wife, Mary."

Fiona's gaze hardened as she looked at Ed. After a few awkward words, he led Mary away.

"There's my sister, Julia," Mickey said, pointing to a young woman entering the dining room from the butler's pantry. "Let's go say hello."

He led Fiona across the room. Julia was arranging platters on the table to make space for more food. Fashionably dressed in high black boots and a hunter green sheath, she had draped a colorful scarf around her neck. She looked up and smiled warmly as they approached.

"So, this is the famous Fiona." She said, embracing her. "Thanks for saving my brother."

After chatting for a few minutes, Julia picked up an empty platter from the table. "Excuse me—I have to bring out more food."

"Let me help," Fiona offered, grabbing another empty dish and following Julia through the narrow butler's pantry into the kitchen. She preferred the seclusion of the kitchen to being paraded around as some sort of superhero.

Typical of homes built when the kitchen was the center of family life, the room was spacious and inviting. The tantalizing aroma of baking pies perfumed the air. A woman stood by the oven, pulling out a pan.

"Ann, this is Fiona," Julia said breezily, depositing the empty platter in the sink.

Ann turned around. "So glad to meet you. My brother's been talking about you nonstop."

"How can I help?" Fiona asked, shifting from one foot to the other.

"Why don't you arrange the cookies on the Christmas platters?" Ann handed her four metal plates decorated with snowmen and reindeer. Julia went into the butler's pantry and returned with several boxes of bakery cookies. As Fiona set up the platters, the two women wandered into the dining room to see what else needed to be done.

Alone in the kitchen, Fiona hummed along with a rendition of "Silver Bells" drifting in from the stereo in the living room.

A sudden cackle shattered the quiet behind her. Startled, she turned around and found herself face to face with a hunched old woman in a loose-fitting black dress. Gnarled fingers clutched a metal cane, which tapped against the linoleum with each uneven step. Beady eyes, set in a maze of wrinkles, studied Fiona with unnerving focus.

"What are little boys made of?" the old woman rasped. "Snips, snails, and puppy-dogs' tails. That's what little boys are made of..." She slammed her cane against the floor to punctuate the rhyme, the sound sharp and jarring.

Julia rushed back into the kitchen. "Granny, what are you doing?"

Granny didn't answer—she simply repeated the rhyme, her voice rising with eerie delight. Julia moved quickly to her side and put her arm around her shoulders. "Don't mind, Granny," she whispered to Fiona. "She probably thinks she's back in the nursery with her children."

The old woman looked confused. Her eyes darted between Fiona and Julia. Then, as if a switch had flipped, she recited in a softer tone, "What are little girls made of? Sugar and spice, and everything nice. That's what little girls are made of."

"So true," Julia said with a warm smile, kissing her grandmother's cheek.

Granny reached up and patted Julia's face with a trembling hand. Her voice dropped to a whisper, laced with warning. "Boys kill birds. They set dogs on fire. They throw kittens in the lake. Be careful of boys, my sweet."

Julia rolled her eyes with affectionate exasperation. “Come on, Granny. Let’s go to the back bedroom and watch a video with your great-granddaughters.”

Fiona stared as Julia maneuvered Granny out of the kitchen. Why did the old woman warn her granddaughter to be careful of boys? What secrets was she hiding?

A chill crept over Fiona. The twinkling Christmas lights, the crackling fireplace, the sweet scent of baking pies—none of it could mask the faint, unsettling undercurrent that pulsed through the house. Something lingered beneath the surface, quiet and ominous.

Chapter 12

Fiona spent the rest of the party in the kitchen helping Mickey's sisters and his sister-in-law, Mary. She preferred the chatter of the women to the boisterous sounds coming from the front rooms. Every so often, Mickey popped in to make sure she was all right.

"Go on," Julia said, waving him off. "We're taking good care of Fiona. Go talk with the guys about the Celtics and the Bruins." She rolled her eyes. "Sports—that's all anyone in this family ever thinks about."

Mary put the dish she'd been drying in the cupboard and moved closer to Fiona. "I hope you've had a chance to meet everyone. After all, you didn't come to the party to work."

"I'm fine," Fiona said with a smile. "I've met most of the family, including your daughter and Ann's."

"It's too bad my son couldn't be here. He had a hockey match at school." Mary glanced at her watch. "We'll have to leave soon to pick him up."

Fiona stared at the dark bruise on Mary's forearm, exposed as she checked the time. "How did you get that bruise?" she asked gently.

Mary's eyes darted around the kitchen. "I…I fell," she murmured, her voice barely audible. Her posture stiffened as she backed away from Fiona. "I should go. My son…the hockey match." She turned abruptly and hurried from the room, tossing hasty goodbyes to Ann and Julia over her shoulder.

Following Mary's retreat, Ann turned to Fiona. "You haven't met my brother Owen yet, have you?"

Fiona shook her head.

“I’m not surprised,” Julia said. “Owen’s a recluse. He’s probably barricaded himself in one of the bedrooms or in the basement doing whatever he does down there.”

“Actually, Owen is with Haim in Dad’s office,” Ann said. “They’re installing some new software on his computer. But Julia’s right,” she continued. “Owen is a loner. He prefers computers to people.”

Julia stared at her sister. “Well, Haim isn’t exactly yucking it up with dad and his cronies either.”

“You know Haim’s uncomfortable around dad and his friends,” Ann said.

Julia lifted her hand to her mouth and announced to Fiona in a stage whisper, “Haim is Jewish.”

Ann frowned at her sister. “My father is a devout Catholic,” she explained. “He was even an altar boy when he was young. He had trouble when I told him I was marrying out of our faith—"

Julia’s mouth dropped open. “Trouble? That’s an understatement. He hit the roof.”

“True. Dad didn’t really accept Haim into the family until after our daughter Rebecca was born.”

A coughing sound from the hallway outside the kitchen made the women turn around. Two men stood in the doorway. “Speaking of the devil,” Julia said. She motioned to Owen and Haim. “Come meet Fiona, Mickey’s friend.”

The men stepped into the kitchen. The tall, slender one with a neatly trimmed beard had a pleasant face. He extended his hand. “Nice to meet you. I’m Haim, the Jew,” he said with a wry smile.

Fiona returned the smile and shook his hand.

She turned to the man beside him—broad-shouldered, dressed in jeans and a Red Sox sweatshirt. “You must be Owen.”

“Guilty,” he said. “Owen, the recluse.”

Julia blushed. “You’ve been eavesdropping on us.”

“Not to worry, sis,” Owen replied. “Nothing we haven’t heard before.”

He studied Fiona for a moment. “You look familiar. Have we met?”

“Only if you’ve robbed a bank or a convenience store lately,” Julia quipped. “Fiona’s with the Belmont P.D.”

Owen rubbed the back of his neck; his face twitched. “Nope. Haven’t done either.”

Haim turned to Julia. “You’d better tell your father it’s time to take Granny back to the home. She’s ranting again. The kids are having a tough time watching TV.”

“I’m leaving,” Owen said. “I’ll tell dad on my way out.”

He slipped through the butler’s pantry and into the dining room, almost colliding with Mickey. “Watch it, bro,” Owen said, side-stepping through the narrow passage.

“I’ve got to move my car,” Mickey told Fiona. “Seems like I’m blocking the upstairs tenant. I’ll be right back.”

“Wait—I should get going. Jasmine needs her walk,” Fiona said.

“Okay,” Mickey replied. “I’ll meet you outside.”

Fiona said her goodbyes to the women in the kitchen. In the living room, she thanked Joe for inviting her, grabbed her coat from the front closet, and stepped out onto the porch to wait.

In the driveway, Mickey was backing out his car alongside two other departing guests. A sudden whiff of cigarette smoke caught Fiona's attention. She turned toward the source and spotted a swarthy-looking man standing in the shadows, dressed in a black ski parka and a knit cap.

"Sorry for trouble," he said in a thickly accented voice, pointing to the driveway. "I have appointment."

"I'm Fiona," she said. "And you are?"

"Leonid. I live upstairs." He took a long drag from his cigarette and exhaled slowly, the smoke curling into the cold night air.

Fiona turned her head and coughed. The cigarette had an unfamiliar odor—stronger and harsher than anything she recognized.

"Smoke bothers you?" he asked.

She nodded.

"Sorry. I put cigarette out."

"You don't have to. I'm leaving."

Fiona said goodbye and went down the steps to Mickey's car. She glanced back at the man on the porch and wondered what kind of appointment he could have so late at night.

Chapter 13

He sat once again at the basement workbench, drilling holes in two thick sticks of wood. After threading white synthetic cord through the holes and knotting the ends, he tucked the garrote inside his backpack.

Earlier that afternoon, he had visited the cemetery where Maureen Doyle was buried, watching as a backhoe clawed into the frozen earth to dig another grave. He debated using the same location, but everything had gone so perfectly the first time. However, as a precaution, he would check beforehand to make certain the area wasn't under surveillance.

He'd wait at the bus stop just as he had for Maureen. His new angel worked at a clothing boutique in Belmont Center. She was younger than his usual choices but had an enticing body. The last time he was in the store, she had worn a white sweater so tight he could see the outline of her nipples. Closing his eyes, he imagined his hands gliding over her curves, his lips brushing her breasts. Aroused, he considered masturbating—but instead, he picked up his backpack and grabbed his parka and knit cap. He didn't want to be late for his date.

***

Minnie Brennan tapped her fingers on the counter as the elderly couple poked through the items on the sales rack. She knew they wouldn't be buying anything. To attract holiday shoppers, the boutique's owner had decided to discount ladies' jeans—none of which would fit over that woman's enormous butt.

She wished they'd hurry. It was two days before Christmas, and she had to get to the mall before it closed. It wasn't that she had procrastinated. To buy her mother and younger brother decent gifts, she had to work overtime. She had just cashed a larger-than-usual paycheck yesterday. The money was in the zipped compartment of her handbag.

Minnie reached into the pocket of her slacks and pulled out her cell phone to call her friend. She eyed the couple still shifting through the racks, still wasting her time.

"Jane, it's me," she said into the phone. "I'm just waiting for some customers to leave, then I'll take the bus home. Pick me up at the bus stop at Cushing Square in about thirty minutes."

She spoke loudly enough so the couple could hear. The woman looked up from the sales rack, clearly catching the hint. "Come, dear," she said to her husband. "I think this young lady would like to close up." Minnie hoped the woman wouldn't tell the owner that she had rushed her out. Her boss would not be pleased.

The woman looped her arm through her husband's. Minnie was right behind them as they hobbled towards the door. Once they were outside, she locked up and flipped the sign in the window to "Closed". After switching off the lights, she grabbed her purse, put the register drawer in the office safe, and exited through the back door.

Compared to the front of the boutique, glowing with Christmas lights and festive decorations, the back alley appeared dark and menacing. She tightened her grip on her handbag and glanced around. All her hard-earned money was in that bag.

She scurried through the alley to the bus stop. *What luck*, she thought. A bus was just pulling up. She climbed aboard and sat near the front. It was just a short ride to Cushing Square.

Minnie was grateful that business had picked up enough so she could work overtime during the holidays. Her mom needed a new purse—something to replace the old plastic one she'd been carrying for years. Minnie had her eye on a soft leather bag, something elegant and durable. No one deserved a nice gift more than her mom.

Since her husband's death three years ago, Mrs. Brennan had worked two jobs. Part of every paycheck went into a college fund for her son and daughter. Minnie, now a senior at the local high school, had earned early acceptance to UMass thanks to her strong grades. She prayed for a scholarship. But if it didn't come through, her mom had vowed to beg, borrow, and steal to pay tuition.

At Cushing Square, Minnie got off the bus and pulled out her phone again to call her friend. "Hey Jane," she said into voicemail, I'm earlier than I thought. I'm heading home from the bus stop. If you get this, come for me now."

She crossed the street and walked alongside the cemetery. Some nights, she ran this stretch, frightened by what might lurk on the other side of the tall hedges. But tonight, her mind was elsewhere—on the mall, on gifts, on the purse she planned to buy for her mom. She didn't have time for ghosts and goblins.

As she neared the end of the block, she stopped. Was the moonlight playing tricks on her? Just ahead, in a break between the hedges, she thought she saw someone watching her—just a glimpse, a shadow, a face. She remembered the woman who had vanished along this very route. Still missing. Still no answers.

Minnie stepped off the sidewalk, intending to cross the street. But she never made it to the other side.

A man burst from the shadows, face obscured by a wool scarf and a knit cap. He lunged at Minnie, grabbing her arm. She kicked and screamed, but a gloved hand clamped over her mouth. She bit down hard on his fingers. He yelled and struck her across the side of the head.

Minnie staggered and fell onto the sidewalk, her handbag landing beside her. The man crouched over her, pulling a garrote from his pocket. He tried to loop it around her neck.

Minnie lashed out, driving her foot into his groin. He doubled over, clutching himself. "Fuck you, bitch."

Minnie scrambled to her feet and bolted. Behind her, she heard his footsteps pounding the pavement, closing in. He caught up, seized her arm, and spun her around. Her back slammed against his chest. In one swift motion, he slipped the garrote over her head, crossed it behind her neck, and began to pull.

She gasped, clawing at the cord, struggling to breathe.

Then—headlights.

A car turned onto the street, beams slicing through the dark and illuminating the scene. It screeched to a stop and pulled over. Jane jumped out.

Cursing, the man loosened his grip. The garrote slid from Minnie's neck. She spun around, coughing, just in time to see him snatch her handbag from the sidewalk and vanish through the hedge into the cemetery.

Chapter 14

Fiona decided to call it a night and began clearing her desk. She'd stayed later than usual at the station to finish writing up the car theft that she and Rick had investigated that afternoon. She was almost to the elevator when her phone rang. Racing back to her desk, she grabbed the receiver. She listened—eyes narrowing, brow furrowed.

"Where did the attack take place?"

She scribbled the address on a notepad.

"Is she okay?" Fiona asked. "I'm on my way."

Skipping the elevator, she bolted down the stairs and out into the parking lot for her car. As she drove, she tried unsuccessfully to contact Rick. She left him a message to call her.

Turning off Trapelo Road onto Elm Street, she spotted flashing red lights a few blocks ahead. As she neared the cemetery, two patrol cars blocked the road. An ambulance idled between them; its rear doors open. Fiona pulled to the curb and got out.

"Hey, Jack," Fiona said to one of the officers. "Where's the victim?" He nodded toward the ambulance.

Fiona approached just as two medics wheeled a gurney around to the back. "Is she all right?" Fiona asked one of the medics.

"She's shaken, but her injuries aren't life-threatening. We're taking her to Mt. Auburn Hospital."

Fiona studied the girl. Her eyes were red and swollen, her face pale. Purple blotches and streaks of blood marked her neck.

"Hi. I'm Detective Sullivan. What's your name?"

"Minnie Brennan."

"How are you feeling?"

"My neck's sore, and it hurts to talk, but I think I'm okay. Did they catch the guy? He stole my handbag."

"Not yet," Fiona said. "But we'll find him."

"Sorry, Detective," one of the medics interrupted. "We're ready to go."

Fiona held up a hand. "Give me one more minute." She turned back to Minnie. "I'll come by the hospital shortly to ask you a few questions. Okay?"

Minnie nodded.

After examining the crime scene and learning what she could about the attack, Fiona headed to the hospital. She'd called Rick to meet her there. He was waiting in the lobby when she arrived. As they made their way to Minnie's room, she filled him in.

"The victim—Minnie Brennan—was attacked in the same spot as Maureen Doyle. According to the first officer on the scene, the perp tried to strangle the girl with what sounds like a garrote. A friend who was coming to pick her up saw the struggle and intervened. The attacker took off."

"She's lucky," Rick said. "It could be the same guy behind Doyle's disappearance."

"You're right. He escaped through the cemetery. I tracked his footprints to the rear exit—then they vanished. He must've had a car waiting."

"Did you find anything else?"

"Only the prints, but with the muddy ground, forensics should be at least able to identify the size and make of his shoes."

When they arrived at Minnie's room, she was lying in bed awake. A gauze collar covered the bruises and cuts on her neck and throat. Her color had returned, and she looked calm--probably due to the medication the nurse had given her. Sitting beside her were her friend Jane and an older woman, presumably her mother.

"Hi," Fiona said. "I'm Detective Sullivan. We spoke earlier at the cemetery. This is my partner, Detective Garfinkel."

The older woman rose to greet them. "I'm Dorothy Brennan, Minnie's mother. And this is her friend, Jane." She placed a hand on Jane's shoulder. "If Jane hadn't shown up when she did, I don't know what would have happened. That monster tried to kill my daughter."

"Your daughter was very fortunate," Fiona said. She turned to Minnie. "How does your neck feel? Are you in pain?"

Minnie touched the bruised area with her fingertips. "It hurts a little, but not too much."

"Do you feel up to answering a few questions?"

Minnie nodded.

"Tell me what happened—from the beginning," Fiona said softly.

"Like I was walking home from the bus stop, thinking about what to get Mom and Jake—my little brother—for Christmas. I'd just finished work. Jane was supposed to pick me up and take me to the mall."

She paused, fighting back tears. Fiona patted her on the arm. "Take your time, it's okay."

Mrs. Brennan handed her a tissue. Minnie blew her nose and continued. "I was passing the cemetery on Elm Street when this man jumped out from behind the bushes and grabbed me. It was horrible. Like I thought I was going to die. He put this thing around my neck. I couldn't breathe."

She dabbed her eyes with the crumpled tissue. "I managed to get loose, but he caught me and put that thing around my neck again. That's when Jane showed up."

"What did he do when Jane arrived?" Fiona asked.

"I guess he got scared. He let go of me and ran through the bushes back into the cemetery. But he took my bag." Minnie sniffed and wiped her nose with the back of her hand. "It had all my money in it. Now I don't have anything to buy Christmas presents with."

Mrs. Brennan quickly stood and handed her daughter another tissue. "Sweetheart, please don't worry about the presents. They're not important. All that matters is that you're safe."

Minnie blinked rapidly, trying to hold back tears. "But I wanted to buy you a new purse…a nice leather one."

Her mother's eyes welled up. She leaned in and kissed Minnie gently on the cheek. "I'm so fortunate to have such a wonderful, thoughtful daughter."

Fiona glanced at the clock, then turned to Minnie. "Can you describe your attacker?"

Minnie's eyes shifted from her mother to Fiona. "I don't know. I really didn't get a good look. Like it all happened so fast."

"Was he tall?"

Minnie rubbed her forehead. "Yeah, I think so."

Fiona turned to Jane. "Did you get a look at him?"

"Not really," Jane admitted. "But he was definitely taller than Minnie. When I first saw them, he was holding her close—she only came up to his shoulders."

"How tall are you, Minnie?" Rick asked.

"She's about five-four," her mother replied.

Fiona jotted down the information. "So would you say he was between five feet ten and six feet?"

Both girls nodded.

Fiona made a few more notes. She turned again to Minnie. "Was he broad-shouldered? Slender?"

"He was wearing a ski jacket," Minnie said. "It made him look kind of bulky."

"What color was the jacket?"

"I think it was black."

"It was," Jane confirmed.

"Was he white?" Fiona asked.

Minnie hesitated. "I don't know. His face was pretty much covered up; he had a scarf wrapped around the lower part and a hat pulled down almost to his eyes." Brow furrowed, seeming to relive the attack, she suddenly cried out. "Wait. I just remembered…I could see the skin around his eyes. He was white."

"What color were his eyes?"

"Black… or maybe dark brown. I'm not sure. They were really scary."

Fiona turned to Jane. “Did you notice?”

“Sorry, I was too far away. I couldn’t see.”

“How about his age? Young? Old?”

Minnie shook her head. “It was hard to tell. Like I said, I couldn’t see his face. I think he was old—like maybe in his thirties or forties.”

“Did he say anything?” Rick asked.

“When I kicked him …you know, down there…he yelled something.” She glanced at those around her. A flush crept across her face. “He said, ‘Fuck you, bitch.’” She turned to her mother. “Sorry, Mom, but that’s what he said.”

Fiona gave a small smile. “You did well. What did his voice sound like?”

“His scarf was pulled up over his mouth,” Minnie said, “so most of the time he was hard to understand. But he did sound like he came from here. I mean, like he didn’t have a foreign accent or anything.”

“Any particular smells?” Rick asked. “After shave? Cologne? Garlic?”

She shook her head. “No.”

“Anything else that might help identify him? Tattoos? Piercings? Scars or moles?”

“Nothing. Sorry.”

“Don’t be sorry,” Fiona said gently. “You’ve given us some good information.”

She reached into her pocket and handed Minnie a card. "If you or Jane remember anything else—no matter how small—please call me."

Fiona tucked her notepad into her purse and said goodbye to the group.

"Detectives," Minnie's mother called as Fiona and Rick turned to leave. "Could I speak with you for a moment?"

Out in the hallway, Mrs. Brennan wrung her hands. "I'm very worried. That man has Minnie's handbag. He knows our address."

Rick offered a reassuring nod. "I don't think he'll come back. But if it'll ease your mind, we'll request a police car patrol to keep an eye on your neighborhood for a while."

Minnie's mother pressed a hand to her chest. "Thank you."

***

Several days later, Minnie's handbag was found in the cemetery. Nothing had been taken.

At first, the killer had considered staging the attack as a robbery. But that idea had quickly unraveled. In the dim light of the basement, wearing rubber gloves, he had emptied the contents of the purse onto the worktable.

A cell phone with a Disney cover— Ariel, the Little Mermaid. A tube of Bonne Bell Strawberry Lip Smacker balm. A small container of Cherry Lifesaver hand lotion. A chartreuse wallet with *LOVE* embossed across the front. A wad of cash tucked into a side pocket. Keys and other items his angel would need.

He rubbed his forehead, a dull ache forming in the back of his throat. He could picture her distress, the way she'd search for her familiar items, the comfort they brought. He hated the thought of her suffering.

The following night, he returned to the cemetery and left the bag where workers would be sure to find it. He was many things, but he was not a thief.

Chapter 15

Fiona decided to spend Christmas with her parents at their home in North Andover, about an hour's drive from Boston. Even though there were just the three of them, her mother had prepared her signature five-course Christmas extravaganza.

"Another helping of plum pudding?" her mother asked.

Fiona braced herself. She knew what was coming.

"This was your sister's favorite dessert."

Clair sighed and wiped away a tear with the corner of her apron. For a brief moment, Fiona and her father held their breath, hoping there would be no further mention of Ciara.

Fiona leaned back in her chair and rubbed her stomach. "I'm so full, Mom. I couldn't eat another bite. Everything was delicious."

Clair turned to her husband. He groaned and shook his head. "I'm stuffed, too. Honestly, this might've been your best Christmas dinner yet—and that's saying a lot."

The praise from her family worked its usual magic. Clair's face lit up as she set down the serving spoon. Fiona was pleased to see her mother smile—smiles had become rare since Ciara's death.

Clair picked up her husband's dessert plate and headed toward the kitchen. Fiona jumped to her feet. "Relax, Mom. You've done more than enough. You and Dad go into the living room and rest. I'll clear the table and do the dishes. As a bonus, I'll even serve you coffee."

"Thanks, sweetheart," her father said, rising, " I'll see what's on TV."

“Just let me pop this dish into the washer,” Clair said. “Then I’ll join your dad.”

In the kitchen, Jasmine rose from the plaid blanket Fiona’s parents had given her for Christmas and padded after the two women. A scrap of food fell from the plate Clair was carrying. Jasmine snatched it up before it hit the floor.

“Don’t you feed this dog?” Clair asked, amused.

“She’s very fussy—especially here. You and Dad spoil her.”

“Well, I’ve got some goodies for Jasmine that you can take back with you,” Clair said, her voice softening. Behind her bifocals, her blue eyes looked misty. “I wish you could stay the night. It would mean so much to your father.”

“I told you—I was invited to Christmas dinner at a friend’s house. When I said no, they asked me to at least stop by for dessert. Hopefully, after the drive back, I’ll have some room.”

“Humph,” Clair muttered as she rinsed the dinner plates.

Hating to see her mom upset, Fiona decided to give her some news she’d welcome. “I didn’t want to say anything because we’ve only known each other a few weeks, but I’ve been dating the fellow who asked me to his family’s dinner.”

Clair turned off the faucet and dried her hands on her apron, eyes glowing. “Well, why didn’t you say so? Who is he? When do we get to meet him?”

“His name is Mickey Foley.”

Clair’s smile widened, clearly pleased by the Irish surname.

“He’s the guy who was in the 7-Eleven when it got robbed.”

“The one who said you saved his life?”

“Yes,” Fiona replied.

“What does he do?”

“He’s a banker.”

“A finance person. That’s good.” Clair said, straightening her glasses. “How old is he?”

“Early thirties. Never been married,” Fiona added, anticipating the next question.

“Well, this is lovely news. I’ll let you finish up in here.” Clair took off her apron and walked briskly into the living room to join her husband.

Fiona lingered in the kitchen and listened as her mother relayed every detail to her father about her new beau. Truth be told, Fiona liked Mickey. He was sweet and considerate, not to mention quite good-looking. Still, it was far too soon to call it serious. But, if nothing else, her mother would stop pressing her to stay the night.

Chapter 16

The clean-up finished, Fiona carried a silver tray bearing three cups of coffee into the living room. She placed two on the coffee table in front of the sofa where her parents sat and set the third on a small side table beside the easy chair near the fireplace.

The scene evoked memories of past Christmases—the crackling fire, the comforting scent of fresh pine, the red and green candles shining on the mantle. Only two things differed from holidays past. Everyone was older, and one person was missing—Ciara.

Deep in thought, Fiona suddenly realized her father was speaking to her. "Sorry, Dad. What did you say?"

"Your mother tells me you have a boyfriend," he said, a twinkle in his eye.

Fiona smiled faintly. "I don't know if I'd call Mickey a boyfriend. We've gone out a few times—movies, dinner, even a Bruin's game."

She caught her mother exchanging a knowing glance with her father and groaned inwardly.

"Mom, please, don't start planning my wedding like you did with the last guy I dated."

"Well, you're not getting any younger…"

Fiona winced.

"I don't know about your college friends," Clair continued, "but most of the girls you went to high school with are married. Remember Susan Whitmore from down the street? She just had a baby girl. Her second." Clair looked wistfully at Fiona. "It must be wonderful to have grandchildren."

She turned to her father, hoping he would intervene. He obliged by changing the topic. "That guy," he said, pointing to the singer on the TV screen crooning White Christmas, "has one hell of a voice."

Clair hit her husband playfully on the arm. "I know when you're trying to change the subject."

"Wait," he said, suddenly serious. "There's a news bulletin." Three pairs of eyes focused on the TV.

"We interrupt this Christmas program to bring you a special bulletin. New forensic evidence has surfaced in the case of the convicted serial killer, Henry Winfield. Several years ago, a jury found Winfield guilty of murdering six women. Now, a coalition of Massachusetts lawyers and law students advocating against wrongful convictions has uncovered evidence suggesting Winfield could not possibly have committed several of the murders. The…"

All color drained from Clair's face. The cup of coffee fell from her hand and overturned as it landed on the carpet.

Fiona's father quickly grabbed the remote and shut off the TV.

"No, turn it back on," Clair said urgently. "I need to know if they're releasing him."

Peter flipped it on, but the bulletin was gone. Regular programming had resumed. He wrapped his arm around his wife. "They can't release him. He was tried and found guilty."

Clair's face crumbled; all signs of Christmas joy vanished. She turned to her daughter, her voice trembling. "But what if they did make a mistake? What if he's innocent?"

"If the new evidence proves he didn't commit the crimes," Fiona said gently, "they'll have to let him go."

Clair rocked back and forth on the sofa, burying her face in her hands. "I can't go through it again," she whispered. Tears streamed down her cheeks. "It's too much, it's just too much."

Fiona moved to the couch next to her mother, placing a comforting hand on her shoulder. "If Winfield didn't do it… Don't you want the police to find the real murderer?"

Peter pulled a handkerchief from his pocket and handed it to his wife. Clair took it with trembling fingers and blew her nose, her lower lip quivering. "I didn't want to live after Ciara died," she said, voice raw. "The only thing that kept me going was the two of you."

She reached out and grabbed their hands tightly. "I was starting to feel okay again. There were days I actually felt happy. And now this?"

Clair looked from Peter to Fiona, her eyes wide with dread. "They'll have to start the search for the killer all over again," she said. "That means more news stories, more headlines, more reporters asking what it's like to lose a daughter."

Fiona squeezed her mother's hand. "Don't worry. I won't let anyone hound you." She glanced at her father. "We'll protect you."

And in that moment, Fiona made a silent vow: she would not rest until Ciara's real killer was found and brought to justice.

Chapter 17

In spite of leaving her parents' home later than planned, Fiona arrived at the Foleys' just before dessert was served. Seven-year-old Rebecca, Ann and Haim's daughter, patted the dining room chair beside her and beamed. "You're sitting next to me, Fiona."

As Fiona took her seat, other family members and Leonid, the upstairs tenant, greeted her warmly. At the far end of the table stood Mary, presiding over an impressive spread of desserts: a pudding made from a potent mix of fruit, Guinness, and rum; a brandy-soaked Christmas cake studded with cherries; and a platter piled high with festive cookies. As Mary began serving, Fiona noticed a faint bruise on her left cheek, not quite hidden by makeup.

Plates bearing generous portions of pudding and cake circulated around the table. For the children, there were cookies. Fiona smiled at the little girl with chestnut curls beside her as she placed the cookie plate in front of her. Rebecca's eyes sparkled.

"We need to thank Granny for most of these treats," Ann said. "The cake and pudding are her recipes." Seated across from Fiona, Granny nodded to the round of applause.

"I brought these recipes all the way from Ireland," she said proudly.

"But they weren't written down, were they?" Mickey asked, already knowing the answer.

"No," Granny replied, tapping her forehead. "I kept them all up here."

Joe, seated at the head of the table beside his mother, gently patted her hand. “My mom could probably recite the recipes right now. Her long-term memory is incredible.”

Granny gave her audience a gap-toothed grin before her expression turned serious. “You can’t make the cake at the last minute,” she cautioned. “I always start days ahead so that the rum has time to soak in properly.”

She glanced around the table. After assuring herself that everyone was listening, she continued. “You need a bottle of rum…um, let’s see. Oh yes—apples, sugar, currents…and,” she paused, squinting, trying to recall the rest. “And other stuff.” Her voice trailed off into silence.

Those at the table exchanged uncertain glances. Joe, with a sad look in his eyes, shook his head gently. “Thanks for the recipe, Mom. Now let’s hold hands again for grace, in honor of our newly arrived guest.”

Everyone extended their arms in an unbroken circle and bowed their heads. All listened as Joe recited the familiar prayer: “Lord, bless this food that we are about to eat. Watch over us and protect us, in the name of the Father, the Son, and the Holy Ghost. Amen.” All except Haim made the sign of the cross.

“This is delicious,” Fiona said after sampling the Christmas cake.

“Thank Mary. She’s the one who made it.”

Mary smiled from the other side of the table, placing a hand self-consciously over her cheek as she turned toward Fiona.

Granny tugged on Joe’s shirt sleeve. “What is it, Mother?” Joe asked.

"Son."

"Yes?" He waited patiently until the disconnect between Granny's thoughts and her ability to express them was resolved.

"Son, who's the little girl?" She pointed to Rebecca.

"That's Rebecca. Your great-granddaughter."

"She's pretty, isn't she?"

"Very." Joe winked at Rebecca, who stared at Granny, her face knotted in confusion.

"Granny, you know who I am."

Ann hugged her daughter. "Of course, she does, sweetheart. But your great-grandmother has an illness that makes her forget things sometimes."

Rebecca smiled at Granny. "I hope you get better soon."

A look of panic crossed Granny's face. She tugged again on Joe's shirtsleeve. "Am I sick?"

"No, Mother. You're just fine."

Granny leaned back in her chair, visibly relieved. Joe stared at the empty plates on the table. "How about seconds, Fiona?" he asked.

"I'm good, Mr. Foley."

"Please call me Joe."

"Okay…Joe."

Leonid stood abruptly. "Excuse me, please. Must go. Thank you for dinner."

Joe rose to see his tenant out, but Leonid was already halfway to the door. As the two sisters cleared the table, the men dove into their favorite topic.

"How about those Bruins?" Ed asked.

"They crushed Minnesota. Total blowout," Mickey said.

Ed turned to Fiona. "Has Mickey taken you to any Bruin's games yet?"

"We saw them play the—who was it again?"

"The Duck's," Mickey answered.

"Yes, that's right. We saw them play the Ducks last week."

Ed grinned. "Watch out, Fiona. If my baby brother takes you to a Bruin's game, your relationship is on a whole 'nother level."

"Can we watch TV?" Rebecca asked.

"Sure," Joe said. "Why don't you take Granny with you?" He turned to his mother. "Would you like to sit in the living room with your great-grandkids and watch some TV?"

Granny looked puzzled.

"C'mon, I'll help you." Joe gently helped his mother from her seat and guided her into the next room, where Mary and Ed's kids were already bickering over the remote.

Ann glanced out the window. "I don't know what's happening to the neighborhood."

"What do you mean?" Joe asked as he returned to the table.

"Earlier this month, your neighbor's house was robbed. And last month, there was that article in the *Globe* about the woman who lives a few blocks from here who disappeared. And now there's the attempted murder of that high school girl on Elm Street."

Joe raised an eyebrow. "You trying to get me to move?"

Ann shook her head. "I know that's not possible. Just be careful, that's all I'm saying."

"Why did your tenant eat and run?" Julia asked.

"He said he had to meet a friend."

Julia frowned. "He always seems to have late-night meetings. What does he do anyway?"

Joe toyed with his spoon. "I'm not really sure. He's involved in some business deals. But I can't complain. He's a good tenant. No trouble. Pays his rent on time."

"He looks and sounds like a member of the Russian Mafia," Julia said.

Mickey glanced at his sister with a mock-serious grin. "Maybe he kidnapped the missing woman and she's tied up right now in his apartment upstairs."

Julia rolled her eyes.

"How long has Leonid been in this country?" Fiona asked.

Joe's eyes narrowed. "Is he a suspect in the disappearance?"

"No. I was just curious," she answered, thinking the question odd.

"About 10 years."

Julia looked surprised. "That long? You'd think his English would be better by now." Ann picked at the crumbs on her plate with a moistened finger. “The paper said the missing woman was twenty-nine and worked in Boston. An analyst for some investment firm.”

“How long has she been missing?” Mary asked.

“Almost a month.”

Fiona lowered her eyes, waiting for the inevitable question.

“And what do the police think?” Haim asked. “Is there a suspect?”

“Sorry. That’s classified information.”

Joe leaned in. “How about that story that’s been on the news? The one that claims that guy, what’s his name? …Winfield… might not have killed those women?”

“I can’t discuss police business.”

Granny shuffled in from the living room, supporting herself by hanging on to the sideboard. “I know who killed those women.” She paused as all eyes turned toward her. “My sons,” she said. “My sons kill.”

Joe’s face drained of color. He jumped up from his chair, took his mother by the arm, and led her gently back into the living room. When he returned, he looked at Fiona. “Sorry for that outburst. My mother just can’t forget that my two older brothers drowned three kittens when they were maybe ten or eleven. Just a boyish prank. I was there, but I only watched. I was six years old.”

“Boys will be boys,” Ed muttered.

Haim shook his head, returning to the Winfield case. “I feel sorry for the victims’ families—having to endure another investigation.”

“How about Winfield?” Julia asked. “Maybe serving time for crimes he never committed.”

Fiona could feel perspiration trickling down her back; her head was throbbing. She didn't want to hear any more about Henry Winfield. "Where's Owen?"

"Our reclusive brother?" Ann replied with a disgusted look on her face. "Seems he can't make time for family gatherings."

"He did drop off his gifts this morning," Joe said.

Ann rolled her eyes. "Snow globes. A lot of thought went into that. And he couldn't even stay long enough to get his own presents. He left empty-handed."

Julia smiled. "At least the gifts were better than last year, when he gave everyone soap-on-a-rope."

Ed glanced at his watch. "Isn't it time to take Granny back to the nursing home?"

Joe looked at his mother sitting peacefully between her great-grandchildren in the living room. "Yeah. I'll get her ready."

Suddenly, a loud thumping sound from the other side of the wall made Julia flinch. "What was that?"

"Just the tenant going downstairs," Joe answered.

Julia shivered. "He gives me the creeps."

Chapter 18

Later that evening, Mickey cruised down Commonwealth Avenue toward Back Bay with Fiona and Julia. At this hour, the streets were quiet—just a few dog walkers braving the cold. If it weren't the holidays, the area would be swarming with barhopping students. They wandered through Kenmore Square. A few blocks later, Mickey turned left and pulled into a parking space in front of a five-story apartment building.

"We're in luck," Julia said. "It usually takes forever to find parking around here."

They climbed out of the car, each carrying a shopping bag containing Christmas gifts for Owen. Inside the foyer, Julia pressed the button next to *Owen Foley*. A loud buzzer sounded. Mickey pulled the lobby door open and held it for the others.

They squeezed into the small elevator and were met with stale odors from cigarettes and pets. Julia pressed the button for Owen's floor. They found him standing in the doorway of his apartment, waiting. Barefoot, dressed in chinos and a navy sweatshirt, he leaned casually against the doorframe. His tousled dark hair suggested he'd just woken up.

"Merry Christmas," Julia said, handing him a shopping bag and pulling him into a hug. Owen returned the embrace.

Before handing over her bag, Fiona introduced herself.

"I know who you are. You're the cop. We met at my dad's party a couple of weeks ago."

"For you," Mickey said as he handed him a third bag. "Merry Christmas."

"Glad to see that Santa's elves make deliveries. C'mon in and sit down."

Mickey, Fiona, and Julia sank into a worn brown sofa while their brother took the shopping bags back to his bedroom. When he returned, he handed each of his siblings an envelope.

"What's this?" Mickey asked.

"Your Christmas presents," Owen replied. "Sorry, Fiona. I didn't know you were coming."

Julia looked perplexed. "What about the snow globes?"

"That's just for the others. I didn't want anyone to know I have favorites in the family."

Julia looked at Mickey and smirked. "Aren't we blessed?"

They opened the envelopes. Inside were fifty-dollar gift certificates to Legal Sea Foods.

"Thanks," they said in unison.

"I love that restaurant," Julia added, smiling.

Owen headed towards the kitchenette. "What would you like to drink?" he called out, opening a cupboard to check his inventory. "I've got instant coffee, a cheap red Merlot, and tap water. No bottled."

"Since it's a holiday, I'll have the Merlot," Julia said.

Mickey and Fiona nodded. "Same here."

As Owen poured the wine, Fiona took in the apartment. The furnishings were a curious mix: two mismatched high stools at the kitchen bar, a small wrought iron end table with a lamp, and a white plastic chair. These stood in stark contrast to the elegant chestnut coffee table and matching console, which held a gleaming 46-inch HDTV.

Julia winced as she took in the furnishings. “You have to give me the name of your decorator.”

“Dissing my minimalist style again, huh, sis?” Owen emerged from the kitchenette, balancing a tray with four glasses of wine. He set it down on the coffee table with a flourish. “Clearly, you missed my latest splurge.” He gestured proudly toward the lone plastic chair.

He sat down on the chair. “*Better Homes and Gardens* did call last week. They wanted to do a spread on the apartment. You know, to show how a successful computer programmer lives.”

His guests laughed.

“No coasters?” Julia asked, raising an eyebrow.

“Oops, hang on.” Owen opened a drawer in the coffee table and produced four coasters, each adorned with a Bud Lite logo.

Julia set her glass down and tapped the table. “This and the TV console are my brother’s pride and joy. He built them himself.”

“I’m impressed,” Fiona said, running her fingers along the smooth chestnut veneer. “They’re gorgeous. You didn’t make them here, did you?”

Julia rolled her eyes. “Instead of socializing like a normal person, Owen spends his free time at Dad’s place, holed up in the basement workshop.”

Mickey turned to Owen. “Not to change the subject, but how was your Christmas?”

Owen shrugged. “It was okay.”

"Dad was pretty disappointed you didn't show."

"He knows I'm not big on family gatherings."

Julia set her glass down with a soft clink. "It'd be nice if you made an appearance once in a while. The kids miss you. And Granny's not going to be around forever."

Owen snorted. "Granny? Are you kidding? First of all, she'll probably outlive all of us. Second, she wouldn't notice if I was there or not. And third, she's got a vendetta against men."

"Yeah, what's with this 'frogs and snails and puppy dog tails' that she was going on about at Dad's holiday party?" Julia asked. "She frightened poor Fiona to death."

Mickey frowned at his sister. "I've seen Fiona in action. Nothing rattles her. Not even Granny."

Fiona smiled and continued to sip her wine.

"What was with Granny tonight?" Julia asked. "That story about dad and his brothers killing three kittens."

Owen placed his wine glass on a coaster. "According to family lore, the Foley boys were absolute terrors growing up. Word is, no cat or dog in the neighborhood was safe."

"I thought they were altar boys," Mickey said.

"They were," Owen replied, "but they had their dark side."

"Well, they have their reasons," Owen said, his eyes narrowed. "According to our uncle, their father was abusive. They blamed their mother for not stopping the beatings. Since their father died when our dad was five, he didn't suffer as much. So, he has a better image of nana."

"I had no idea," Julia said, shaking her head. Mickey put his arm around his sister. No one spoke.

Fiona took the opportunity to ask a question that had been on her mind. "I heard that on your father's street, it's common for the kids to live upstairs, above the parents. Why do you all have separate places?"

Mickey shifted uncomfortably. "The house holds bad memories for us. Our mom died there."

"We've tried to get Dad to move," Julia said. "But he won't. His father bought that house, and I think he feels tied to it. Maybe after Granny's gone, he'll finally let it go."

Fiona hesitated, then asked gently, "How did your mom die?"

Owen looked away. Fiona noticed his leg twitching.

"Tell her," Julia said. You were there when it happened."

"*After* it happened," Owen said. He picked up his drink and took a deep breath. "I was twenty-four and still living at home. I cut out early from work that day. Dad and I were going to a Red Sox game. Mom's car was in the garage, so I figured she was home."

He rotated his glass slowly between the palms of his hands, a pained expression on his face. "When I didn't see her, I called out. There was no answer. I went into the kitchen and noticed the basement door was open. I looked down the stairs…and there she was, lying at the bottom of the steps. The laundry basket she'd been carrying was overturned, clothes scattered everywhere."

His voice dropped. "I ran down and checked for signs of life…"

He paused, eyes distant. "It's been almost eleven years, but I can still see her—right there on the basement floor. Her head encircled by blood."

"We were in college then," Mickey added. "I was twenty-two. Julia was twenty."

"What was the cause of death?" Fiona asked.

Mickey shrugged. "A concussion, I think."

Fiona rubbed her thumb against her chin, deep in thought. She instinctively shifted into police mode. "Was there an autopsy?"

Owen looked confused. "Why would there be? It was obvious she fell down the stairs."

"Did investigators determine what caused the fall?" Fiona asked.

The three siblings exchanged uncertain glances.

"Was it a worn stair runner? Something left on a step?"

"Don't know for sure," Mickey said. "We think she was coming up the steps. The laundry was already folded, ready to be put away."

Julia shook her head. "There wasn't any real investigation. It was ruled an accident."

"Where was your father?" Fiona asked.

"He was on his way home from work," Owen replied. "He got there just a few minutes after I did."

Fiona's brow furrowed. "What did he do for a living?"

"At the time, he ran a watch repair shop in Cushing Square," Owen said. "Sold it about a year after mom died. Now he works part-time fixing watches at Sears, over at the Burlington mall."

Julia's eyes filled with tears. "Mom's death shattered him. They really loved each other."

A heavy silence settled over the room. Fiona glanced at their grief-stricken faces, suddenly regretting the direction of her questions. The years hadn't dulled the pain—it lingered, raw and unresolved.

Chapter 19

It was nearly two a.m. when the group finally left Owen's apartment. Mickey dropped Julia off in Cambridge, then retraced his route back to his father's house, where Fiona had left her car.

"It would have been easier for you to have dropped me off before your sister," Fiona said as they pulled into the driveway.

"I know," Mickey replied. "But I wanted a moment alone with you so I could give you your Christmas present."

Fiona rubbed the back of her neck, looking sheepish. Mickey gave her a sideward glance. "What's the matter?"

"You didn't say we were exchanging gifts. I didn't get you anything."

Mickey gave her a playful grin. "Don't worry. You can make it up to me with an extra-special gift next year."

At his dad's house, Mickey helped Fiona out of the car. "I don't want to give you your present here. Mind if I follow you home?"

Fiona nodded, and they drove separately to her place. Once there, Mickey parked and waited by the side of his car.

"Do you want to come upstairs?" Fiona asked.

"I thought you'd never ask."

As soon as Fiona opened the apartment door, Jasmine darted out to greet them.

"Why don't you make yourself comfortable?" Fiona said, clipping on the dog's leash. "I'm going to take Jasmine out for a quick walk."

"Mind if I join you?"

"Sure."

Outside the house, Fiona and Mickey watched as Jasmine sniffed around and marked her territory. "What were you doing at the 7-Eleven that night?" Fiona asked. "It's pretty far from where you live."

"I was picking up some beer for my dad. His poker buddies were coming over, and he'd run out."

"Your father seems nice."

"He is," Mickey said with a nod. "He's had a hard time of it with Granny. Most of his money goes toward keeping her in the nursing home."

Fiona opened her mouth to ask another question but decided not to. She didn't want Mickey to feel like he was being grilled. For the rest of their walk, she let him ask the questions.

When they returned, Fiona unclipped Jasmine's leash and headed into the kitchen to fill her water bowl. Walking back into the living room, she found Mickey standing by the fireplace, studying a photo of her and her sister when they were little girls.

"You were just as pretty as a child as you are now. Just one question—where did all the freckles go?"

"I hated those brown dots all over my face," Fiona said. "Every night I prayed to God to make them disappear. I guess He listened. They're pretty much gone now."

"How about your sister? Does she still have hers?"

Fiona lowered her eyes. "My sister's dead."

Mickey's voice dropped. "I'm sorry. I didn't know."

“How could you have?” Fiona murmured. “I never told you.”

He put his finger under her chin and lifted her face. Tears filled her eyes. Mickey wrapped his arms around her and pulled her close.

“Do you want to tell me about it?” he asked.

Fiona hesitated. She preferred asking the questions rather than answering them. But after a moment, she shrugged her shoulders. “I suppose so. After all, you told me about your mother’s death.”

Mickey took her hand. “Let’s sit on the couch.”

Curled up beside him, Fiona rested her head on his shoulder. “Ciara was two years older than me, but we were really close.” She pulled a tissue from her pocket and blew her nose. “It happened on Tuesday, October 15, 2000—a date I’ll never forget. Ciara was a sophomore at B.U. She and her boyfriend used to jog four to five evenings a week to stay in shape. But on that night, he had to study for an exam, so she went alone.”

Tears streamed down Fiona’s cheeks. “They found her the next morning beside a boathouse. She’d been raped and stabbed to death.”

“How horrible.”

Fiona’s chin trembled. “My parents had to go to the morgue to identify her. When my mother saw Ciara, she fainted.”

“Is that why you became a detective?” Mickey asked.

“Probably,” she said quietly. “At the time I swore I’d find her killer and put him away for life.”

“Did you?”

She shook her head. “No. A man confessed to killing her—and five others.”

"Not that Winfield guy?"

"I'm afraid so. But if his attorneys are telling the truth, then Ciara's actual killer is still out there."

Mickey slid down on the couch and pulled Fiona close. He wrapped his arms around her, stroking her hair. "It looks like you might get your chance to catch him after all."

***

The oak mantel clock struck three. The unfamiliar chimes stirred Mickey from sleep. He sighed, relieved to find Fiona still nestled in his arms. It hadn't been a dream. She was unlike anyone he'd ever met. Tough as nails, when she needed to be, yet sweet and almost naive when she wasn't wearing her badge.

Worried that she might be uncomfortable, Mickey carefully shifted out from under her, nearly tripping over Jasmine in the process. The dog yelped. Fiona's eyelids fluttered.

"Go back to sleep," Mickey whispered.

Tiptoeing into her bedroom, he pulled down the blanket and top sheet. Returning to the living room, he gently lifted her up and carried her to the bed. He laid her down, removed her shoes, and paused—considering whether to take off her dress. He decided against it. After tucking her in, he kissed her forehead and made his way back to the couch. He didn't want to leave her—not tonight. Wrapping himself in his parka, Mickey lay back down on the couch. Just before falling back to sleep, he remembered: he still hadn't given Fiona her Christmas gift.

Chapter 20

Fiona awoke to the rich aroma of coffee drifting in from the kitchen. Blinking against the morning light, she realized with a start that she was still wearing the outfit from last night's Christmas party. She sat up slowly and padded toward the kitchen, where Mickey was busy preparing breakfast.

"What time is it?" she asked bleary-eyed.

"About ten thirty," he replied, glancing over his shoulder.

"You shouldn't have let me sleep that long."

"You looked so peaceful. I didn't have the heart to wake you."

Fiona looked at Jasmine, whose nose was buried in her food dish. "Don't worry," Mickey said. "Jasmine's taken care of. We went for an early walk to the bakery and picked up some pastries. You don't have much food in the house."

Grateful, Fiona walked over to Mickey and gave him a kiss on the cheek. "Why don't you sit down. The coffee's just about ready," he said.

Fiona sat at the wrought iron bistro table. Between the two place settings sat a small box wrapped in gold foil, tied with a ribbon of silver, white, and gold.

"Is this for me?" Fiona asked.

"Who else?" Mickey said, placing two steaming mugs of coffee on the table before sitting down beside her. "I meant to give it to you last night."

Fiona's eyes sparkled as she untied the ribbon and opened the box. Inside lay a gold and diamond heart infinity necklace. "It's so beautiful," Fiona whispered, unclasping it and slipping it around her neck. "Thank you."

Mickey smiled, clearly pleased. "If you don't like it, you can exchange it."

"No," she said, gently touching the pendant. "I love it."

Over a second cup of coffee, they talked about their families, their aspirations, and their dreams. The conversation flowed easily. They lingered at the table, ignoring the pastries except to offer occasional bites to Jasmine, who wandered between them with hopeful eyes. When the mantle clock chimed one, Mickey stood up to leave.

"Do you have to go?" Fiona asked, her voice tinged with disappointment.

"I feel skuzzy. I'm still in the same clothes I wore yesterday." Fiona's shoulders drooped. "Tell you what, I'll go home, shower, change, and be back by three."

Her face lit up. "Sounds good. That'll give me time to clean up, too."

From the living room window, she watched as Mickey opened the door to his Prius. Before getting in, he looked up, saw her watching, and waved. Fiona fingered her new necklace. Mickey Foley was becoming someone very special in her life.

Chapter 21

Mickey returned to Fiona's later that afternoon. Together, they decided to take Jasmine on a long walk through the neighborhood.

"How long have you had her?" Mickey asked, watching Jasmine trot ahead with her tail wagging.

"About four years," Fiona replied. "I got her from a shelter. It was love at first sight."

"She's a great dog."

"I know," Fiona said, smiling. "She's come a long way. When I first brought her home, she'd panic at the slightest noise. She'd hide whenever anyone came over. The guy at the shelter told me she had been abused as a pup."

"You'd never guess that now."

"Nope. These days, she'll lick you to death. However, she seems to have a sixth sense about people. She reacts instantly to anyone she doesn't trust. Like that night at the 7-Eleven. She knew something was off in the store even before we walked in."

"And she didn't cut the thief any slack."

"I didn't have to tell Jasmine to sic him. She knew instinctively what to do."

"She seems pretty comfortable with me," Mickey said, glancing down at Jasmine, who was now walking between them.

Fiona slipped her hand into Mickey's. "You've passed the Jasmine test with flying colors."

As they neared Cushing Square, Mickey's phone buzzed in his pocket. He pulled it out and glanced at the screen.

"It's my dad," he said, answering the call.

"What's up?" Mickey asked.

He listened for a moment, then covered the mouthpiece. "My brother Ed was supposed to go to my dad's this afternoon for poker. Something came up, and he had to cancel. Dad wants to know if I can take his place. We're only a couple of blocks away. Want to drop by?"

"What about Jasmine?" Fiona asked.

Mickey relayed the question to his dad. "He says Jasmine's always welcome. She helped save his son's life, after all."

Fiona hesitated. "Could I play poker, too?"

"Hey Dad, Fiona wants to know if she can play, too."

"He says fine but be prepared to lose money. He and his friends have been playing for a long time."

"I've played a little," Fiona said with a shrug.

Mickey passed on the information to his father.

"They're going to play Texas Hold'em. They each put in one hundred bucks."

"That's okay," Fiona said.

Mickey spoke into the phone again. "Dad? Fiona's in—she'll play, too."

He ended the call and slipped his phone into his pocket. "You sure you want to do this?"

"Like I said, I've played a little. I know Texas Hold'em. Plus, I'm feeling lucky today."

As they neared the Foley house, Jasmine's behavior shifted. Her steps grew erratic, her body tense. The closer they got, the more agitated she became. A low rumble began in her throat, escalating into sharp, persistent growls.

"What's wrong with Jasmine?" Mickey asked, concerned.

"I'm not sure," Fiona replied. "Maybe she's reacting to the plastic Rudolph on the lawn."

When Joe came to the door, Jasmine barked vociferously. Fiona grabbed her collar and dragged the dog into the house. In the dining room, Leonid and Denny, the next-door neighbor, sat at the table. The leaf had been removed, making the table more compact. At the sight of the men, Jasmine pulled against her collar, lips curled in a snarl.

"I'm so sorry," Fiona said, wrestling with the dog. "She doesn't usually act like this."

She turned to Mickey, her voice low. "I think I'd better take her home."

"Stay," Joe said. "Leonid, can we leave Jasmine upstairs in your place?"

Leonid's dark eyes studied the dog. "I don't know. Will it behave?"

"I think so," Fiona said, not at all convincingly.

Leonid mulled over the request, then gave a resigned shrug. "Give me a minute to shut the doors. Dog stay in the kitchen."

A few minutes later, Fiona led Jasmine upstairs to Leonid's apartment. Low growls sounded in her throat as they entered the apartment. Eyeing the dog warily, Leonid made a wide berth around Jasmine.

In the kitchen, Fiona unclipped the leash and turned to leave. As she passed through the living room, she glanced around. Three televisions—why would a man living alone need that many?

Back downstairs at the table, Fiona winced at Jasmine's sporadic barking. She thought about leaving, but her competitive nature got the best of her. She was looking forward to the poker game.

Joe pulled his billfold from his pocket. He placed five crisp twenty-dollar bills in the center of the table. "Alright, everyone, ante up." He looked at Fiona. "You sure you want to play?"

She nodded and reached for her wallet. Fortunately, her father had slipped her some cash on Christmas. She didn't usually carry around a hundred dollars.

Once everyone had contributed, Joe gathered the money and distributed chips to the players. He turned to Fiona. "We're playing Texas Hold'Em. Want me to go over the rules?"

"Sure," she said.

While Fiona listened, Denny glanced at Leonid and nodded towards the sole female at the table. His smirk said it all: *Easy pickings.*

Joe dealt two cards to each player. As the dealer, he tossed a one-dollar chip into the pot to start the round. Leonid, seated to his right, matched the bet, followed by Mickey. Fiona hesitated for a moment, then anted up. Denny folded without playing.

Joe burned three cards, then flipped the next three face-up on the table: the three of hearts, the jack of spades, and the nine of spades. Each remaining player added another chip to the pot.

Fiona leaned toward Joe. “Can you remind me which hands beat which?”

Joe gave a quick rundown while the others waited. Then he turned over the fourth card: the four of spades. Joe and Mickey folded. Leonid pushed a ten-dollar chip into the pot.

Fiona frowned, glancing at her cards. “What do I do now?”

“If you’ve got nothing,” Joe said, “it’s best to fold. If you’ve got something decent, you match his bet. If you’ve got something strong—a flush, straight, or two pair—you can raise.” Fiona’s eyes lit up. She slid two ten-dollar chips into the pot. Leonid’s gaze shifted from his cards to Fiona. He added a ten-dollar chip to match her bid.

Joe revealed the fifth and final card: the king of clubs. Fiona couldn’t contain her excitement. She grinned and reached for another chip, but Mickey grabbed her arm. “Wait your turn. Let Leonid decide first.”

Leonid glanced once more at his cards, then at Fiona’s beaming face. He grunted. “I fold.”

“What happens now?” Fiona asked.

Joe smiled, “You won the pot.”

Eyes sparkling, Fiona slid the chips over to her side of the table. “This is fun.”

Leonid glared.

Chapter 22

By late afternoon, nearly all the chips were stacked in front of Fiona. "That wipes me out," Denny said, pushing back from the table.

Mickey shook his head. "I'm ready to quit."

"How about you, Leonid?" Joe asked.

"I'm out."

Joe smiled at Fiona. "Looks like you're the big winner."

"Beginner's luck," she replied, a smug expression on her face as she cashed in her chips. "I'll go get Jasmine. She's been awfully quiet. I hope everything's okay."

She followed Leonid up the stairs. As they approached his apartment door, Jasmine barked sharply. Fiona could hear her thumping against the door. "She must've gotten out of the kitchen."

Leonid opened the door slowly. Fiona reached for Jasmine's collar. As they entered, they were greeted by a foul odor. On the rug, in the center of the living room, was a dark, wet circle of dog urine.

On the walk back to her apartment, Fiona recounted the scene to Mickey. "Was that Jasmine's way of protesting?" Mickey asked, clearly amused by the dog's parting gift.

"Leonid hit the roof," Fiona said. "If he had a gun, I swear he would've shot her."

"You came downstairs pretty fast. I guess you didn't clean up the mess."

"No. Leonid just wanted Jasmine out of there. I'll call him tomorrow and offer to pay to have the rug cleaned."

"Speaking of clean, you really cleaned up this afternoon. Not bad for a beginner."

Fiona hesitated, then grinned. "I've a confession to make. This isn't the first time I've played. I'm in a regular Thursday night game with the guys at the station."

"So, you're a ringer," Mickey said, raising an eyebrow.

Fiona smiled.

"What were you holding in that first hand? You were practically jumping out of your seat. A flush? A straight?"

"A pair of fours."

Mickey's jaw dropped. "Seriously?"

"I was bluffing. I saw Leonid and Denny exchange glances like I was an easy mark. So, I leaned into it."

Mickey shook his head, laughing. "You're amazing."

Chapter 23

The first day back at work after Christmas, Fiona went to Chief Mahoney's office, carrying a basket of cookies. She paused at the door, peering through the glass. The Chief was on the phone; his chair swiveled toward the back wall. She glanced at his desk. Unlike hers, which was cluttered with papers and files, his was orderly—only one sheet of paper was visible. He turned around, saw Fiona, and held up his hand signaling her to wait.

After a few minutes, he hung up and waved her in. She sat down and slid the basket of cookies across his desk. "From my mom. She baked these just for you."

Mahoney smiled. "How thoughtful. Tell her thank you. Hope your family had a nice Christmas."

Fiona squirmed in her chair and bit her lower lip. "That's actually what I came to talk to you about."

Mahoney folded his hands on the desk. "Go ahead."

"We got some bad news."

The chief cocked his head to one side.

"You probably know that my older sister, Ciara, was raped and murdered by a serial killer."

"Yes," he said softly. "That came up during your background check when you were hired."

"A drifter named Henry Winfield confessed. He's serving life without parole at Shirley."

"I remember the trial. That was what—seven, eight years ago?"

"My family and I attended every court session. We were there for the sentencing." Fiona paused, tears in her eyes. "And now, some legal students are questioning whether Winfield actually committed the crimes."

"I know," Mahoney replied. "I heard it on the news."

"Even back then, watching the trial unfold, I wasn't convinced he was guilty. I was still in college and thought maybe I just didn't understand everything."

Mahoney nodded slowly. "It was a strange trial. Just between us, there were rumors that it was rigged. The good citizens of Belmont wanted a quick conviction so they could feel safe again. Evidently, Winfield obliged. He offered nothing to his defense team that would get him off. Seems like he almost wanted to be found guilty."

"I had the same impression," Fiona said. "He looked almost relieved when the verdict was read."

The two were silent. Fiona leaned forward. "I have a favor to ask."

"Go ahead."

"I know Boston PD is handling the case. I called them. They told me that one of their lawyers, Paul Bentley, is going to Shirley tomorrow to speak with Winfield and his attorney. I'd like to be at the meeting."

Mahoney rubbed his forehead, clearly uneasy. "I don't know, Fiona. That's a tough request."

"My sister and I were very close. When she was killed, I swore I wouldn't rest until her killer was brought to justice."

"What good would it do for you to see Winfield?"

"I don't want to wait years before his case goes through the federal justice system only to find out he was innocent."

"I don't know—"

Fiona straightened up. "I have a reason to be there."

"What's that?"

"The Maureen Doyle and the Minnie Brennen investigations. The girls fit the profile of the victims in the Winfield case. They're young, fair-skinned, attractive, slender, middle-class, and Irish or Irish-looking. If Winfield isn't the murderer, then that means a serial killer is on the loose. A serial killer who might have lain low for a period to let everyone think the murderer had been caught."

Mahoney nodded. "That argument might work. Let me give it a try. I'll let you know as soon as I find out."

"Thanks. I really appreciate it."

"And Fiona, if I do succeed in getting them to take you along, don't mention your sister."

Chapter 24

Fiona pulled into the parking lot in front of the Souza-Baranowski Correctional Center. Located in Shirley, Massachusetts, the maximum-security facility boasted one of the largest camera matrix systems in the country. As she walked toward the entrance, she knew that one, likely several, of the center's 366 surveillance cameras were trained directly on her, recording her every step.

Despite the cloudless sky and bright sun overhead, the prison looked foreboding. It wasn't just the barbed wire fence that surrounded the center or its isolated setting. A feeling of doom and desperation radiated from the stark white building.

A tall, slender young man holding a battle-scarred briefcase waited at the entrance. "Fiona?" he asked as she approached.

She nodded and extended her hand. "Nice to meet you, Paul. Thanks for letting me sit in."

"Your chief said that this case might be related to one you're working on now."

"That's right."

"Hopefully, we can be of help."

Paul held the door open for Fiona. After signing the visitor sheet, they proceeded to the metal detector. Paul removed his black wool coat, a gray suit jacket, and a thin black belt, and put them in a bin. Fiona followed, placing her outerwear and bag in a container. Once past the detector, an officer escorted them to a conference cell. In the center stood a long table surrounded by a few chairs—the only furniture in the cell. They took seats next to each other, facing the entrance.

"Who's representing Winfield?" Fiona asked.

"George Slaughter, a top-notch litigator. He's part of a Boston group that advocates for the wrongly accused. Apparently, Winfield reached out to them a few months ago, claiming he was innocent. After reviewing his case, George agreed to represent him."

The sound of footsteps cut their conversation short. Two guards entered, escorting Henry Winfield and his attorney. Shackled at the wrists and ankles, Winfield shuffled into the room and took a seat across from Fiona and Paul, with George Slaughter beside him.

Fiona studied Winfield's face. Surprisingly, prison suited him. He no longer had the scruffy, dazed appearance of an alcoholic. Cleaned up, one might even call him handsome, although he still possessed the pained look of a defeated man.

George introduced himself to Fiona. He and Paul exchanged a nod of familiarity. "Now that my client is sober and his memory has improved," George began, "he believes he may have been wrongly convicted—at least in some of the cases."

He opened his briefcase and placed a file on the table. "For example…" He paused to flip back the file cover. "In the case of Ciara Sullivan..." Fiona could feel her face flush at the mention of her sister's name. "At the estimated time of her murder, my client was in the E.R. at Mass General, receiving treatment for a fall that occurred at the shelter where he was staying that night."

George took several papers from the file and handed them to Paul. "These are from the hospital. They show that my client was checked into the ER at 5:00 PM. He saw the doctor who diagnosed a broken ankle at 6:48 PM. By the time he was X-rayed and his leg had been set, it was after midnight. The coroner placed the time of Ciara Sullivan's death as being between 10:00 PM and midnight."

Paul looked over the documents, then handed them to Fiona. He turned to Winfield. “Why did you confess to the crime?”

Winfield glanced at George, who gave a subtle nod.

“I’m an alcoholic—or I was. I’ve been in recovery for years now. At the time of the murders, I was drinking heavily. Half the time, I was in a blackout. I had no idea what I was doing or what I had done. When I was found next to the dead girl in the park, I assumed I must have murdered her, or why would I be covered in her blood? I was asked about the other murders, girls who had been killed in a similar fashion. I felt so guilty about the dead girl, I said yes to the five other crimes.”

“Do you think you killed any of the victims?” Paul asked.

Winfield slowly shook his head. “Now that I’m in recovery and have had many years in solitary confinement to think about the crimes, I don’t think I’m capable of murder.”

“How about the girl in the park?”

“I don’t know. I probably just lay down to sleep it off. Drunk like I was, I might’ve thought the girl was lonely and got down next to her. She had been raped. The rapist must have worn a condom. There was no sperm found to do a DNA test. All the evidence against me was circumstantial.”

“And the other murders?” Fiona asked.

Winfield’s attorney pulled out other files from his briefcase and placed them on the table. “For two of the remaining cases, we have eyewitnesses who saw my client elsewhere at the time the crimes occurred.”

Fiona turned to Winfield, her brow furrowed. "I still don't understand why you would confess to crimes you had no memory of committing."

Winfield lifted his head, an anguished look on his face. "I wanted to be punished. Not necessarily for these murders, but for something else I did."

"What?" Fiona asked.

Winfield hesitated, then spoke, his voice barely above a whisper. "Believe it or not, I once had a pretty normal life. I was married to a wonderful woman, had a decent job as an insurance adjuster, and ..." His voice cracked. "I had a beautiful little boy, Bobby."

Tears welled in his eyes. He dropped his head into his hands. Fiona took a Kleenex from her purse and passed it to Winfield.

"Thanks," Winfield said as he took the tissue and blew his nose. "Bobby was the greatest little kid, smart, active as hell, a joy to be around."

He closed his eyes as if picturing his little boy. "My wife and I both worked. A babysitter picked Bobby up from daycare—he was three—and waited with him until one of us came home. That Friday, I came home early—straight from a very liquid lunch—to take Bobby to the doctor for a check-up."

Winfield shut his eyes and pressed his lips together. He rubbed his hands up and down his trousers. "I was drunk. The babysitter noticed. She even offered to take Bobby to the doctor herself. I should've let her. We were running late, so I put him in the front with me instead of in his car seat in the back. I wrapped the seatbelt around him. It was just easier than messing with the straps of his car seat."

He paused, his voice quivering. “Bobby thought riding in the front seat was the greatest. ‘I’m a big boy,’ he told me, ‘Just like Daddy’.”

Once again, Winfield stopped, tears careening down his cheeks. “I wasn’t paying attention and ran a red light. A car slammed into the passenger side, right where Bobby was sitting. The airbags deployed…they were just too much for him.”

He buried his face in his hands and sobbed.

The room fell silent. Fiona blinked back tears. Winfield’s attorney placed a comforting arm around his client’s shoulders. After a moment, Winfield sat upright again, his face pale and drawn.

“My wife left me. It was my first DUI. I guess the judge felt I had suffered enough. My license was revoked, and I spent a weekend in jail. But none of that mattered. I couldn’t live with what I’d done. I killed my little boy.”

Winfield shook his head and grimaced. “When the police woke me in the park next to the dead girl, I figured I’d finally get the punishment I deserved. I wanted to go to jail. I didn’t deserve to be free. That’s why I confessed to the other murders.”

“Then why change your plea now?” Paul asked.

“When my attorney,” he glanced at George, then back to Paul, “showed me evidence that proved I wasn’t guilty, something changed. I realized there was someone far worse than me—a monster who raped and murdered six women. A monster who was still out there and could murder more young women.” He lowered his head. “I just don’t want to be responsible for any more deaths.”

Outside the prison, Paul walked Fiona to her car. “What do you think?”

She unlocked her car with her remote. “What a heartbreaking story. But no, I don’t think he killed those women.”

“Neither do I,” Paul said. “Winfield needs to be retried and freed before the real killer strikes again.”

Fiona slid into the driver’s seat, her expression grim. “Unfortunately, he already has.”

Chapter 25

Mahoney waved Fiona and Rick into his office. They pulled up seats in front of his desk.

"What's up?" Rick asked.

The chief peered over the rims of his wire-framed glasses. "The funeral thief has struck again. Just got a call from a Mr. Apostolos on Waverley Street. His house was broken into last night while he was at his mother's funeral. The thieves took some silver and jewelry." He handed Rick a slip of paper. "Here's the address. I need you to check it out."

Rick tucked the note into his pocket. "Maybe it's time to put out flyers again," he said, "or put something in the newspaper. You know, advise the family of the deceased to have their home looked after while they're at the funeral."

"Good idea," Mahoney said. "Fiona, why don't you take care of that?"

Fiona frowned. After they left the office, she complained to Rick. "Why do I always get the grunt work? It was your suggestion; you should do it."

"Obviously, the chief thinks I have more important things to do."

"Like napping at your desk? I saw you yesterday."

"The kids kept me up all night with their hacking."

Fiona looked concerned. "Are they sick?"

"We kept Peter home from school. Jeanne is taking him to the doctor."

They left the building, walked to the parking lot, and climbed into the patrol car. “When you have kids,” Rick said, starting the engine, “you’ll be sleeping at your desk, too.”

“That’s not happening anytime soon.”

Rick pulled out of the parking lot. “By the way, I owe you an apology.”

“For what?”

“I heard the news that Winfield might not be the serial killer.”

Fiona smiled at her partner with an I-told-you-so look. “Yesterday, I was with the prosecuting attorney at Shirley. We spoke with Winfield.”

“And?”

“He did not kill my sister.”

Fiona stared out the window. Belmont was at its least attractive the week following a snowfall. White flakes mixed with mud, pet urine, and other debris sullied the sidewalks. Pedestrians in dark attire trudged along, reminding her of old black and white photos of the town. Thoughts of Ciara weighed heavily on her.

Rick pulled up in front of a small white cottage with a brick façade and a wide bay window. The detectives got out and walked up the freshly shoveled path to the front door. A short, stocky man with an olive complexion opened the door.

“Mr. Apostolos?” Rick asked.

The man nodded.

“I’m Detective Garfinkel, and this is my partner, Detective Sullivan,” Rick said, flashing his badge. “We’re here about the burglary.”

“Come in,” the homeowner replied, stepping aside.

After taking down pertinent information and obtaining a list of the items stolen, the detectives checked the back of the house. The thief or thieves had broken a window in the rear door to make their entry.

“Same pattern as the other robberies,” Rick muttered.

Fiona examined the area around the back porch while her partner dusted for fingerprints. Kneeling, she spread apart the blue needles of a Juniper shrub. A piece of gold foil caught her eye. She called Rick over.

“What is it?” he asked, crouching beside her.

With a gloved hand, she picked it up and placed it in an evidence bag. “It looks like a cigarette butt. Not one that I’ve ever seen before. It’s black with gold foil around the top.”

“Let’s see,” Rick said, taking the bag from her and examining the contents. “This cigarette is called a Sobranie Black Russian. It costs an arm and a leg. Weird that thieves would smoke such an expensive brand.”

“Maybe they have a Black Russian addiction and rob to support their habit,” Fiona said with a smirk.

Rick grimaced and handed the bag back to Fiona. “If you thought that remark was funny, it wasn’t.”

“Does that mean I have no hope of becoming a stand-up comic?”

“Stick to your day job,” Rick said, moving toward the back door. “Let’s see if Mr. Apostolos smokes these.”

Once inside, Rick asked the burglary victim if he smoked. “I used to years ago but gave it up. Filthy habit.”

“Could any of your visitors have smoked?”

“No. Not in my house. I don’t allow it.”

“Could someone have gone out on the back porch to smoke?”

“I suppose so, but I don’t remember anyone doing it. Why?”

Fiona held up the plastic evidence bag. “We found an unusual cigarette butt in the backyard near the porch. Does anyone you know smoke these?”

“They’re Sobranie Black Russians,” Rick added.

Mr. Apostolos shook his head. “Never seen them before.”

“It’s possible it belongs to the thief,” Rick said. “We’ll send it to the lab for a saliva test.”

Before leaving the area, Rick and Fiona canvassed the neighbors, asking if they had seen or heard anything unusual the night before, about the time of the burglary. Most had been at the funeral. The few who were home reported nothing out of the ordinary.

“Let’s file this report and get the cigarette butt to the lab,” Rick said. “Then we’ll check the local pawn shops to see if anyone’s been trying to fence the stolen objects.

Chapter 26

Ed Foley rolled onto his back, drained but content.

"How was it, baby?" Sally asked, elbow propped up on the bed.

"Fantastic, as always."

Ed wondered what his life would have been like if he had married Sally instead of Mary. He'd dated Sally in his twenties, and reconnecting with her had felt like fate. A few weeks ago, he'd googled her name on a whim and discovered she lived in Cambridge—less than ten miles away. She'd been divorced for three years.

They met at a coffee shop near her home, and fifteen minutes later, they were in her bed. It was like they'd never been apart. She was the best lay he ever had. Quite a contrast from Mary. On the rare occasions they made love, she was so unresponsive he could barely get it up.

Ed sat up and pulled out a cigarette from the pack lying on the nightstand.

Sally frowned. "I thought we agreed you wouldn't smoke in the apartment."

In response, he ran his fingers over Sally's breasts. Her nipples hardened. "You really want me to stop playing with your boobs and leave?"

"I didn't say anything about you leaving."

"If I have to get dressed to go outside to smoke, I might as well leave."

"You are so unfair," she said, lying back down on the bed.

Ed set the unlit cigarette back on the nightstand and moved toward Sally. He ran his hand over her angular face. She was still a pretty woman. From a distance, with her slender build, large, uplifted tits, and long dusty blond hair, she could easily be mistaken for someone in her twenties—the age they were when they first started fucking.

Back then, they had had a tempestuous relationship. They'd either fight or make love. Sally had wanted to get married, but Ed felt he was too young. Besides, she wasn't Catholic. He knew his dad wouldn't approve.

His hand moved slowly down her neck, over her breasts, and between her legs. She was aroused. Ed rolled onto his back as Sally climbed on top of him, sliding sensuously down his body. *What the hell*, he thought, *gettin' head was better than a cigarette any day.*

***

"Where the heck is he?" Mary muttered after another failed attempt to reach Ed on his cell.

She shut off her phone and pulled the Honda Civic into the garage. His car wasn't there.

"Thanks, Mom," Sean said, pulling his hockey gear from the trunk.

"Sorry you had to wait. I don't know what happened to your father."

"That's okay."

Mary glanced into the family room. Emily was curled up on the couch, watching a Hannah Montana video.

"Did your father call?" she asked.

"No."

"Did anyone call?"

"Just some lady from the PTA to remind you that you volunteered to help chaperone the class trip to some museum."

"The Gardner Museum?"

"Yeah, that's the one."

Mary went into the kitchen and set the kettle on the stove. "Where could he be?" she murmured, spooning instant coffee into a mug.

The kettle whistled. She poured the hot water into her cup and sat at the table, inhaling the pungent aroma of the coffee. She couldn't ignore the signs. This was the third time in two weeks that her husband was "unavailable." Her elbows on the table, raised hands encircling the coffee mug, Mary felt a tightening in her chest. Her husband had found himself another whore.

Chapter 27

"Shit," Ed muttered as he listened to his voicemails inside his new silver Corvette—a fortieth birthday gift to himself. He could picture Mary's pinched face as she left her fifth message. "Where are you? Sean's been waiting over an hour for you to pick him up at the hockey rink."

On the drive from Cambridge to Belmont, Ed concocted and then rejected a number of excuses. He finally settled on one and telephoned his friend Larry.

"Larry, I need a favor."

"Shoot."

"I'm going to tell Mary I was with you tonight. That we played pool at McGinty's."

"Sure, what's up?"

"I was getting a piece of ass and forgot to pick up Sean at the rink."

Larry chuckled. "No problem. You owe me, though."

"Anytime."

With that settled, Ed pulled a cigarette from his jacket pocket and lit it with the car's lighter. He pulled into his driveway. The house was dark. Hopefully, everyone was asleep. With any luck, the confrontation with Mary wouldn't take place until the next morning.

Inside, he slipped off his shoes and crept up the stairs. The bedroom door was closed. Good sign. He eased it open, wincing at each squeak, and tiptoed toward the bathroom.

Suddenly, the room lit up. Startled, Ed turned toward the queen-size bed. Mary sat propped up, her arms folded tightly across her chest. “Where have you been?” she asked, her voice low but firm.

Beads of perspiration formed on Ed’s forehead. “With Larry at McGinty’s. I lost track of the time.”

Mary’s eyes narrowed; her eyebrow arched.

“What? You don’t believe me? Call Larry, he’ll tell you.”

“I did. Hours ago. His wife said he was home alone on the couch, watching a Bruins game.”

Ed’s face reddened.

Mary threw off the covers, slipped into her bathrobe, and headed toward the bathroom. Ed blocked her path, grabbing her by the shoulders. “His wife’s a fucking liar,” he growled, thrusting his phone toward her. “Here. Call Larry.”

Mary recoiled, trembling. “We can’t call him now. It’s two in the morning.”

“Why don’t you ever do as I say, bitch?” Ed felt the anger rising from his gut. No longer in control, he flung the phone across the room, lifted his hand, and slapped his wife hard in the face. Mary staggered backward, hitting the dresser. Before she could recover, he punched her in the stomach. Mary crumpled to the floor, her elbow slamming against the bed frame. Wide-eyed, she stared up at her husband, a look of shock and fear on her pale face.

Chapter 28

It was three weeks into the new year. He had laid low since the attack on the high school girl, waiting for the uproar to fade. No mention of the incident had appeared in the local press or on the nightly news for over a week.

He sat at the same table in the restaurant that he'd taken for the last few days. He knew it was her station. She glanced at him and grinned. "I'll be right with you."

His eyes followed her as she moved between two other tables, serving drinks and chatting with ease. He didn't mind waiting. It gave him more time to watch her. He closed the menu. He'd have his usual, a hamburger and extra crispy fries.

"Welcome to Smiley's," she said, placing a glass of water in front of him.

"I'll have the usual, Amanda."

"You remembered my name."

He had, but he wasn't about to tell her it was printed on her nametag. Instead, he smiled. "I'll take a coffee with that, as well. Make sure--."

"I know," she said. "Make sure it's piping hot."

He grinned, watching her as she bounced back toward the kitchen. She was perky. Perky was something he usually found tedious, but on Amanda, it worked. It suited her short athletic build.

She returned with the coffee and a small pitcher of milk. There were benefits to having the same waitress. Amanda knew he liked his coffee really hot and preferred milk to those tiny containers of whitener. A broad smile appeared on her angelic face. He wanted to touch her clear, perfect skin, kiss her full red lips, and run his fingers through her long blond hair.

"I'll be right back with your meal."

She bounded back towards the kitchen, hips swaying rhythmically from side to side. It wasn't a seductive walk. She was too innocent, too peppy for that. He imagined she'd been a cheerleader in high school. Yesterday, she told him she was in college. She wanted to be an elementary school teacher. That would be a perfect match for her personality. Her students would adore her—especially the little boys. Too bad she'd never get the chance to teach.

Amanda emerged from the kitchen carrying a platter. She set a plate down in front of him. "A burger with extra crispy fries."

"Perfect," he said, resisting the urge to add *just like you.*

He was glad he had come to Lexington to find his next angel. He noticed a number of young women who would fit the bill, so to speak. Plus, there was a cemetery not too far away on Bedford Street. He had passed by earlier and noticed a fresh grave being prepared for a burial the following day. Everything was falling into place.

"Can I top off your coffee?" Amanda asked, holding a pot.

"Thanks." He poured some milk into the freshly filled cup. "Do you have classes this afternoon?"

"No. Tonight's my late night. I work until eight."

"Do you drive yourself home?"

"I don't have a car. I walk home. I live pretty close."

"Eight o'clock… It's pretty dark at that time. Does your boyfriend walk with you?"

"I don't have a boyfriend. Between school and work, I don't really have time to date."

"Well, be careful. You never know what kind of crazies are out there, prowling around for someone like you."

"Maybe in Boston," she said with a laugh, "but Lexington is really safe."

He smirked as Amanda walked away. His questions were just to make conversation, just a way to reconfirm her schedule. He already knew she worked late tonight and that she'd be walking home alone. He had spent the last week stalking her. Stalking—such an unpleasant-sounding word. He preferred *getting to know her better* to *stalking.*

Amanda returned to place the check on the table. "Just pay this whenever you're ready. No rush. Oh," she continued, "the register's broken. We can only take cash."

He took his wallet out and checked. "I'm good." Then he leaned back in his chair and smiled. "I don't know what I'll do when you're gone."

"Don't worry," she said brightly. I'll be here a long time. I don't finish college for another two years."

Oh, Amanda, he thought. *So beautiful but so naïve. I'm afraid this will be your last day at Smiley's.*

Chapter 29

He waited for Amanda in a vacant lot on Forest Street, concealed from view behind a dense screen of shrubbery. It was just past 8:15 in the evening. Clouds masked the moon. No streetlight pierced the blackness. Dark and desolate. This was the perfect place to meet his angel.

After subduing Amanda, he would place her body in the white van parked just in front of the vacant lot. He would drive the few blocks to the rear entrance of the Westview Cemetery and carry his angel to the open grave. His backpack, filled with the necessary tools, was already in the van.

A dog yelped. He crouched lower. Through the branches, he spotted an elderly woman hobbling by.

"What's the matter, Precious?" she cooed, bending down to pick up a silky, long-haired Yorkie. She adjusted the pink bow on its head. "Is my little poopsie scared?"

Cradling the dog, she toddled past the lot. When she put it down, the Yorkie tugged at the leash, nose pointed toward the shrubbery. A low growl followed, then a burst of yelps. Pulling the dog behind her, the woman continued on and quickened her pace.

He removed his wool cap and used it to wipe the sweat from his brow. Dogs didn't like him. The feeling was mutual. Maybe he should use the garrote on Precious. A silly thought. The anticipation of Amanda's body beneath his stirred his senses. Reflecting on what would soon happen in his *underground love nest*—he preferred this designation to hollow grave—he felt his penis harden.

Headlights from an approaching car illuminated a figure on the sidewalk. Amanda moved toward him as if in slow motion. His heart beat rapidly. He could scarcely breathe.

He picked up the garrote lying beside him, pulled up his scarf to conceal his face, and repositioned his cap. The sound of her footsteps on the pavement grew louder. She walked by the vacant lot.

He sprang from behind the bushes. Coming up behind her, he wrapped the cord around his hands, slipped the garrote over her head, and pulled hard. Taken by surprise, Amanda had no time to react. She opened her mouth to scream but uttered no sound. After several minutes of struggling, her lifeless form fell back against his chest.

Suddenly, he heard voices down the street. Panicked, he dragged the body back behind the bushes. Too late, he noticed Amanda's pocketbook on the sidewalk.

A group of four teenagers sauntered into view. They stopped in front of the large black bag, its contents strewn on the sidewalk.

"What's this?" one of them asked.

A girl bent down and picked up the bag. She gathered a tube of lipstick, some dollar bills, and change from the sidewalk and put them back inside the purse.

"Looks like someone dropped it," she said.

"Strange," said a boy in a high school varsity jacket. "Wonder why she didn't pick it up."

"Maybe she was mugged."

Her friends laughed. "Sara the dramatic," one teased. "Maybe she was walking her dog and didn't notice."

"How could she not notice?" Sara shot back. "She would've heard the bag hit the ground. I think we should take it to the police."

"Sara's right," one of the boys said. He raised his hands and wiggled his fingers in a grotesque fashion. "There's a mugger lurking on the streets of Lexington."

The girls shrieked.

"Let's get out of here," Sara said. "Before he returns."

Laughter, screams, and nervous giggles accompanied the teens as they continued on their way. He waited until he could no longer hear them, then crept toward the road. After looking up and down the street, he unlocked the van and opened the rear doors. Returning to the bushes, he lifted Amanda's body and placed it gently inside. He had lined the floor of the van with a plastic sheet to prevent soiling the interior. Still, he'd take the van to be washed in the morning. He wanted no loose ends.

In the driver's seat, he removed his cap and used it once again to wipe the sweat from his brow. Damn those kids. If they hadn't come along, her handbag would be in the van with him now—not on its way to the police station.

Driving to the cemetery, he decided to forget about the slight glitch in his plans, focusing instead on the pleasures to come. In any event, even if the police did have her pocketbook, no one would ever find his angel in the grave, buried beneath a casket.

Chapter 30

Only two mourners stood at the gravesite when he arrived at the cemetery the following afternoon. He hesitated. Perhaps he should leave. He risked standing out in such a small group. One of the mourners, a frail elderly woman, supported by a cane on one side and a young man on the other, stared at the stranger. Too late, he thought. He would be more conspicuous leaving than staying.

Following the brief service, the old woman hobbled over to him as the young man held her arm. “I don’t recognize you. How did you know my brother?” she asked cocking her head to one side.

He removed his hat and ran his fingers through his hair, shifting uneasily. “I didn’t know him well, just casually. I came to pay my respects.”

“Thank you,” the young man said. “We appreciate your coming. My uncle didn’t have many friends, after—well, you know—the conviction.”

“I should be going,” the man said, backing away. “My deepest sympathies.”

Turning around, he hustled up the path toward the parking lot, not waiting to see the coffin lowered into the grave as he usually did. At home, he checked the paper to see whose funeral he had attended. He googled the name. The deceased, a 75-year-old man, was a convicted pedophile.

A chill ran through his body. His poor angel was buried beneath a child molester. He would have to be more careful in the future. He owed it to his women to screen those with whom they would spend all eternity.

Chapter 31

Fiona and Rick wasted no time getting to the Crime Scene Substation on Albany Street in Boston. They took the elevator to the second floor. “May I help you?” the receptionist asked.

“I’m Detective Garfinkel, and this is my colleague, Detective Sullivan. We called your office earlier this morning. We’re here to check out that handbag that was found last night in Lexington.”

“Please take a seat, and I’ll tell the officer in charge that you’re here.”

The two thanked the receptionist and sat down. After several minutes, a uniformed man appeared. “Hi,” he said, extending his hand. “I’m Officer Bradshaw. You’re here about the handbag those kids turned in last night, right?”

Rick nodded. “Yeah. We’ve had a couple of missing women cases in Belmont and just learned about this new one in Lexington. We’re hoping the purse will help us in the investigation.”

“Follow me,” the officer said, leading them down a dimly lit hallway. Inside a small room, Officer Bradshaw retrieved the handbag and placed it on a metal table.

“The handbag belongs to an Amanda Tierney, “he said. “She works at the Smiley’s on Bedford Street. She never showed up at the restaurant this morning for her shift.”

“You checked her home?” Rick asked.

“Yes. The superintendent let us into her apartment,” Bradshaw said. “It didn’t look like she slept there last night.”

“How about the area where the purse was found?” Fiona asked.

"The kids found the pocketbook on the sidewalk on Forest Street between Elm and Whitacre in front of a vacant lot. There were some broken-down bushes. No footprints. The ground was frozen hard."

Fiona eyed the bag. "Did the lab turn up anything?"

The officer shook his head. "No. The only prints on the bag were from the kids and the owner. It wasn't a robbery. The missing woman is a waitress. There were a lot of loose bills and coins still in the purse."

"Was there a cell phone?" Rick asked.

"Yes. We checked it out. So far, no unusual calls have been received or sent. The calls were primarily to her friends and family. We're still working on it, though."

"Keep us posted if anything turns up," Rick said.

"Will do."

Fiona pressed her lips together. "Mind if we take a look at the pocketbook?"

"Sure, go ahead," the officer said, moving to the side.

Rick and Fiona slipped on latex gloves and carefully examined the contents of the purse. Nothing they found inside provided any additional information about the missing woman.

Fiona turned to Bradshaw. "Would it be alright if we spoke with the kids who found the purse?"

"Of course. Wait here, and I'll get you their names and phone numbers." He returned in a few minutes with the information.

"Appreciate it," Rick said, as he and Fiona headed toward the elevator.

Chapter 32

In the car, Fiona suggested they check out the spot where the pocketbook had been found. But as they drove into downtown Lexington, she suddenly changed her mind. "There's the Smiley's where Amanda worked. Let's stop here first and see if we can find out anything."

Rick pulled into the parking lot. Inside, the restaurant buzzed with the late lunch crowd. Fiona approached the hostess stand, where a young woman with purple-streaked hair and a nose piercing greeted them. "Did you know Amanda?" Fiona asked.

"Just from work," the girl replied. "She was sweet. The customers liked her. She had a few regulars."

"Do you remember any of them?"

"I don't know their names. But there was this older couple. They'd come in about five o'clock, two or three times a week."

She paused, a pensive expression on her face. "Oh yeah. There was this guy who's been coming in for lunch for the past week. Amanda said he kept trying to talk to her. It made it hard for her to take care of her other tables."

Fiona pulled out her notepad. "Do you remember what he looked like?"

"He was tall—maybe 6 feet."

"Was he Caucasian?"

"Cau—what?"

"His race," Fiona clarified. "Was he white, African American, Hispanic?"

"White."

"Thin? Heavy?" Fiona asked.

"I don't remember exactly, but he didn't seem overweight."

"How old would you say he was?"

"Not young."

"Was he in his forties? Fifties?"

"Maybe forties," she said with a shrug. "I didn't really look at him that closely."

Fiona looked up from the notepad. "How about hair color?"

"He wore a wool cap when I seated him."

"And when he took it off?"

The hostess gave a tight smile. "Look, I just seat the customers. That's all I'm supposed to do. We're pretty busy here at lunchtime. I don't have time to check out their hair color."

Fiona sighed. "Anything else you can remember?"

The hostess rubbed her chin, thinking. "No," she said slowly. "Wait a minute, he liked his coffee really, really hot. One day, Amanda told me he sent it back three times because it wasn't hot enough. He told her he liked it 'piping hot'."

Rick stepped forward. "We'd like to check your cash register receipts."

The hostess scrunched up her face. "Why do you want the receipts?"

"In case he paid by credit card," Rick said.

"He didn't."

Rick tilted his head. “How do you know?”

The hostess pointed to a sign by the cash register. “It’s been cash-only the past couple of weeks. There’s something wrong with our register.” She lowered her voice. “The boss isn’t in a rush to fix it. Cash means more money in his pocket. And honestly, most customers haven’t complained.”

Fiona closed her notebook and put it back in her pocket. “Thanks, you’ve been very helpful.” She pulled out a card and handed it to the hostess. “If you remember anything else, or if the guy who likes his coffee ‘piping hot’ comes in again, please give us a call.”

After leaving the restaurant, Rick drove to where the pocketbook had been found. Fiona stayed in the car, finishing a phone call with one of the teenagers who had found the purse.

A few minutes later, she joined Rick on the sidewalk. “When we’re done here,” she said, “let’s head over to Best Buy at the Burlington Mall. One of the kids, Christopher Abrams, will see us in an hour.”

“Sounds good,” Rick replied from behind a cluster of bushes. “C’mer, I think this is where our kidnapper was hiding.”

Fiona examined the site. “Looks like he crouched here. There are a lot of broken branches.”

Rick examined the area from the sidewalk to the bushes. “From the way the shrubbery is chewed up here, he might’ve dragged the victim back behind this clump.”

Fiona studied the space between the sidewalk and the curb. “And then out again, back over the sidewalk and—to what? A vehicle parked about where our car is?”

Rick nodded. “I’m guessing the kids interrupted the attack. The perp pulled the victim back behind the bushes where he was probably hiding initially, waited for the kids to go by, and then loaded the woman into a vehicle.”

Fiona’s eyes narrowed as she visualized the scenario. “If that’s how it went down, he saw the kids pick up the purse. Maybe he even heard what they were going to do with it.”

“If he did hear something,” Rick said, “he’ll probably lay low. I doubt the hostess at Smiley’s is going to call us to say the guy who liked his coffee ‘piping hot’ just walked in.”

Chapter 33

After a few more minutes of checking the area, the detectives returned to their car and headed for Burlington Mall. At Best Buy, they waited until Christopher finished helping a customer.

Rick flashed his badge. "Detectives Garfinkel and Sullivan. We'd like to ask you a few questions about the purse you found."

"Sure," the young man said, slipping his hands into his pockets.

"Can you tell us where you found it?"

Christopher explained how he and three of his friends were walking down Forest Street the previous evening, when they found the bag and brought it to the Lexington police station.

"Thanks for doing the right thing," Fiona said. "Did you and your friends discuss what to do with the handbag when you found it, or did you decide to turn it in after you left that location?"

"We decided to turn it in right away."

"So, if someone, let's say, was hiding in the bushes nearby, he could've heard you talk about taking it to the police?"

Christopher nodded.

Fiona jotted down some notes. "Were there any vehicles parked in front of the lot?"

"Yes, there was a van, a light-colored one…white or gray… can't remember. It was parked by the sidewalk."

"Do you know the make?"

"No. I really didn't get a good look at it. Maybe one of my friends did."

Rick handed his card to Christopher. “Can you give us their names and phone numbers?”

“Sure,” Christopher said, taking the card. “By the way, did the police return the bag to the woman?”

“Not yet,” Fiona replied, looking away.

Chapter 34

January in Boston was dreary and cold. Christmas trees lay abandoned on curbs awaiting pickup, their former splendor reduced to a few strands of tinsel clinging tenaciously to withered branches. Fiona trudged along Stuart Street, pulling her charcoal cap down over her ears. Mickey's sister Julia had invited Fiona to have lunch with her and her sister-in-law, Mary. They wanted to get to know Mickey's girlfriend better.

Fiona regretted not wearing earmuffs. The frigid air penetrated her woolen coat and fleece-lined boots. Pushing against the piercing wind, she was relieved to see the Legal Seafood sign—a welcome refuge from the bitter cold.

Inside, the hostess led her to a booth where Julia and Mary were already seated. Fiona removed her coat, greeted the women, and slid in next to Julia.

"Your cheeks are like ice," Julia said, placing her palm against Fiona's crimson face.

Fiona rubbed her hands together. "My fingers are even colder. I can barely feel them."

She turned to Mary, surprised to see her left arm in a cast cradled by a sling around her neck. "Mary, what happened?"

Mary shifted in her seat. Her hand shook as she pushed back her hair. "I fell outside the house. I slipped on the ice and broke my arm."

Fiona narrowed her eyes, a flicker of disbelief crossing her face.

"That's how it happened, really," Mary insisted. "I was lucky Eddie was home. He drove me to the ER."

Just then, a waitress approached their table. “Have you decided what you’d like?”

After ordering, Fiona found herself staring at Mary, only half-listening to Julia jabbering on about the fantastic New Year’s Eve party she’d missed. Mickey had invited her, but Fiona had decided to usher in the New Year with her parents in North Andover. Her mother was still struggling to accept the possibility that her daughter’s alleged killer might be innocent.

“Fiona, you haven’t heard a word I said,” Julia said, her tone tinged with annoyance.

Fiona’s eyes flitted from Mary to Julia. “I’m sorry. I’ve been waiting for Mary to tell us what really happened.”

Julia frowned. “But she did. She fell on the ice in front of her house. That’s what happened, isn’t it, Mary?”

Mary looked from one woman to the other. Her eyes filled with tears, and her lower lip quivered. Fiona moved to Mary’s side of the booth and put her arm around her shoulders.

“Please,” she said softly, “Tell us what really happened. I can help you.”

Mary covered her face with her good hand and sobbed. Fiona continued to hug the distraught woman. Julia sat and stared, a stunned expression on her face.

Reaching into her purse, Fiona pulled out a tissue and gave it to Mary. Out of the corner of her eye, she noticed the waitress standing nearby, unsure whether to interrupt. At neighboring tables, diners had paused mid-meal, their attention drawn to the emotional scene unfolding in the booth.

Mary blew her nose and dabbed at her eyes with a trembling hand. "I'm so sorry," she murmured, catching the curious glances from nearby diners. "I didn't mean to make a scene."

"Mary, please tell me what happened," Fiona said. "Believe me, it will only get worse. I've seen this before."

Mary sat in silence; hands clasped tightly in her lap. Tears glided down the crevices of her thin face. The waitress brought the lunches over to the table, setting plates down gently, sensing the tension. None of the three women made a move to eat.

"You mean you didn't fall on the ice?" Julia asked, her brow furrowed.

With a resigned expression on her face, Mary shook her head. "I wasn't even outside. I was in the bedroom."

Fiona's voice dropped to a whisper. "Did Ed do this to you?"

Mary nodded, eyes downcast.

Julia's jaw dropped. "My brother?"

"This isn't the first time, is it?" Fiona remarked. She knew she was in drill mode but didn't really care.

Mary hesitated before she spoke. "No. It's been going on for years. But that night, he was especially vicious. After he broke my arm, he burned my back with his cigarette."

Julia's eyes opened wider. "Ed did this to you? I can't believe it."

Ignoring Julia, Fiona turned to Mary. "What triggered the attack?"

Once again, Mary hesitated before answering, her voice barely audible. "I think he's seeing someone else. He didn't come home that night until two in the morning. When I wouldn't believe where he said he was, he…he just snapped."

Fiona watched as Mary wiped the tears from her face with the edge of her napkin. "It was my fault, Mary whispered. "I shouldn't have said anything. But I don't know what to do anymore. I'm so afraid."

Julia shook her head. "I'm so sorry, Mary. Do you think that if I get my dad involved, it'll help?"

Mary's eyes widened in alarm. "Please don't. If Eddie finds out I've told anyone, he'll kill me."

"There are a number of shelters for battered women," Fiona said. "I suggest you take the children and go to one of them."

"I don't want to uproot their lives," Mary said, shaking her head. "They've already been through so much."

"Then what about a restraining order?" Fiona asked.

Mary looked down. "Eddie would be furious. I don't think it would help. He'd probably just ignore it."

"Then he'd risk going to jail."

"I can't let that happen. The children… they need their father."

Fiona leaned closer to the distraught woman her voice steady. "Mary, this is serious. These attacks won't stop on their own. If you won't act now, promise me next time—and there will be a next time—call me. Or call 911."

She reached into her purse and handed Mary a business card. "Please. Don't wait until it's too late."

Chapter 35

Later that day, back at the office, Fiona studied the murder board she had assembled. Her fingertips touched the first photo—Ciara. Her eyes grew misty. She remembered when Ciara's boyfriend had taken the picture. They were helping her sister move into her dorm at B.U. for the start of her sophomore year. It had been a gorgeous September day.

Fiona closed her eyes, letting the memory wash over her. She used to love early fall. For her, this was the best time of year in Boston. Windows were opened, allowing cool breezes to dissipate summer's musty odors. Trees displayed foliage of a deep emerald green, a last hurrah before morphing into autumnal hues. Fresh-picked apples greeted customers in bins outside grocery stores. Students engaged in animated conversations with friends not seen since spring. Until Ciara's death, Fiona eagerly awaited fall. Now it was tainted by the memory of her sister's murder.

Her gaze moved down the board. Lined up after Ciara's photo were the faces of five other victims:

- Karen O'Sullivan, 23, Boston
- Maureen Kelly, 28, Cambridge
- Deirdre Walsh, 25 Cambridge
- Peggy Connolly, 24, Boston
- Caroline Lynch, 26, Cambridge

A ten-year gap separated these women from the next cluster of victims: Maureen Doyle, Minnie Brennan, and Amanda Tierney.

"Any connection?" Rick asked, handing Fiona a cup of coffee.

"Thanks," she said, taking the cup. "Other than the obvious—young, pretty, Irish descent—nothing ties them together. In all but one of the earlier cases, the killer raped the victim. According to the pathologist, the rapes occurred after they were killed. So yeah...we're likely dealing with a necrophiliac."

She took a sip of her coffee. "His M.O. for the first six was the same. He waited for them near vacant lots or parks late at night, then stabbed them to death. With the exception of Peggy Connelly, they were all raped."

Rick studied the board. "Someone might have interrupted the attack on Connelly, and he took off."

"Makes sense. But we don't know any more about the murders than we did before the Winfield trial. We're still looking for a serial killer who murders and then rapes young, attractive women of Irish descent."

"The chief isn't one hundred percent convinced that the same person is responsible for both sets of attacks," Rick said. "You have to admit there are some major differences."

"Like what?" Fiona asked.

"The weapon, for starters. He stabbed his first victims to death and left them where they fell. We don't know how he killed, or even if he killed, the two missing women. He tried to strangle Minnie with what sounds like a garrote. No knife. No stabbing. What makes you so convinced that it was the same guy?"

Fiona's jaw tightened. "He's operating in the same general geographical area. His assaults are all carefully planned. He knows the routines of the women he targets. The attacks are always in a deserted place—a vacant lot, a park, a cemetery. Plus, to not raise suspicions about Winfield's alleged guilt, he'd probably make some changes—such as a garrote instead of a knife."

"It would help if we had the bodies."

"They'll turn up," Fiona said confidently. "They always do.

Chapter 36

The weekly poker game had shifted venues—from the Foley's to the Wysocki's house next door. When Mickey and Fiona arrived, the rest of the group—Joe, Leonid, Ed, and Denny—were already gathered around the table.

Dressed in a purple pantsuit, clearly purchased when she was several sizes smaller, Angela Wysocki brought chips and dip to the table. She leaned close to Mickey. "What can I get you to drink?"

"Coffee would be great. I need to stay awake tonight." He cast a sideward glance at Fiona. "The competition's gotten tougher."

Angela turned to Fiona, her tone noticeably cooler. "And you?"

"I'll have the same. Thanks."

By the time Angela returned with two steaming mugs, Denny had distributed the chips and shuffled the deck. "Okay, everyone, time to ante up."

The players tossed in their chips. Denny dealt two cards to each. Fiona glanced at her hand: jack of clubs, queen of hearts.

"Do you remember how to play?" Ed asked Fiona.

"I think so," she answered, sounding not quite convinced.

"If you have any questions, just ask," Joe offered.

Ed smirked and nudged Denny. Fiona kept her eyes on her cards, pretending to concentrate.

Denny discarded three cards and turned over the next three: a two of clubs, an eight of diamonds, and a ten of spades. A wide smile on her face, Fiona upped the ante by a dollar.

"You sure you want to do that?" Denny asked.

"I've got a pretty good hand," Fiona said confidently.

Ed rolled his eyes. "So much for a poker face."

"Shouldn't I have said that?" Fiona asked.

Mickey frowned. "C'mon, guys, give her a break."

After a few more rounds of betting, only Fiona and Leonid remained in the game. Denny turned over the final card. Fiona put one chip into the pot. Leonid saw her bid and slid his remaining chips into the center of the table. All eyes were on Fiona.

"Now what?" Fiona asked Mickey.

"If you have a good hand and want to stay in the game, you need to go all in or Leonid wins the pot."

Fiona bit her lower lip and slowly pushed her remaining chips forward.

"Pair of nines and a pair of sixes," Leonid said, revealing his hand.

Fiona shifted in her seat. "I don't really have anything. I was just bluffing."

"Let's see your cards," Mickey said.

When Fiona turned over her cards, Leonid's jaw dropped. Mickey's eyes lit up. He arranged her cards around the ten on the table. "You have a straight. Eight, nine, ten, jack, queen."

"Is that good?"

"Yes. A straight beats two pairs. You win the pot."

Leonid sat back in his chair and folded his arms across his chest. Through narrowed eyes, he glared at Fiona. She opened her arms wide and pulled the chips onto her side of the table, thrilled to have taught Ed and Denny a lesson again.

Ed sneered. "Yeah, like you didn't know you had a straight."

Fiona smiled sweetly at him. One person at the table was finally onto her.

Denny handed the cards to Mickey, the new dealer. After he shuffled them, he paused to take a sip of his coffee. He grimaced.

"What's the matter?" Denny asked.

"The coffee is cold. Guess I let it sit too long."

Denny leaned back in his chair. "Hey Angie!"

Angela appeared from the back of the house. "What's the matter?"

"Mickey's coffee's cold."

She shuffled over to Mickey and whacked him playfully on the back of his head. "So, why'd you wait so long to drink it?"

Mickey shifted in his seat. "Sorry, but I like my coffee piping hot."

Fiona looked up abruptly from stacking her chips. She turned sideways and studied Mickey's face.

Angela grabbed the cup. "I'll zap it for you, but this time, drink it before it turns into iced coffee."

Chapter 37

On the drive back to Fiona's, Mickey brought up the poker game. "You're taking us to the cleaners," he said with a grin. "Honestly, I thought it would be worse after that first haul."

Fiona stared out the window, Mickey's "piping hot" comment still echoing in her head. "I was having trouble concentrating."

"What's the matter?"

"Nothing really."

They rode in silence until Mickey pulled up to Fiona's house. He shifted in his seat. "So… am I coming up?"

"Not tonight. I have to get up early tomorrow. Next time."

Mickey raised an eyebrow. "Tomorrow's Saturday."

"I'm working this weekend," Fiona said quickly. Her face turned bright red, as it always did when she lied.

Mickey pulled Fiona toward him and tried to kiss her. She turned her head.

"What's the matter?" Mickey asked.

"Have you eaten at a Smiley's in Lexington lately?"

"I don't think so," Mickey said. "I had to go to our Lexington office a few times, but I don't remember eating at a Smiley's. Why?"

"No reason. My partner thought he saw you there last week."

"Last week? It definitely wasn't me. I haven't been in Lexington for at least a month."

Fiona looked relieved. *I guess more than one person can prefer their coffee "piping hot"*, she thought.

Chapter 38

Fiona fed Jasmine, then took her for a short walk before heading to bed. She had just dozed off when the phone rang. 11:42 p.m. *Who could be calling at this hour?*

Picking up the receiver, she heard Mary's panicked voice. "Please help me. I'm afraid Eddie's going to kill me."

"I'll send a patrol car right away." Fiona hung up and dialed the Belmont police.

By the time she arrived, two patrol cars were already parked in front of Mary's gray clapboard house. Attracted by the sirens and flashing red lights, neighbors and passersby watched from the sidewalk.

Fiona squeezed her car into a tight spot and hurried up the porch steps, taking them two at a time. Inside, Mary sat on the couch in the front room next to an officer who was jotting down notes. Ed glared at Fiona from the hallway. He stood between two officers, his hands manacled behind him. Watching from the top of the stairway, Mary's son and daughter stood in their nightclothes, their faces ashen. Sean had his arm protectively around his younger sister. Emily's face was streaked with tears, her lips trembling.

Fiona turned to the officer beside Ed. "Everything under control here, Mark?" Mark nodded.

Ed's eyes narrowed. "So, you're the one who called the cops." He lowered his voice and spoke between clenched teeth. "What goes on in this house is none of your fucking business, cunt."

Mark cuffed the back of Ed's head. "Hey, watch your mouth. You're talking to an officer."

Sean led his sister down the stairs. As they passed their father, Sean's eyes narrowed, his lips pressed into a hard line. Emily kept her head down and scooted as far away from Ed as possible—away from the man who had just beaten her mother.

Mark and his partner shoved Ed toward the door. "We're taking him down to headquarters and booking him," Mark said.

"I'll be down as soon as everything's settled here," Fiona replied.

"You'd better watch yourself, girlie," Ed snarled as he passed her. "You'll regret this."

The two officers pushed Ed outside onto the porch. The sound of the door closing behind them caused Mary to look up. She smiled at Fiona through missing teeth. What a sad family portrait, Fiona thought. Mary, her face bruised and battered, sat next to her eleven-year-old daughter, whose head rested against her shoulder. On the other side was Mary's thirteen-year-old son, arms folded across his chest, face twisted in silent rage.

The officer questioning Mary stood up. "I'm done here," he said to Fiona. "You can talk to her now."

"Thanks, Bobby." Fiona took a seat on the couch next to Mary. Close up, her wounds looked worse. In addition to the missing teeth, Mary's nose appeared to be broken.

Fiona took Mary's trembling hands in hers. "You need to go to the hospital." She glanced at the children. "Is there anyone who could stay with Emily and Sean?"

Emily sat up and looked at her mother. "Could we stay with Nana?"

"Is that okay with you, Sean?" Mary asked. Her son nodded.

She turned to Fiona. “My mother lives in Newton Highlands. It’s not too far from here.”

Fiona gave Mary’s hands a reassuring squeeze. “If you give me your mom’s number, I’ll call to let her know we’re on the way.”

***

It was 11 p.m. when Fiona pulled up to the emergency room at Mount Auburn Hospital in Cambridge. They had stayed at Mary’s mother’s home until the children were settled. Horrified when she saw her daughter’s battered face, Mary’s mother confessed to Fiona after Emily and Sean were in bed that she was not surprised. Even though Mary had remained silent on the subject, she had seen enough to know Ed was an abusive husband.

Fiona waited with Mary until she was admitted, and a nurse took her through the security doors. There was nothing more she could do tonight.

Chapter 39

Early the following morning, Fiona drove to Newton Highlands with Julia in tow. She'd debated whether to bring her, but ultimately decided someone from the family needed to see what Ed had done to his wife.

At Mary's mother's house, Fiona rang the doorbell. No one answered. Fiona knocked on the door. She noticed someone peering at them from behind lace curtains.

"Mary, please let me in. It's Fiona."

"Who's with you?" a voice asked.

"Julia."

"Anyone else?"

"No."

Fiona heard the sound of multiple locks being opened. Mary's face looked worse than the previous night. Julia gasped at the sight of her sister-in-law, both eyes blackened, welts on her cheeks, nose set in an odd contraption, front teeth missing. Once inside, she hugged Mary. "Did Ed do this to you?"

Mary nodded. Her mother stood beside her. "Please come sit down," she said, motioning toward the living room.

"What happened?" Julia asked once everyone was seated.

Mary looked at her mother, who nodded, encouraging her to tell her story. "I was going through the bills we had, and I noticed Eddie bought an expensive diamond bracelet last month. My birthday's not for another six months, our anniversary had just passed, so I knew it wasn't a gift for me."

Mary pulled a tissue from her pocket and wiped her eyes. “After the kids had gone to bed, I asked Eddie about the purchase. He got angry and accused me of spying on him. I told him I had the right to know if he was cheating on me. That’s when he asked what I would do if he were seeing someone else. I told him I’d leave and take the children with me. He started yelling at me, screaming, ‘No, you won’t, bitch.’ I went upstairs to the bedroom, pulled my suitcase from the closet, and started packing.”

Mary was silent for a moment. A pained look crossed her bruised face as she opened her mouth to continue. “He walked over to me and threw the suitcase off the bed. Then he started beating me, punching me in the face. I guess my screaming woke up the kids. Their knocking on the door probably saved my life. While Ed went to deal with them, I ran into the bathroom with my purse and locked the door. I didn’t know what to do. I was so afraid Ed would take his anger out on the children. Fortunately, my cell phone was in my purse. That’s when I called Fiona.”

Julia, who sat next to Mary, put her arm around her shoulder. She hugged her tightly. “I’m so sorry. I can’t believe my brother would do something like this.”

“What do you plan on doing?” Fiona asked.

Mary looked down her voice barely audible. “I don’t know. I’m afraid. I don’t even want to think about what he’ll do to me when he finds me.”

“Is he in jail?” Mary’s mother asked.

Fiona pulled her phone from her pocket. “He was this morning. Let me check if he’s still there.”

Following a brief conversation with headquarters, Fiona turned to Mary. “He’ll be arraigned this afternoon. The officer-in-charge told me his father plans to bail him out as soon as the judge sets the amount."

Mary trembled. "He'll come here after me. I know he will."

"You need to contact an attorney and get a restraining order," Fiona said firmly.

"What good will that do?" her mother asked.

"A restraining order will prevent him from getting close to your daughter. If Ed violates the order, he can be jailed."

Mary rubbed her hands together anxiously. "What about my children?"

"Your attorney can take steps to ensure he stays away from them, too."

Mary's voice dropped to a whisper. "He has guns. If he gets drunk, he'll come after us."

"I'll make sure you and the kids are safe," Fiona said.

Mary shook her head, concern on her face. She looked as if she doubted that anyone could protect her from Ed's wrath.

"Do you need the name of an attorney?" Fiona asked.

"I spoke to an attorney the last time Eddie beat me," Mary said softly. "She suggested a restraining order just like you did, but I chickened out."

"In the meantime," Fiona said. "I think you and the children should stay at one of the shelters for abused women."

Mary looked at her mother. "But the kids are so comfortable here. I don't want to take them to a shelter."

"You know the risks," Fiona said. "At a shelter, you would be safer."

Mary stuck out her chin defiantly. "I'm staying here. My children will be better off in their Nana's home."

Chapter 40

Ed Foley paced the 6x8 holding cell at the Nashua Street jail. Where the hell was his father? He'd been stuck in this fucking hellhole the whole night. It had been over eight hours since he had contacted his father to post bail. He sat down on the edge of a long bench and punched his closed fist repeatedly into the palm of his other hand. He badly needed a cigarette.

His mind replayed the events of the previous night. Who the hell did that cunt detective think she was? What happened in *his* house was *his* business. Maybe he was a bit rougher on Mary than he should have been, but Fiona—or whatever the hell her name was—had no business sending in the cops. Once he got out, he'd teach her and his bitch wife a lesson they wouldn't forget.

Ed stood and began pacing again. He kicked the tray of untouched breakfast food lying by the cell door. How did they expect him to eat that crap? He had tried, but the gruel was thick and lumpy. He peered through the bars. Where the hell was his father?

***

After he'd received the 2 a.m. call from his son from jail, Joe Foley called a friend who was an attorney. The lawyer advised posting bail. The court system was so backed up that it would be unlikely that his case would go to trial, especially if Mary didn't press charges. The whole thing might disappear within a year, unless Ed was to get into trouble again. Then both the first charge and the second would be considered.

Joe's next call was to the jail. The police had contacted the clerk magistrate, and bail had been set at $20,000—the standard amount for a felony domestic violence case. To secure Ed's release, he'd need to put up ten percent of the bail. Joe checked his bank account: $900. Most of what he earned working at Sears, plus the rent from his tenant, went toward paying for his mother's nursing home. He didn't want to borrow against his house. He finally owned it free and clear.

Picking up the phone, he decided to call his kids. If they all chipped in, Ed could be out by the afternoon.

Chapter 41

Julia, Mickey, and Owen sat at the dining room table as Joe told them he needed money to pay Ed's bail. "I hate to ask you, but if I can't get you to help, I'm going to have to refinance the house. And damn it," he said, shaking his head," I just paid the mortgage off."

Owen stood and slipped on the jacket that had been draped over the back of his chair. "Sorry, Dad. That's not good enough for me. Maybe jail time will make him treat his wife better."

Joe lowered his head as Owen strode to the door. "Don't get up, Dad. I'll let myself out."

The three remaining family members sat in silence as the front door slammed shut. Joe finally spoke. "Look, if you kids don't want to help your brother, I'll take out a mortgage on the house. I'll do whatever's necessary to bail Ed out."

Julia, seated beside her father, placed her hand gently over his. "I'll help you, but just so you know, this is for you, not for Ed. It's going to take Mary months to recover from what he did to her."

Mickey pulled out his checkbook. "I'll help, too," he said. "I know how hard you worked to pay off your mortgage. I don't want you taking out a new one."

Joe smiled at both of them. "Thanks."

"How much do you need?" Julia asked, pulling her checkbook from her purse.

"With the cost of Granny's nursing home, I can only put in six hundred dollars. If you could each give me seven hundred, that would do it. I'll try to give you some money back when I get paid next week."

"You don't need to reimburse me," Julia said to her father, handing him the check.

"Me neither," Mickey added, sliding his check across the table. "Only tell Ed I'd better be getting one hell of a birthday present this year."

Chapter 42

Mahoney pulled down the shade in his office. Returning to his desk, he sat down, grabbed a cloth wipe from a drawer, and cleaned his glasses. He held up the spectacles to the overhead light and checked the lenses. Satisfied, he slipped them on, folded his hands, and fixed his gaze on the two detectives seated in front of him.

"Fiona, fill me in on this domestic violence case."

"Mary Foley called me at 11:42 p.m. Friday, asking for help. She was afraid her husband was going to kill her. I contacted the station and asked them to dispatch a patrol car. When I arrived, Mary was talking to an officer about what had happened. Two others had subdued and cuffed her husband, Ed Foley."

"Why did —," Mahoney opened the file in front of him to see the name. "Mary Foley call you?"

Fiona squirmed in her seat. "She's a friend of mine. I'm dating her brother."

Mahoney leaned forward and narrowed his eyes. "Was everything handled properly?"

"By the book, sir," Fiona said. "Every step."

"Where is the husband now?"

"His family posted bail for him Saturday afternoon. I imagine he's home."

"And his wife?"

"His wife and kids are staying with her mother in Newton Highlands. Mrs. Foley filed a restraining order." Fiona decided not to mention that it took her and Mary's mother working together, nearly all day Saturday, to convince her to file the injunction.

Mahoney closed the file and opened another folder. He removed his glasses and looked at the detectives. "There's been another burglary," he said. "This time, while the family was attending their mother's wake."

Startled, Fiona looked up, eyes wide. "You're kidding. I had flyers distributed. I even ran a notice in the local paper warning people not to leave their homes empty."

"Apparently, it didn't work," Mahoney said flatly.

Fiona frowned, frustrated by the wasted effort. "So, what now?"

"I'm getting a lot of heat about the robberies from the mayor's office. Since the victims are ignoring our warnings, we need to ratchet this up a level."

"A stakeout?" Rick asked.

Mahoney nodded. "Let's give it a try."

Chapter 43

Rick reached into the back seat of the unmarked patrol car and pulled out a thermos. "More coffee?"

Fiona held out her cup. "What time is it?"

"About eight-thirty."

"The wake's over in about an hour. Looks like another wasted evening."

They sat parked across the street from a modest two-family home, where an elderly widow had recently passed away. The daughter and her family lived on the second floor of the house. An obituary had been placed in the paper naming the deceased, her address, and the hours of the wake at a local funeral home. The house was dark except for a dim front porch light.

For the past week, Rick and Fiona had staked out homes left empty during funerals. On three of the five nights, two other unmarked cars had joined them, monitoring similar locations based on published obituaries. But with resources stretched thin, the police chief had pulled the extra units.

Rick rubbed his eyes. Suddenly, he jumped up, almost spilling his coffee. "Check out the back windows of the house. I think I saw a flashlight beam."

Fiona followed his gaze. "You're right."

She put her drink into the cupholder between their seats, then checked for the gun inside her pocket. "I'm ready. Let's move."

They got out of the car and crossed the street, taking advantage of dark shadows and shrubbery for cover to reach the back of the house. The porch steps creaked as they made their way to the back door. A glass pane of the partially open door had been shattered. Guns raised, Rick and Fiona slipped inside the house and into the kitchen.

Platters of food covered the countertops and kitchen table, prepared for the mourners who would be returning to the house after the funeral. Guided by the narrow beam of a prowler's flashlight, Rick pointed toward the front room visible through the butler's pantry. Fiona tiptoed across the kitchen and slipped through a side door into a hallway leading to the dining room. At the same time, Rick moved through the butler's pantry.

Fiona froze. Light from the full moon streaming through the dining room window revealed a large dark form about twenty feet in front of her. Face covered by a ski mask, the prowler was emptying the contents of a sideboard drawer into a sack. Fiona could also make out a second figure in the living room, unhooking the TV.

Suddenly, a loud thud echoed from the butler's pantry. Both thieves turned toward the sound. Fiona ducked back into the kitchen.

"Police, freeze," Rick shouted. A shot rang out from the living room. The thieves grabbed their satchels and bolted out the front door. Fiona rushed into the hallway, but she was too late—they were gone. She started to chase after them, but stopped when she heard a moan from the pantry. Rick lay on the floor, blood spewing from a wound in his thigh.

"You're hit," she said, dropping to her knees beside him.

"Nice going, Sherlock."

"Are you okay?" Fiona asked.

"Yeah. I'll survive. Go after those bastards."

"And leave you here alone? Not happening." Fiona pulled out her phone. "This is Sullivan. Need back-up. We've got a 10-30 at 260 Abbot Way. Officer down. Send a bus. I repeat, officer down."

She raced to the front porch and looked up and down the street. There was no sign of the intruders. Back inside, she grabbed a throw pillow from the living room sofa and placed it under Rick's head. She dampened a paper towel in the kitchen and swabbed Rick's leg wound.

"How's your leg?"

Rick winced. "Hurts like hell, but I'll be okay."

"What happened?"

Rick gestured toward a nearby object. "I tripped over that damn step ladder."

His broad frame filled the narrow butler's pantry. Like the kitchen, the countertop was cluttered with food containers. Fiona folded the stepladder and moved it out of the way. Someone had probably been using it to remove dishes from the upper cupboards. She peeked into the dining room. Plates, glasses, and silverware covered half the table; the other half awaited the platters from the kitchen. Unfortunately, since the room was now part of a crime scene, no one would be eating in this house tonight.

Fiona knelt beside Rick again. "How are you holding up?"

"I'm okay," he said through gritted teeth. Go get those bastards."

"They're gone. I'll stay with you until the ambulance gets here. Want me to call Jeanne?"

Rick shook his head. "No. She'll only worry. I'll call her from the hospital."

Moments later, red lights flashed as two patrol cars and an ambulance pulled up in front of the house. Fiona guided the medics to Rick. She quickly briefed the officers, instructing them to canvass the area for the two suspects—armed and likely on foot.

After the medics took Rick out on a gurney to the ambulance, Fiona ran yellow tape around the front and back porches. Two additional patrolmen arrived, dusted the house for fingerprints, and searched for any clues that might have been left behind.

On the back porch, Fiona spotted a cigarette butt—black with a gold foil. A Sobranie Black Russian. She placed it in a plastic evidence bag. She'd send it to the lab to see if any DNA could be found on the butt. She suspected there would be a match with the DNA taken from the cigarette found at the Apostulos break-in.

Back in the car, Fiona called the hospital to check on Rick. He was in surgery to remove the bullet from his thigh. She'd go see him after she turned in her report of the break-in at the station. On an impulse, she drove past the Foley house. The blinds were up, and a TV was on in the lower unit. She could see the back of a man's head, probably Joe's, watching from the couch. The second-floor windows were dark. But hidden behind a curtain, someone watched as her car made its way down the street.

Chapter 44

The February wind whipped across the hospital parking lot as Fiona stepped out of her car to visit Rick. She clutched the bouquet of flowers tightly to her chest. Overhead, a gold and blue "Get Well" balloon jerked violently in the gusts, its ribbon straining. She quickened her pace, eyes looking upward, willing the balloon not to break free.

Inside, she set the flowers and the balloon on the admissions counter. Unwinding her plaid wool scarf, she pulled off her hat and gloves, fingers stiff from the cold. The receptionist glanced up.

"I'm here to see Rick Garfinkel."

The receptionist ran her finger up and down a list of names. "When was he admitted?"

"Last night. He had surgery. His wife said he's out of recovery and in his room, so it's okay to visit."

"Could you spell that name?"

Fiona held back her frustration. She resisted the urge to say that it was spelled exactly like it sounded. Instead, she replied evenly, "G as in George, A as in Ann, R as in Ralph, F as in--."

"Found him," the receptionist interrupted as the line of waiting visitors grew. "He's on the second floor. I'll need to see some ID."

Fiona pulled her police ID from her pocket and handed it to the woman.

The woman raised an eyebrow. "You're with the police, too?"

"Yes."

A hush fell over the people waiting behind Fiona—no doubt hoping to hear the lurid details of a crime.

"Here's your sticker. It's good for the day."

Fiona took the sticker from the woman and pressed it onto her jacket. She picked up the flowers, the balloon bobbing cheerfully above, and headed toward the elevator.

Although the door to the room was open, Fiona knocked. A tall, slender woman set aside her knitting and rose from the chair beside Rick's bed.

"Hi Jeanne," Fiona said, handing her the flowers and balloon. "How's our patient?"

She heard a familiar growl from the bed. "If I weren't hooked up to all these machines, I'd be back at work already."

Fiona looked at her fallen giant, right leg wrapped in bandages, arms tethered to IV lines. "You don't look ready to go."

"Looks can be deceiving," Rick muttered.

"How's the leg?"

Jeanne, who had resumed her post at her husband's side, turned to Fiona. "Rick will tell you everything is okay, but it's not."

Rick opened his mouth to protest, but Jeanne's voice rose above his as she continued. "The operation went well. The surgeon managed to clean out the bone and bullet fragments, but the fracture impacted the knee joint. It's possible Rick will need a knee replacement."

Rick gave a snort that translated said his wound wasn't as severe as his wife indicated.

"How long will he be laid up?" Fiona asked Jeanne.

"Several months at a minimum. But then he'll need physical therapy."

Fiona smiled sympathetically at her partner. "Looks like I'll be riding solo for a while."

"I heal fast. I'll be back in no time. Besides, I have a debt to settle." Rick grimaced as he shifted in the bed. "Any word on the thieves?"

"Not yet. But the DNA on the cigarette butt I found on the back porch matched the one we picked up at the Apostulos break-in. Looks like we're dealing with the same guys."

"No surprise there," Rick muttered.

Jeanne rose from her chair, walked over to the bed, and patted her husband's arm. "Since Fiona's here, I'm going to grab something from the cafeteria downstairs. I haven't had lunch yet. I also want to check on the kids and make sure your sister can stay the rest of the afternoon."

"Go ahead," Fiona said. "I'll stick around till you get back."

After Jeanne left, Fiona settled into the vacated chair. Rick's upbeat expression faded, replaced by a downturned mouth.

"What's the matter?" she asked.

"Jeanne wants me to ask Mahoney for a desk job. She freaked out when she heard I was shot—even after I told her it was just a leg wound."

"What do you want to do?" Fiona asked.

"I don't know," he sighed. "She told me her worst nightmare is getting a call in the middle of the night to tell her I've been hurt…or worse."

"You can't blame her," Fiona said. "It's got to be tough married to a cop—especially with kids in the picture."

"I'll be stuck at the station anyway. At least until my leg heals."

"Who knows? You might end up liking it."

"I won't," Rick said flatly. "I joined the force to avoid sitting behind a desk."

He turned his gaze away. Fiona reached out and took his hand. "I'll miss my partner."

Chapter 45

Although Mickey and Fiona saw each other two to three times a week, their relationship remained strictly platonic. Mickey pressed for more, but Fiona was reluctant to take the relationship further after her role in his brother's imprisonment.

On a Friday evening in mid-February, Fiona checked her image in the full-length bedroom mirror. It was poker night. She initially told Mickey she couldn't make it—Ed might be there. But after several calls from Joe, she relented. Besides, without the Foleys, her social life was nonexistent. Always somewhat of a loner, especially after Ciara's death, her evenings were either spent at karate class or curled up by the fireplace with a book.

The doorbell rang. Jasmine sprang into action, barking furiously. Fiona grabbed her purse, patted the dog on her head, and went downstairs to greet Mickey.

"Hi," he said, kissing her lightly on the cheek. "You look ready for action."

"I'm rarin' to go."

He held her arm as they walked down the front steps. There was a time when she would have pulled away. But tonight, she rather enjoyed being treated like a lady.

"Are we playing at your dad's or Denny's?"

"My dad's."

"Who'll be there?"

"I'm not sure. Probably the usual guys…" He winked at Fiona, "and gal."

Fiona preferred Joe's place. She was uncomfortable at Denny's house. His wife was barely civil to her. Did she think she was interested in her husband?

As they drove down Christian Way, Fiona spotted a white van parked in the Foleys' driveway. "Is that your father's van?" Fiona asked as Mickey pulled up in front of the house.

He looked in the direction Fiona indicated. "No, that's Angela's."

"What's it doing in your father's driveway?"

"He or Leonid probably borrowed it. The Wysocki's are very generous with the van. They lend it to anyone in the neighborhood who needs it."

"What does Denny do for a car?"

"He has that red Ford Fiesta parked in front of his house. The van was his father-in-law's. He passed away a few years ago. Owned a hardware store and used the van for deliveries."

"Who took over the store?"

"Angela's brother. But he already had a van, so he gave this one to his sister."

"What does Denny do?"

"He's a plumber. Does all right for himself."

The front storm door was unlocked. Mickey held the door open for Fiona as the two stepped inside.

"It's about time you got here," Denny yelled from the dining room table. Fiona nodded to him, Joe, and Leonid, then froze as the man at the end of the table turned around.

"Who the fuck invited her?" Ed snapped.

Joe's eyes flashed with anger. "That's no way to greet a guest."

Ed mumbled and stared at the table.

"I should go," Fiona said quietly, turning to Mickey.

Ed jumped up, knocking his chair to the floor. "No, I'm going." He glowered as he strode by Fiona, grabbed his parka from the front hall closet, and slammed the storm door behind him.

Joe got up, righted the overturned chair, and shook his head. "I'm sorry that happened."

As she took her place at the table, a refrain went through her head: *"What are little boys made of? Snakes and snails and puppy dog tails..."*

Chapter 46

On Monday morning, Fiona backed her Mini Cooper out of the garage and headed for the station. She missed riding with Rick in the patrol car. On the drive to work, they would plan their schedule for the day, barring any emergencies. Although her partner was doing well, it would be at least four or five months before he'd be able to return to active duty—that is, unless Jeanne had her way and he remained at a desk job.

Pulling into the station lot, Fiona spotted an open space on the right marked for police personnel. A black car that she didn't recognize had stopped opposite the space. She flipped on her blinker and pulled into the parking space. As she stepped out and headed toward the station, the driver of the black car leaned out his window. "Hey, you."

Fiona bristled. "Are you talking to me?"

"Yeah. What's the idea?"

"What idea?"

"I was waiting for you to pass so I could take that spot."

Fiona walked over, sizing him up. Olive-skinned with thick, black, wavy hair and dark brows, he looked like an extra from *Jersey Shore*. She narrowed her eyes. "I'm not a mind reader. If you wanted the spot, you should've put your turn signal on. Besides, if you had read the sign, you would have noticed these two rows are reserved for employees."

"I am an employee," he said, voice clipped.

"Oh, really? I haven't seen you around before."

"This is my first day. I appreciate the warm welcome."

"If you hadn't acted like a jerk, you might have gotten one." Fiona spun on her heel and strode toward the station. The driver scowled at the departing figure, muttering under his breath as he shook his head.

Inside the station, Fiona dropped her briefcase on her desk with a thud. Still fuming, she poured herself a cup of coffee and tried to calm down. *What an obnoxious jerk*, she thought as she booted up her computer to check her emails.

By the time she finished her coffee, the parking lot incident had faded from her mind. She pulled out the files on the murders still pinned to Henry Winfield. She studied each case, once again searching for a pattern, something that would provide a link between the victims. Although all six young women had similar appearances and lived in the Boston area, there seemed to be no other connection. No shared college, no common workplace. She planned to investigate any clubs or associations they might have joined, though the trail was cold. Too much time had passed since the first wave of killings.

Deep in thought, Fiona did not notice Mahoney and another officer approach her desk. "Good morning, Fiona," the chief said.

She looked up, startled. "Hi, Chief."

"This is detective Vinnie Mancini."

Fiona's mouth fell open. Standing beside Mahoney was the man from the parking lot. He was about five-eleven, with dark eyes, olive skin, and a gym-honed physique that didn't go unnoticed. He gave her a half-smile.

"We've already met."

"Good to hear," Mahoney said. "Rick mentioned he's aiming for a desk job when he gets back, right?"

"Yeah," Fiona replied. "But I'm sure he'll change his mind."

Mahoney shrugged. "We'll see. In the meantime, Vinnie's your new partner. He's transferring in from the Worcester station."

Fiona's eyes narrowed. "But..."

Mahoney didn't wait for Fiona to finish. "If Rick decides he wants to go out again, I'll reevaluate."

Fiona's jaw clenched. How could she possibly work with this jerk?

"I'm taking Vinnie to his desk. Once he's settled, bring him up to speed on your current cases."

Vinnie flashed a parting smile, winked at Fiona, and swaggered behind Mahoney across the room toward the empty desk by the window.

Chapter 47

He watched captivated as the hairdresser, dressed in black tights and a low-cut top that slipped off one shoulder, went about her business. Perched atop five-inch platform heels, she leaned forward to trim the neckline of the man in her chair, exposing her ample bosom. Once finished, she circled the chair seductively. Wiggling between the client's knees, she proceeded to trim his bangs.

He thought about requesting the young seductress for his next haircut, but he had been a client of Roberto's, the owner, for several years. It wouldn't be appropriate to ask for another stylist, especially since he liked the way Roberto cut his hair. No, he'd have to settle for watching the little flirt in action and fantasize about cupping her breasts in his hands and feeling her body beneath his.

Her name was Muriel. Roberto had hired her about three months ago. Best thing he ever did. According to him, business was up almost twenty percent—mostly from middle-aged men who enjoyed Muriel's full-service haircut.

Muriel wasn't the type of woman he normally chose—although she did have red hair and green eyes. She had a small ring above her right eyebrow and multiple ear piercings. A large tattoo of an angel was partially visible on her exposed back and shoulder. He preferred his women demure and innocent, but for Muriel, he'd gladly make an exception.

Eager to talk about his new hire, Roberto had shared that Muriel lived near the Alewife subway station in Cambridge. He'd driven her home a few times, and he insisted their relationship was strictly professional. No roommates—just Buttercup, her miniature poodle. He remembered the tiny dog from his last visit, dressed in a pink sweater with matching bows on her ears. Muriel had left her previous job, Roberto said, after a romantic entanglement with the owner went south.

For the past two weeks, he had skipped out of work early to follow her. Most evenings, she went straight home, a predictable routine he had come to rely on. Tonight, he waited for her at the Alewife station, his face hidden behind dark glasses, an upturned collar, and a dark knit cap pulled low. Occasionally, she'd stop at a Domino's pizza for takeout. He had tried to follow her on Sunday and Monday, her days off, but her schedule was too erratic, too unpredictable. Their encounter would not take place on those days.

He planned their rendezvous for the end of the week, on Thursday or Friday. Even though it was not the closest cemetery available, he settled on the one in Newton. In warmer months, its streams and ponds meandered through manicured lawns and well-tended flower beds. It was a place of serenity mixed with vibrant color. Muriel would like it. It was a class above the cemeteries located in her neighborhood.

Chapter 48

Driving the white van toward Cambridge on Thursday, his heart beat wildly. Just the thought of that evening's pleasures aroused him. This time, he had planned better than with his last angel. Muriel's grave mate would be an 82-year-old war hero. According to the obituary, he was survived by five children, twelve grandchildren, and sixteen great-grandchildren. Unlike the prior funeral, there should be plenty of relatives and friends at the gravesite.

He was uneasy. The abduction would be tricky. Muriel's walk home from the subway offered no cover—no vacant lots, no thick shrubbery to conceal him. Somehow, he'd have to coax her into the van.

Earlier that day, he'd stopped by a Salvation Army and purchased a floral-print armchair. Now, parked in front of a brick house on the first residential block after the subway station, he waited. The armchair sat on the curb behind the van's open doors.

"Damn," he muttered, as an old woman wrapped in a black wool shawl emerged from the house behind him and settled into a rocker on the porch. He considered packing up and moving to the next block when he spied Muriel approaching. *Too late*, he thought. He dabbed at his face with a handkerchief. He would make the old crone part of his act.

As Muriel approached, he put his hands on his hips and stared at the armchair, shaking his head in mock frustration. She paused when she came upon the scene. With jaws constantly in motion, chewing a wad of gum, she surveyed the situation.

"What's the matter?" she asked.

“I just bought this chair for my mother from the old lady over there,” he said, nodding to the porch where the woman sat watching. “I didn’t think about how I’d get it into the van. Figured the seller would help—but turns out she can barely walk.”

Muriel tilted her head, her two-inch silver earring almost touching her shoulder. She was silent. Did she suspect something was wrong? Maybe she didn’t buy his story.

She stared at him, cracking her gum. “Hey, don’t I know you?”

Finally, she wasn’t the sharpest gal he’d ever met. He feigned recognition. “You work at Roberto’s, don’t you?”

“Yeah.” She chomped on her gum. “I thought you looked familiar. You were just there last week.” She smiled, probably amused by the coincidence, seemingly forgetting the chair dilemma.

“Say, maybe you could give me a hand—unless you’re in a rush,” he said.

“I’m just heading home. I live pretty close.”

“Tell you what,” he said. “Help me get the chair into the van, and I’ll give you a ride home.”

Muriel eyed the chair. “It isn’t too heavy, is it?”

“Here’s an idea—why don’t you climb into the back of the van? I’ll lift it up, and you can pull it inside.”

She hesitated, a flicker of doubt crossing her face. “Sure. Why not?” She studied the van. “How do I get in?”

His heart pounded at the thought of touching her. “I could lift you up.”

“Okay.” She placed her shoulder bag on the floor of the van and positioned herself with her back facing the opening. He stepped in front of her, their bodies almost touching. He could feel his cock throb.

Muriel smiled, seeming to enjoy the effect she was having. She stood on tiptoes and looped her arms around his neck. He caught the lingering scent of salon products on her skin, intoxicating and close. He shut his eyes, lost in the moment.

"Well," she teased. "Are you going to lift me up or not?"

The spell broken, he put his arms around her slender waist and hoisted her into the van.

By the time they maneuvered the chair into the back of the van, he could barely contain himself. He slammed the rear doors shut and locked them. Muriel had already slid into the passenger seat, flashing him a flirtatious glance as he climbed in.

Although he knew the answer, he asked her where she lived. They said little during the short drive. He drove with his right hand on the wheel. With the left, he pulled the garrote from his jacket pocket.

There was no one in sight as he pulled in front of Muriel's apartment building. She placed her hand on the door handle, then turned to say goodbye. Before she could open her mouth, he lunged towards her, wrapping the garrote around her neck. She shrieked. Twisting violently, she clawed his face with her nails. He reached back and grabbed a lead pipe from behind his seat that he kept for emergencies.

Muriel pushed away, then dove for the door. With the pipe in his hand, he raised his arm and swung. The pipe struck the side of her head with a sickening crack. Blood sprayed. She collapsed against the seat, motionless.

Once again, fortune favored him. The street was empty—no witnesses in sight. He started the car, flicked on the headlights, and pulled away from the curb. As he drove toward the cemetery, his hand drifted to Muriel's lifeless thigh.

***

As was his ritual, he attended the graveside funeral the following afternoon. He watched as two servicemen in military garb folded an American flag and presented it to the grieving widow of the World War II vet. After joining the other mourners offering condolences to the family, he sat on a bench in front of a leafless oak tree several hundred feet from the grave. From there, he observed the final moments—the lowering of the casket, the quiet dispersal of mourners.

Only when the cemetery had emptied did he rise. As he walked toward the exit, his fingers toyed with the silver earrings tucked in his coat pocket.

Chapter 49

Seated at her desk, Fiona looked up as Vinnie made his usual grand entrance into the room. For the past week, Vinnie had followed the same routine. He'd pause at the department secretary's desk to check for messages. Beth, flustered by his presence, would immediately stop whatever she was doing. Perched on the edge of her desk, Vinnie would chat while Beth gazed at him adoringly, a moon-struck expression on her face.

Barring any phone interruptions, the two would converse for five to ten minutes, completely oblivious to the others in the room. Their flirtation ended, Vinnie would strut to his desk, winking at every female he passed. The water cooler buzzed with talk of the handsome, unattached new detective.

Fiona had to admit he was good-looking, but so far, she was not impressed. They hadn't interacted much since the incident in the parking lot. He spent most of the day shadowing Mahoney, learning the ropes. Today would be their first assignment as partners.

She got up from her desk and walked over to Vinnie's. He was engrossed in the sports pages of the *Globe.* She cleared her throat.

Vinnie glanced at her. "Hi. What's up?"

"The chief wants us to look into the latest disappearance."

Vinnie folded the newspaper and set it aside. "What disappearance?"

"I thought Mahoney filled you in—two women have gone missing."

"He did," Vinnie said, becoming more focused.

"There's been a third possible abduction," Fiona said. "A woman named Muriel Donahue never showed up for work yesterday at Roberto's Hair Salon in Belmont Center."

Vinnie raised an eyebrow. "And we're jumping straight to abduction?"

"Roberto, the owner of the shop, notified the police. Said it was completely out of character. She never misses work without notice. The police checked her apartment. She didn't come home Thursday night."

"How old is she?"

"Twenty-two."

Vinnie leaned back in his chair. "Maybe she went out partying, met someone, and he got lucky."

Fiona shut her eyes and counted to ten. She did not want to get into an argument with this prick.

"Her dog hadn't been fed or walked," she said evenly. "The officers spoke to the neighbors. If Muriel ever stayed out overnight, she always asked one of them to take care of the dog."

Vinnie shrugged. "I say we give it a few days. She'll probably show up."

Fiona's jaw tightened. "I don't know how you did things in Worcester, but here, when someone goes missing, we first try to rule out foul play. Given the similarity between Muriel's profile and the other missing women, we don't have the luxury of waiting."

Vinnie studied her for a moment, then nodded. "So, what do you propose?"

"Start with the owner of the salon," Fiona said. "If Muriel were abducted, the kidnapper could be a customer. Next, check the route from the Alewife Station to her apartment, see if anything stands out."

Vinnie frowned. "The Alewife Station's in Cambridge? Why aren't their detectives working on this?"

"They're short-staffed. And since this case lines up with the others we've been working on, they told Mahoney they'd welcome our help."

Vinnie grabbed his jacket, his displeasure obvious. As they passed Beth's desk, he flashed a wide grin. "We'll be out for a while. I'm expecting some calls."

"Don't worry." She picked up a yellow Post-it pad. "If anyone calls, I'll leave the message on your desk."

Vinnie winked. "Thanks, doll."

In the parking lot, Fiona unlocked the patrol car.

"I'll drive," Vinnie said, walking over to the driver's side.

"I've got it," Fiona replied, already sliding behind the wheel. "I know the city better."

Vinnie muttered something under his breath and climbed into the passenger seat, arms folded, scowling. Fiona hummed a tune as they drove, her mood light in contrast to his brooding silence.

Inside the salon, the detectives questioned Roberto. The receptionist provided a list of Muriel's customers along with their phone numbers. Vinnie checked out Muriel's station, examining her beautician's license and a few photos taped beside it—Muriel smiling with friends, one of her holding a small dog.

"She's a pretty sexy broad," he said.

Fiona rolled her eyes. What was wrong with this guy?

"I'd like to take the photos," she said to Roberto. "Someone might've seen her at the subway station."

Back in the patrol car, photos tucked in her bag, Fiona drove the mile and a half to the Alewife Station. "According to Roberto, Muriel left the salon around seven on Thursday night. She would've taken the red line. Maybe someone working at the station saw her."

Vinnie shrugged. "We don't even know if she took the subway that night. Maybe she met up with friends after work in Belmont. Maybe someone gave her a ride home."

"She told Roberto she was heading home. He saw her digging in her purse for her monthly subway pass."

Vinnie leaned back. "Hey, whatever you say. You're in the driver's seat."

Yes, I am, Fiona thought. *And you'd better get used to it.*

Chapter 50

Inside the Alewife station, the detectives met with a transit security officer. He made copies of Muriel's photos to distribute to the employees on the evening shift. With luck, someone might remember seeing her Thursday night.

Muriel's apartment was just a few blocks from the T station. Fiona and Vinnie carefully checked the route she would have taken but came up empty-handed.

"This was a waste of time," Vinnie said.

Fiona ignored his remark. "There's quite a lot of foot traffic on this street. Maybe someone saw or heard something unusual."

Vinnie sighed. "So, what now?"

"We start knocking on doors. Ask the locals if they noticed anything Thursday night."

Vinnie rolled his eyes and held out his hand. "Give me the keys. I'll wait in the car."

Fiona reached into her pocket and handed them over. "Thanks, partner."

"Don't mention it." Vinnie turned and walked toward the station where they had parked the car. "Just don't be too long or I might take off without you."

"Very funny."

Fiona decided to start her inquiry with the first house on the same side of the street as the T station. She would work methodically down the block. After ringing the bell at three homes with no answer, doubt crept in. Maybe Vinnie was right.

At the fourth house—a tidy brick one with lace curtains—she spotted movement behind the window. An elderly woman opened the door.

"Good morning. I'm Detective Fiona Sullivan with the Belmont Police. I'd like to ask you a few questions."

The woman's blue eyes opened wide; her lips trembled.

"Don't worry. You're not in trouble," Fiona assured her, "I'm investigating the disappearance of a young woman Thursday evening, around rush hour. Did you hear or see anything unusual that afternoon or evening?"

The woman put a finger on her chin. "There was something odd."

Fiona pulled out her notepad.

"A white van was parked in front of my house for quite a while. The driver pulled out an armchair, which was upholstered in a floral design, and set it behind the van. Then someone walking by stopped and helped him load it back in."

"Did you see what that person who helped him looked like?"

"Not really. It was getting dark and I've got cataracts. But I'm sure it was a woman. She wore very high heels."

Fiona leaned in. "What happened after they got the chair in the van?"

"It took off."

"Was the woman inside the van?"

"I think so. I didn't see her walk away."

Fiona took down the woman's name and phone number, then thanked her for the information. The encounter reaffirmed what she already knew—her instincts were worth trusting, no matter what her partner thought.

When Fiona got back to the patrol car, she saw Vinnie in the driver's seat, a smug expression plastered across his face.

Chapter 51

It was the first Friday evening in March. Outside, gusting winds slapped tree branches against the side of the Foley house. The blustery weather swept away winter's stale air, promising fresh starts and the resolution of old issues.

Inside, Joe and his poker group sat in the living room, waiting for Mickey and Fiona to arrive. Ed Foley paced back and forth, fists clenched, his jaw tight. "So, I've been replaced by the cunt detective."

Joe watched his son, his red face ready to explode. "Don't be ridiculous. You haven't been replaced. There's room at the table for both of you."

"You know I don't want to be in the same room as that bitch. She's wrecked my life."

"If we get a vote," Denny said, "I'd rather have Ed here than the cop. No one's been able to win a damn thing off her."

Ed glared at Denny. "What's that supposed to mean? She's a better player than me?"

Denny held up his hands. "Hey, I'm just kidding. I don't like being in the same room with a cop, let alone playing poker with one."

"Same here," Leonid added.

"But Mickey's really smitten with her, and besides," Joe winked at the group. "I'd rather look across the table at a sexy broad than at you guys."

Ed scoffed. "If all you want is eye candy, I can find someone to join the game."

Denny chuckled. "Sounds good to me. Could you make that two?"

Joe shook his head. "Then Mickey would be upset. Look, I can't make everyone happy."

Ed dropped into the chair beside his father, his voice low and bitter. "No surprise there. Whenever it's between Mickey and me, you always pick him."

Joe sighed. "You know that's not true. Besides, you owe your brother. He helped bail you out."

The two were silent. Ed cracked his knuckles; Joe tapped his fingers on the table. "How's it going with Mary?"

Ed's jaw tightened. "She's seeing a fucking attorney. She won't divorce because of the church. He's got her asking for a legal separation."

"You got a lawyer?" Joe asked.

"Not yet. I'm thinking about asking your buddy—Mike Donovan."

"He's good. Whose Mary got?"

"Bruce Schwartz."

Denny whistled. "From what I hear, he's one of the best divorce lawyers around. One of Angie's friends hired him. She cleaned up."

"Man, that makes me feel really good," Ed replied.

Joe stood and headed into the kitchen. He returned with four bottles of beer, handing one to each of the men. Ed twisted off the cap and took a long swig, then wiped his mouth on his sleeve and set the bottle on the coffee table—ignoring the coaster Joe had put down for him.

"Are Mary and the kids back in the house?" Joe asked.

"Yeah, the bitch kicked me out."

"Do you want to stay here?"

"Thanks, but Sally's putting me up."

Leonid raised an eyebrow. "You've already got another woman? That was fast."

Ed smirked and clinked his beer bottle against Leonid's. "And she's some looker."

Joe leaned forward, "Do you think staying at Sally's is a good idea while you're negotiating a separation agreement?"

Ed's eyes narrowed. "I really don't give a fuck."

"Suit yourself," Joe said, reaching for his beer.

Ed took a long drink from his bottle. "The bitch has even turned the kids against me. I wanted to take Emily out last Saturday. She made up some lame excuse why she couldn't go."

"How about Sean?"

"He's okay. I took him to a Bruin's game."

Joe checked his watch. "Mickey and Fiona should be here in a few minutes. Sure, you won't stay?"

"If I did, I'd probably do serious damage to Mickey's broad."

Tilting back his head, Ed chugged the rest of the beer. He got up and carried the empty bottle into the kitchen, returning to the living room just in time to see Mickey and Fiona through the front window, sauntering up the walk. “Shit, they’re here.”

He grabbed his jacket from the front closet. “Bye, Pop. I’ll call you during the week.”

Throwing open the door, he bounded down the steps—right into Fiona. She slipped and fell with a startled gasp.

“Damn it, bro, watch where you’re going,” Mickey snapped.

Grinning broadly, Ed apologized and offered a hand to help Fiona up. She grasped his arm as she rose and pulled on it hard while sticking out her leg. Ed tripped and landed face-first on the sidewalk.

“So sorry,” Fiona said sweetly as Mickey rushed to help his brother.

Face red as a beet, blood trickling from a cut on his chin, Ed leaped to his feet and lunged at Fiona, who deftly side-stepped her attacker. Watching from the house, Denny, Leonid, and Joe bolted outside to restrain Ed, who was on the ground, cursing Fiona. The three men half-carried, half-dragged the battered attacker to his car. Mickey rushed Fiona inside the house for safety.

As Ed’s car pulled away, Mickey turned to her. “Where did you learn that move?”

“Karate class,” she said with a smirk. “I’m a black belt.”

He shook his head. “Guess I’d better watch out.”

Chapter 52

Fiona was having a good evening. Not only had she decked a man more than twice her size, but she was also winning handily at poker. As she pulled in her fourth big pot, Leonid pushed back his chair. He took a pack of cigarettes from his pocket and offered them to the group. Denny took one.

Fiona's eyes widened as she examined the package. "Can I have one?" she asked.

Leonid handed her a cigarette. Fiona turned it over in her fingers, inspecting the black cylinder with its gold foil filter.

"You don't smoke," Mickey said.

"I know. I just wanted a closer look. I've never seen a cigarette like this. What kind is it?"

Leonid puffed up his chest. "It is Sobranie Black Russian. Superior to American cigarettes."

Twisting the cigarette between her fingers, Fiona studied it. "Is that so?" She didn't mention that the cigarettes were actually made in England.

"Yes. Sobranie Black Russians are one of the oldest in the world. Very expensive. One carton costs more than three times the price of American cigarettes."

"Makes me almost wish I hadn't quit," Joe said.

Denny got up from his chair. "Be right back. I'm going to savor this delicacy on the porch. You joining me, or are you just going to sit here and tell everyone how much better this cigarette is than American smokes?"

"Coming right out," Leonid said, pushing back his chair.

As Fiona watched them leave, a quiet urgency settled over her. Somehow, she had to get her hands on the butts of the cigarettes they were smoking.

Chapter 53

Mahoney peered over his glasses at Fiona, seated across from him. His thick fingers held a plastic evidence bag, which he studied briefly before tossing it onto the desk.

"So, what is this?"

Fiona leaned forward, eyes shining with excitement. "Sobranie Black Russians."

"And why are these cigarette butts important?"

"I found others like them behind two of the houses that were broken into. It was the first time I'd ever seen one."

Mahoney picked up the bag again and examined the contents more closely. "They are pretty distinctive."

"The ones in front of you came from Jim Foley's front porch. I managed to pick them up after a poker game on Friday. I told the group I wasn't feeling too well and needed some fresh air. So, while they got ready for the next game, I slipped outside."

"Let me guess—the DNA from the saliva matches what you found on the cigarettes at the crime scenes."

Fiona smiled smugly. "Yes, it does."

"So, what's your conclusion?" Mahoney asked.

"One of the cigarettes was smoked by Joe Foley's tenant, Leonid, and the other by his next-door neighbor, Denny Wysocki. Our thief is most likely one of them—or maybe both, considering there were two perps when Rick got wounded. But if it's just one, I'd bet on the tenant. Wysocki was a victim himself. But," she added, "he might have staged the burglary to throw us off the track."

"Possibly," Mahoney replied.

"At one point," Fiona added, "I thought it might be an insurance scam."

Mahoney leaned back in his chair and folded his hands over his chest. "How long since the last break-in?"

"It's been around a month now—the night Rick was wounded."

Mahoney nodded slowly. "I want you and Vinnie to stake out this guy Soldatenkoff."

Fiona grimaced.

"What's the problem?"

"I'd rather do it myself," she said.

"You don't trust your partner?"

"We got off on the wrong foot, and it's only gone downhill from there."

Mahoney took off his glasses and rubbed his eyes. Setting them on the desk, he held his head in his hands. After a long pause, he looked up, a stern expression on his face. Fiona bit her lower lip. This was not a good sign.

"I'm not letting you do this solo. Look what happened last time—and you weren't even alone then. You had Rick."

"But…"

"I don't care if you don't like Mancini," Mahoney said firmly. "You'd better get used to him. He's going to be around for a while."

Frowning, Fiona picked up the plastic bag from Mahoney's desk.

"How're the missing women cases coming along?"

Fiona debated whether to tell the Chief about the disagreement with her partner during the Alewife Station investigation. She decided against it. "We found something that connects two of the victims."

Mahoney leaned forward. "What's that?"

"In both of the most recent disappearances, witnesses reported seeing a white van."

"Still no bodies?"

"No. If the kidnapper used the van to transport them, their remains could be anywhere."

Mahoney exhaled sharply. "How about that guy who's in prison?"

"Henry Winfield?"

"Yeah."

"His attorney is compiling evidence to show he couldn't have committed at least four of the murders he confessed to."

Mahoney rubbed his forehead. "All hell's going to break loose if they find he's innocent. People are already panicking over the missing women. The mayor told me he gets from three to five phone calls a day demanding to know why we haven't caught anyone yet."

"The kidnapper will slip up. They always do," Fiona said, not at all convinced that he would.

Chapter 54

Sally stood in the living room, lip curled, hands planted firmly on her hips. She glared at Ed, sprawled on the couch with his feet up on the coffee table. "You promised you wouldn't smoke in the house anymore."

Ed pulled the cigarette from his mouth, letting a trail of ash fall onto the beige carpet. "C'mon, baby, gimme a break, it's cold outside. I'll freeze my ass off on the porch."

"Better your ass than my carpet."

With the cigarette still dangling from his lips, Ed half-heartedly brushed the ashes under the couch. "While you're up, grab me a beer."

Sally gave Ed a withering look. But she returned a few minutes later with a glass and a can of beer.

"You know I don't use any glass. Just give me the can."

Without a word, Sally placed a coaster on the coffee table and set the beer down, stepping between Ed and the TV. He waved his arm impatiently.

"C'mon, Sal, I can't see the fuckin' game."

Sally winced, reached for the remote, and shut off the TV.

Ed shot up from the couch, knocking over the ashtray. He grabbed her arm. "What the hell, Sally? You knew I was watching that!"

Standing as tall as her five-foot-three-inch frame allowed, Sally glared at him. "I'm sick and tired of spending Sundays with you glued to the TV while I serve you food and drink and watch you destroy my house. I'm not your waitress."

Ed loosened his grip, his voice defensive. "I work hard all week. I need the weekends to unwind."

Sally's chin lifted defiantly. "I work hard all week, too," she snapped. "And I don't enjoy spending my free time catering and picking up after you."

"So, what are you saying?"

"I'm saying this arrangement isn't working anymore."

"I thought you loved me."

"I thought I did, too."

Ed seized Sally by her arms, pulled her toward him, and kissed her hard on the lips. She tried to pull away. "Let go. You're hurting me."

"C'mon, baby," he said as he drew her closer. "You know you want me. You know you like my big dick."

"Let go of me," she said, twisting and turning to get loose.

His grip tightened. Ignoring her protests, he dragged her from the living room toward the bedroom.

That was the last thing she remembered.

***

When Sally regained consciousness, she put her hand up to her face. She felt something wet and sticky around her nose and mouth. Was it blood?

She propped her nude body up on one elbow. In spite of the pain in her shoulder, she managed to flip on the nightstand light. She got up, pulled a hand mirror from the drawer, and gasped. Not only were there blood and bruises on her arms and black and blue marks on her thighs, but her face looked like it had been used as a punching bag.

She lay back down on the bed and tried to remember what had happened. She recalled being dragged into the bedroom. Ed had ripped off her clothes, pushed her down hard on the bed, struck her again and again—and then…and then… Tears streamed down her face.

Hearing a noise in the hallway, she pulled the covers over her head.

"So, you're finally awake," Ed said from the doorway.

He stepped into the room and approached the bed. Sally lay still.

She felt the mattress dip as he sat beside her. Only the crown of her head peeked out from beneath the blanket. He reached out and stroked her hair.

"Don't touch me," she said, her voice low and firm.

He withdrew his hand. "Don't you want to see what I bought you?"

"No."

"C'mon, baby. I'm sorry. I didn't mean to hurt you."

"Get out of my house."

"You don't mean that."

"If you're not out of this house in two minutes, I'm calling the police."

Sally felt the mattress jolt as Ed sprang to his feet. "You're no different than my bitch wife," he yelled, flinging his offering on the bed.

Moments later, she heard the back door slam and the rumble of a car engine in the driveway. Slowly, she pulled the covers down from her face. Strewn across the bed and spilled onto the floor were two dozen long-stemmed red roses.

Chapter 55

When Joe Foley answered the doorbell later that evening, Ed stood before him holding a suitcase. Joe sighed and shook his head. He didn't need an explanation—he already knew.

"That cunt kicked me out," Ed muttered.

"Which cunt?"

"This isn't a joke," Ed snapped, his face flushed, his eyes bloodshot.

"I wasn't joking. C'mon in."

Joe gave his son a reassuring pat on the back as he stepped inside. Ed dropped the suitcase with a thud. "I could use a beer."

"You know where they are. Grab me one too."

Ed returned with two bottles and handed one to his father. They popped off the caps and drank in silence for a few minutes. "Mind if I stay with you for a few days?" Ed asked. "Just 'til I find a place."

"Of course. You know you're always welcome."

"Think I'll look for something in Quincy. One of my buddies lives there. His place isn't much to look at, but, hey, I don't need much—just somewhere to sleep."

"Want me to come with you to check out apartments?"

Ed shook his head. "I'll handle it myself. I'll need your help later, though—furniture, maybe a couple of bucks."

"Do you want to take some of my furniture?"

"Nah. I'll hit the Salvation Army, pick up something cheap."

"What can I do?"

"Could you borrow Denny's van? Maybe you and he could help me move the stuff."

"Sure." Joe finished the last sip of his beer and set the bottle down. "I think I'll be heading to bed. It's almost midnight. Need anything before I turn in?"

"Nah, I'll just grab a blanket and pillow and crash on the couch. Mind if I watch TV for a while?"

"Not at all." Joe turned to go but paused. "Just one thing."

"What's that?"

"No smoking in the house."

Chapter 56

Fiona pulled two grocery bags from the trunk of her car. She had stopped at the convenience store on her way home from work. As she unlocked the apartment door, she was greeted by Jasmine's barks. She nudged the dog away with her knee and stepped inside. The blinking light on the telephone caught her eye.

After feeding Jasmine and putting away the groceries, she pressed the button to check her messages. About to refill the dog's water dish, she recognized Julia's panicked voice.

"Please call me as soon as you get this."

Fiona instantly dialed her number. "Julia, it's Fiona. What happened?"

"I got a bizarre email."

"What did it say?"

"It said I'm going to be this person's 'next sweet angel' and I should say my prayers. What does that mean? It sounds so scary."

Fiona took a deep breath and closed her eyes. This could be the break she'd been looking for. "You didn't delete it, did you?"

"No."

"I'll be right there."

Thirty minutes later, Fiona stood outside Julia's Cambridge apartment building, ringing the doorbell.

"Who is it?" Julia asked through the intercom.

"It's me—Fiona."

“Thank God. I’ll buzz you in.”

Inside the building, Fiona took the elevator to the third floor and knocked on Julia’s apartment door.

“Is that you, Fiona?”

“Yes.”

Fiona heard the clicking of locks and the rattle of a chain being removed. Julia opened the door and gave her a sheepish look. “Sorry—I knew it was you. But this email has me really rattled.”

She ushered Fiona into the living room. “I’ll get the email.”

Fiona settled onto the couch, taking in the space. The apartment was a stark contrast to her brother’s minimalist style. A plush taupe sofa rested atop a striking carpet with a bold geometric design. Vibrant accent pillows echoed the colors of the carpet and picked up the colors of the rug. The Brazilian rosewood floors added warmth to the room.

Face flushed, Julia raced back into the living room. “Here’s the email.”

Fiona took the printout and read the message: *u r my next sweet angel…don’t forget to say ur prayers.*

A chill ran down her spine as she read and reread the cryptic message. “Can I keep this copy?”

“Of course. Do you think it’s serious?” Julia asked.

“I don’t know, but we’re not taking any chances. I’m getting a police tail on you.”

Julia’s face went pale. “So, you think I’m in danger?”

"The disappearances of those three women have been all over the papers for weeks. It could be someone's sick joke, but I doubt it's the same person behind the abductions. The police checked the victims' computers—no emails, no contact attempts of any kind."

Fiona folded the printed message and slipped it into her jacket pocket. "Have you given your email address to anyone recently?"

"No, but it's not hard to find. It's on my Facebook page."

"Have you friended anyone new recently?"

"Yes, but only people I know. I'm careful about who I let in."

Leaning back on the couch, Fiona assessed the situation. Julia fit the victim profile: attractive, Irish descent, mid-twenties. Like Maureen Doyle, the first victim who vanished, she worked at an investment firm. Although it didn't fit the perp's profile, the email concerned her, in particular the email address of the sender 'tsk10@gmail.com'"

"I'll take this over to forensics tomorrow," Fiona said. "Let's see if we can trace the sender."

"Do you think 'tsk' could be his initials?"

"I don't know."

"What about the 10? Could it be a year?"

"Possibly."

Fiona didn't want to tell Julia what ran through her mind. If it were the serial killer, Julia would be his tenth victim—six confirmed murders that Winfield had stood trial for, plus the three missing women. And "tsk"? Could it stand for "the serial killer"?

"If it's the same guy who's responsible for the other three disappearances, he usually targets women on their way home from work. Make sure you're not alone when you walk home from the subway, even if it means taking an alternate route. And if you pass any vacant lots or places where someone could be hiding, cross the street."

Julia's blue eyes opened wide. "I thought you were assigning a policeman to follow me."

"I am, but I want you to take some precautions, too. I don't know how long the chief can spare someone. We're stretched pretty thin."

Julia buried her face in her hands. Getting up from the couch, Fiona walked over, sat down beside Julia, and put an arm around her. "Nothing's going to happen to you," she said gently. "Here—take my card. It has my direct line at the station and my cell. Call me anytime. I'll let you know as soon as the tail's in place. I should be able to get someone on it today."

Julia wrapped her arms around her friend. "Thank you. You've been such a blessing for this family."

Fiona returned the hug, then got up from the couch. "I have to head out now. Make sure you lock the doors behind me."

Chapter 57

As soon as Fiona arrived at the station, she called Mahoney from her desk.

"I need to see you. There's been a new development in the missing women case. Can I come up?"

"Sure. Is Mancini around?"

Fiona glanced over. Vinnie waved from his desk. "Yes, he's here."

"Bring him with you. He needs to be kept in the loop."

"Okay," Fiona said, her jaw tightening.

She hung up and motioned to Vinnie. "Come on. The Chief wants to see us."

"What's going on?"

"New lead. He wants you there, too."

They walked in silence to the elevator. Once inside, Vinnie turned to Fiona. "Word is you're a black belt in karate."

She nodded.

"So am I. We'll have to spar sometime."

"Why?"

"To settle who drives."

Fiona gave Vinnie a puzzled look.

"Whoever wins," Vinnie said with a grin as the elevator doors opened, "drives the patrol car."

"I'll think about it."

The two waited outside Mahoney's office until he got off the phone. After hanging up, he waved them in. "It was the mayor again. Says he's getting a lot of heat about the funeral robberies as well as the missing women. Wants to know why we don't have a suspect in either case."

"Did you mention the cigarette match-up?" Fiona asked.

"I just told him we were getting close. No point in raising expectations just yet."

Vinnie leaned forward in his chair his jaw tight. "What cigarette match-up?"

Mahoney grimaced and shook his head. "Don't you two communicate? You're partners for Christ's sake."

Fiona handed the Chief the message Julia received. "A friend of mine received this email last night."

Mahoney scanned the message, then passed it to Vinnie.

"Julia Foley," Fiona continued, "matches the victim profile. She's scared, and rightly so. I told her I'd ask about assigning a tail."

Mahoney adjusted his glasses and flipped through the duty roster. "I can spare someone for a few days. After that, we'll have to reassess."

"Thanks, Chief. Here's her work, home, and cell numbers so your officers can reach her directly."

Mahoney took the slip of paper, nodding. "Maybe this is the break we've been waiting for." Then he turned to Fiona, his eyes narrowing. "Now, bring your partner up to speed on the break-ins."

Fiona turned to Vinnie, a flush creeping up her face and neck. “I picked up two cigarette butts smoked by two people I know that are similar to the ones found at the crime scenes. The lab ran saliva tests—there’s a match.”

Vinnie’s brow furrowed. “So, we know who did it?”

“We’ve narrowed it down to two suspects: Denny Wysocki and Leonid Soldatenkoff. They live next door to each other.”

Mahoney folded his arms across his chest and peered over the rims of his glasses. “I want the two of you to stake out Soldatenkoff’s place. Starting tonight.”

Fiona’s lips tightened. She started to protest.

Mahoney leaned forward, his voice firm. “Starting tonight, Fiona. No arguments.”

The meeting finished the detectives rose to leave. Vinnie opened the door and, with a ceremonial wave of the hand, followed Fiona out. Mahoney watched them go, shaking his head. Maybe keeping those two together had been a mistake after all.

Chapter 58

That evening, Vinnie and Fiona sat in an unmarked car parked down the street from where Leonid Soldatenkoff lived. They munched on the hamburgers and fries they had just picked up at McDonald's. Fiona sipped her coffee, missing the thermos Rick's wife used to pack for stakeouts—strong, hot, and comforting. Vinnie stuffed the last of the burger into his mouth, wiped his hands on his navy pants, and let out a loud belch.

"Excuse me," he said, glancing at Fiona behind the wheel.

"Glad to see you enjoyed the meal," she said dryly.

"Sorry 'bout that. It's a guy thing, you wouldn't understand."

Fiona shot him a look. "Try me."

"I've never partnered with a female. When I was on a stakeout with the guys, burping and farting came with the territory."

"If you're going to expel gas, let me know in advance so I can at least open a window."

She picked up her cup of coffee from the holder between the two seats and took a sip. "If you'd rather partner with one of the men, I'm sure Mahoney can make that happen."

Vinnie shook his head. "Actually, I prefer working with you."

Fiona rolled her eyes. "Yeah, right."

"No, really. You're more interesting and way better looking than the guy I was stuck with in Worcester."

Fiona waited for the dig, but when none came, she shrugged and resumed eating. Vinnie picked up his cup and drank the last of his coffee.

"Why'd you leave Worcester?"

"I've always wanted to work on the Boston force. Belmont's a lot closer to the city than Worcester."

Finished with her burger and fries, Fiona wiped her hands on a napkin and put it and the wrappers in the empty McDonald's bag. "So, what made you decide to be a cop?" she asked.

"My dad was on the force. Ever since I can remember, he'd bring me down to the station. I never wanted to do anything else."

"He must be proud of you. You're a sergeant, right?"

"Yeah, but he never saw me get promoted. He was killed during a bank robbery about five years ago."

"I'm sorry," Fiona said softly.

They sat in silence, eyes fixed on the house down the street.

"What about you?" Vinnie asked. "Why'd you become a cop?"

Fiona swallowed the coffee she was drinking and placed her cup back in the holder.

"I thought criminology was interesting. That's all."

Vinnie gave Fiona a sideward glance. "Someone told me your sister was murdered. Is it true?"

She drew in a deep breath. "Yes."

"I guess you don't want to talk about it."

Fiona took another sip of her coffee. Vinnie's eyes shifted to the home under surveillance. No one spoke.

"My sister was murdered by a serial killer," Fiona said, after a long pause.

Vinnie looked at her tear-filled eyes and squirmed uncomfortably, as though he wished he hadn't brought up the subject.

"We thought the killer had been caught. A guy named Henry Winfield confessed to all six of the murders. But now he claims he didn't do it. There's a group of attorneys and law students who believe him. They're working on an appeal."

"Do you think he did it?"

"I had doubts during the trial. My family and I were there every day." She paused and stared out the window. "I visited Winfield at Souza-Baranowski two months ago. Winfield's alibi for where he was when my sister was killed checked out."

"So, her killer's still out there?"

"I think he's the one behind the missing women."

Vinnie nodded slowly. "Interesting."

Fiona gave a faint smile. "And to answer your first question—yes, that's why I became a detective."

Suddenly, Vinnie reached into the back seat and grabbed the binoculars. "Whoa. There are two guys coming out of the house."

He handed the binoculars to Fiona. "That's Joe Foley and his son, Ed. They're not the two we're looking for."

"You know them?"

“Mickey Foley, one of Joe’s sons, and I have been seeing each other. I play poker with him most Friday nights. His dad joins in. So do…” Fiona hesitated, “The two burglary suspects.”

Vinnie’s head jerked back. “Wait, what?”

“I didn’t know they were thieves when I first joined the poker group. Denny happens to be Joe Foley’s neighbor, and Leonid is his tenant. They have no idea I’m onto them.”

“Let’s hope it stays that way.”

Chapter 59

Two hours passed. Aside from Joe and Ed, who had returned home, no one had entered or exited the house under surveillance.

"It's ten," Vinnie said, glancing at the dashboard clock. "How much longer do we wait?"

"At least until eleven," Fiona replied. "If you're tired, take a nap. I'll keep watch."

"Nah, I'm good."

Suddenly, Fiona's phone rang. Answering it, she recognized Julia's voice.

"We'll be right over," Fiona said, sliding the key into the ignition.

"What's going on?" Vinnie asked.

"It's Julia Foley. She just got another threatening email."

When they arrived at Julia's apartment, Fiona heard the familiar click of locks and chains being undone. Dressed in a pink robe and a diaphanous nightgown, her hair in disarray, Julia opened the door. Upon seeing Vinnie, she quickly tied her robe. "I thought you'd be alone."

"This is my partner, Vinnie Mancini."

Julia ran her fingers through her long hair. "I must look a mess."

Vinnie winked. "If this is a mess, I can't wait to see you all dressed up."

Fiona glared at Vinnie, then turned to Julia. "Let's see the email."

"It's on my computer," Julia said. "There are attachments. I couldn't bring myself to download them—they're revolting."

The detectives followed Julia into her bedroom. Fiona was struck by the contrast. Unlike the sleek, modern aesthetic of the rest of the apartment, this room had a soft, old-fashioned feel. With its four-poster bed, muted colors, and traditional oak armoire, dresser, and nightstands, the room, like Julia, was very feminine.

Vinnie glanced at the bed and then at its owner, a slap-worthy expression on his face. Fiona shook her head. *Damn Mahoney,* she thought. *Why had he partnered me with the Don Juan of the Belmont PD?*

On the other side of the bed, tucked into an alcove, Julia's laptop rested on her desk. She sat down and opened the email. It was from *tsk10.*

The cops can't watch you 4ever. Take a look at ur future.

There were three attachments. Julia turned her head. "I can't look at these again."

Fiona had Julia get up. She took her seat. "Let me open them."

She clicked on the first file. The image loaded slowly, then it appeared: a nude body sprawled on a blue blanket in a grassy clearing, surrounded by dense brush. Through the foliage, Fiona glimpsed water. Was it a stream? The edge of a lake? Strands of red hair covered the victim's face. Blood trickled from the side of her mouth.

Fiona enlarged the photo and gasped. She recognized the location instantly—the bank of the Charles River. Even before she studied the partially visible face, she knew who it was—Ciara.

Face ashen, her body shaking, Fiona rose from the chair. Vinnie rushed to her side, grabbing her arms to prevent her from falling. He guided her gently to the bed, then glanced at the photo. "It's your sister, isn't it?"

Tears streaming down her cheeks, Fiona nodded. Julia rushed to her side. "I didn't know your sister was one of the killer's victims. I'm so sorry."

Fiona drew a shaky breath, trying to pull herself together. She was a detective. She had to compartmentalize the grief if she was going to bring her sister's killer to justice.

"It's not your fault," she said to Julia. "You couldn't have known."

Standing up, she made her way back to the computer. Vinnie stepped in front of her. "I'll take it from here," he offered.

"No," Fiona said, her voice steadier now. "This is something I have to do." Nonetheless, she said a silent thank you to Vinnie for having replaced her sister's photo with that of the next victim.

The second attachment opened to a similar scene: a body with long ash-blond hair, partially obscured by a bush. She wore only a blouse. Fiona clicked on the third file. A brunette lay naked on the ground, arms folded across her chest, one leg crossed over the other. Large hazel eyes stared into the camera.

"It looks like the killer posed her," Fiona murmured.

Standing behind her, Vinnie studied the image. "From the way her limbs are arranged, it's like he was aiming for modesty. He's some twisted dude."

"I'm forwarding these to my computer," Fiona said. "Maybe Boston's high-tech crime unit can pull something from these images."

When they returned to the living room, Julia looked beseechingly at Fiona. "Please don't leave yet. I'm terrified."

"Do you have anything to drink?" Vinnie asked. "Might help take the edge off."

"There's wine in the cabinet next to the fridge," Julia offered.

"I'll get it," Vinnie said, disappearing into the kitchen.

After several minutes of banging cupboard doors, he returned with three glasses of merlot. He handed a glass to Julia and one to Fiona. The two women took a seat on the couch. "Just another service of the Belmont PD," Vinnie said. "Although don't tell anyone. I could get into trouble."

Sitting on the couch, feet curled up under her, Julia looked pale. Fiona moved next to her. "I know the email is upsetting, but there is still an officer assigned to you." She decided not to mention that she hadn't seen him outside the building when they had pulled up earlier.

Julia reached to set down her glass, her hand shaking so badly she spilled some wine on the table. "But what happens when he's no longer there?"

With the image of her sister still in her head, Fiona patted Julia's hand. "Don't worry. I'll make sure you're protected—even if I have to do it myself."

Chapter 60

The following morning, seated at her desk in the police station, Fiona called Julia to make sure she was all right.

"I'm doing fine," Julia said. "Things are less scary in the daylight. Thanks so much for coming over last night."

"Any more emails?"

"No. Thank God." She paused, then added, "But how are you doing? I still can't believe it was your sister's body."

"I'm okay. It was a momentary shock. If I'm going to catch her killer, I have to put things like that behind me."

"Well, I still feel guilty."

"Don't. You didn't know. I'm just glad you're feeling better this morning. I'll talk to you later."

"Fiona, wait."

"Yes?"

"Your partner—what's his name again?"

"Vinnie."

"He's a hunk. Is he married?"

"Don't think so. Are you interested?

"Maybe. Does he have a girlfriend?"

"I don't think so."

"Can you find out?"

Fiona clenched her jaw. What did Julia think she was—a matchmaker?

"Okay."

"Talk to you later," Julia said.

After the call ended, Fiona opened her desk drawer and retrieved the copies of the photos Julia had sent—the images of her sister and the two other women. She crossed the room to the murder board and began comparing them to the victims' photos. Even though the images were grainy, she was able to match them to two of the women from the first set of murders for which Henry Winfield had been imprisoned—Maureen Kelly and Caroline Lynch. The threats Julia had received didn't align with the killer's usual pattern, but no one else could have taken these photos.

Fiona shuddered. Those emails were not empty threats. Julia was in real danger.

Chapter 61

At eleven thirty the following morning, Vinnie sidled over to Fiona's desk. "Got lunch plans?"

"Thinking of grabbing a burger at the diner across the street," she responded.

"Mind if I tag along?"

"Sure. Just give me a couple of minutes to finish what I'm working on."

As Vinnie turned to leave, she added, "Let's invite Garfinkle."

He shrugged his shoulders. "Why not? The more the merrier."

"Wait here—I'll go get him.

Fiona sprinted down the steps to the floor below. She found Rick, a scowl on his face, sitting at his desk, shuffling papers.

"You don't look like a happy camper," she said.

"This desk job has me batty. I never should've promised Jeanne I'd give it a shot."

"Give it a chance. You might end up liking it."

Rick grimaced. "Not on your life. I'm built for the field, not for sitting at a desk all day. It's damned uncomfortable."

Fiona chuckled. "Well, I hope Jeanne relents. You left me with—pardon my French—a real piece of work for a partner."

"Still butting heads with Mancini?"

"It's a little bit better," Fiona said, "but I definitely prefer my former partner."

Rick smiled, apparently happy to be missed.

"Speaking of Mancini," she continued, "he asked me to go to lunch. Seems like he's making an effort to be friendly. We're just going to the diner across the street. Do you want to come, too?"

"Wished you'd asked me sooner. I brown-bagged it today. Sitting makes me hungry. I polished off my lunch at nine thirty."

"Too bad. I'll ask you earlier next time."

At the diner, Fiona slid into the red vinyl booth and glanced at the menu, although she already knew what she wanted. After the waitress took their lunch order, the conversation shifted to Julia.

"Wonder why the guy sent Julia those pictures. That's not his usual M.O., is it?" Vinnie asked.

"That's what I was wondering. Maybe to let us know he's serious and that a serial killer wannabe didn't send the emails."

Vinnie nodded. "And since Winfield's still locked up, those photos are more proof he's not the guy. No way he sent them from prison."

Fiona raised an eyebrow. "Wow. Great observation. Can I quote you on that?"

Vinnie shot her a look. "Just when I thought we were starting to get along."

Fiona lowered her eyes, wishing she had kept her mouth shut. Their relationship was getting better. Things between them were finally improving. Was she trying to mess that up?

"A little off-topic," she said after taking a bite of her burger that the waitress had just brought, "but a friend of mine wants to know if you're married or have a girlfriend."

Vinnie raised an eyebrow. “What friend?”

“Not important.”

He smirked. “Negative on both counts.”

Vinnie took a sip of his soda, then leaned back. “So, are we still having our match?”

“What match?” Fiona asked.

“Karate. Winner gets to drive the getaway car.”

She grinned. “Sure.”

“When?”

“After we crack the missing women case.”

Vinnie shrugged. “Why wait?”

Fiona smiled. “I like being in the driver’s seat.”

Chapter 62

Storm clouds gathered in the dark sky. Wind whipped through tree branches, decapitating burgeoning buds. The unmarked police car skidded on the slick pavement as it turned onto Christian Way. Behind the wheel, Fiona squinted to see the road through the thick mist that engulfed them. Suddenly, she slammed on the brakes. Propelled forward in his seat, Vinnie's coffee splattered onto the dashboard and his shirt.

"Damn it, Sullivan. What the hell was that?"

"There's a cat crossing the street. I didn't want to hit it."

In the glare of the headlights, a large black tabby with white paws froze mid-road, stared at the car then darted to the other side. Shaking his head, Vinnie pulled some napkins from the McDonald's bag to wipe his shirt as the nutty aroma of the spilled coffee filled the car.

"That coffee was really hot. What were you trying to do? Scald me?"

"It had nothing to do with you. It's pitch black out, and in case you missed it, so was the cat. I didn't see him until he was right in front of us."

Annoyance visible on his face, Vinnie crumpled up the napkins and threw them on the floor.

Fiona glanced at him. "Did anything spill on the file?"

He picked up a brown folder and checked it. "Nope. All clear."

"How many funerals are there tonight?" Fiona asked.

Vinnie opened the file. "Three."

"Do we know where the immediate families live?"

"Yeah. I had Beth call the funeral homes." He flipped through the pages using a flashlight to find the addresses. "Let's see—one family is on Ash, another on Trapelo, and the third lives on Lewis."

Fiona drove a few more blocks, then parked the car a couple of houses down from where Leonid and Danny lived.

"Not a great start to our stakeout," Vinnie muttered. "A black cat crossed our path, and now a Nor'easter's rolling in."

A loud clap of thunder sounded overhead, followed by a flash of lightning. Pebble-sized raindrops hammered the windshield. Fiona turned on the ignition, dimmed the headlights, and switched on the wipers.

Vinnie peered through the binoculars. "Tough to see in this downpour."

Fiona squinted through the rain. "Is that a white van in their driveway?"

"Yeah, it is."

"Then they're moving tonight."

The two detectives ate their burgers and fries in silence, taking turns watching the house. Fallen branches littered the street. Rainwater surged past clogged gutters. Another flash of lightning lit up the road—just long enough to reveal two figures climbing into the van.

"There they go," Vinnie said.

Fiona eased the car into drive without turning on the headlights and crawled out of the space. She waited until the van pulled away, then followed at a cautious distance. At the end of the block, she turned left onto Belmont Road.

At the first intersection, she flicked on the headlights. The van had turned right. By the time she made the same turn, several cars had slipped between them. Headlights and taillights stood out sharply against the black night. After a few blocks, Fiona spotted the van's left turn signal blinking.

"They're turning onto Lewis Street," she said. "That's one of the three streets you mentioned. What's the number?"

"Two-forty"

The van was already halfway down the block when Fiona made the turn.

Vinnie squinted to read the house numbers. "That gray one's 216. The one we're looking for should be midway down the block on the right."

Fiona slowed to a crawl, letting Vinnie scan the addresses. "There it is," he said. "The white two-family up ahead."

Fiona parked a few houses back, killed the engine, and dimmed the lights. She studied the house through the rain-smeared windshield. "Dark as a dungeon. Not a glimmer of light anywhere. Might as well hang a sign that says, 'rob me.'"

They watched as the van sped down the block, made a sharp U-turn, and pulled into the driveway of 240 Lewis Street. Two figures exited the vehicle and disappeared around the back of the house.

"Call for backup," Fiona said.

Vinnie grabbed his phone and dialed the station. "Good news—Mahoney's sending a unit. Bad news—he's short-staffed. He's pulling the officer tailing your friend."

Fiona exhaled slowly, her jaw tight. “We don’t have a choice.”

She stared through the rain-streaked windshield, silently willing the night to pass without incident. *Please let Julia be safe.*

Chapter 63

"They're in the house," Vinnie said as he and Fiona darted across the street. "See the flashlight in the rear window?"

"Be careful. They're probably armed. I'm not losing another partner."

"So, you'd miss me?" Vinnie asked.

"Like gonorrhea."

They circled behind the house two doors down, slipping through unfenced backyards and hiding behind the detached garage at 240 Lewis Street. The house sat on a slope—street-level in the front, basement-level in the back. Peering around the side of the garage, they noticed the basement door was ajar, and a shattered pane of glass glimmered in the moonlight.

Fiona covered Vinnie as he crossed the back lawn and headed for the house, his Glock drawn. He nudged the door open and stepped inside, sweeping the room with his flashlight. No immediate threat. He signaled Fiona, who dashed across and entered carefully, avoiding the shards of glass.

In the darkness, they could hear the thump of boots on the hardwood floors above. Vinnie scanned the basement with his flashlight. Usual stuff. Washer-dryer, unemptied moving cartons, and what looked like a woodworking bench in the far corner.

He trained the light on the staircase and whispered, "Let's go up. Sounds like one guy is near the front, the other is in a back bedroom. I'll take the front. You get the one in back."

Fiona nodded, frustration simmering. *Where the hell is backup?* She dialed again.

With Glocks drawn and flashlights cutting through the gloom, she and Vinnie crept up the basement stairs, pausing at every creak. No sound from the first floor. They pressed on. The door squeaked slightly as they eased it open and stepped into the kitchen. Vinnie nodded to Fiona and crept toward the front of the house. Fiona, heart pounding, moved silently down the hallway toward the bedrooms.

The hallway was dark and narrow. A carpet runner muffled her steps. She paused outside the first door, peered around the frame—and froze. A burly figure in a ski mask stood with his back to her, rifling through a dresser drawer. A pistol bulged from his rear pocket.

Fiona stepped into the room. One hand flipped the overhead light; the other kept her Glock trained on the intruder.

"Police. Hands over your head," she commanded.

The man spun around, reaching for his weapon. A shot cracked through the room. He staggered, clutching his shoulder as blood sprayed across the dresser.

Gunfire erupted from the front of the house. Sirens wailed outside. Backup had finally arrived.

Someone pounded on the front door. Fiona heard boots thudding up the back steps. She turned as a uniformed officer appeared in the hallway.

"You, okay?" he asked.

"Yeah," she said, lowering her weapon. "What took you so long?"

"We were in Cambridge. Got here as fast as we could."

He motioned to the thief to turn around and lie flat on the floor. Pulling out a pair of handcuffs, he placed one knee on the intruder's back and cuffed him.

Fiona stepped forward and retrieved the gun from the crook's pocket. With a swift tug, she yanked off the ski mask.

"Denny Wysocki," she said coldly. He shut his eyes, unable to meet Fiona's gaze. The officer lifted him upright and shoved him toward the door.

"Ow," Denny winced. "You're hurting my shoulder."

"So sorry," the cop muttered, pushing him harder.

In the living room, another officer stood over the second burglar, already cuffed and facedown. The front door was wide open. Through the window, Fiona watched two policemen unfurl yellow crime tape across the yard. Neighbors had begun to gather, drawn by the flashing lights and noise. Some were clustered on porches; others lined the sidewalk.

Fiona's eyes landed on the man on the floor—thick black hair, a pack of Sobranie Black Russians beside him. She shook her head. "Smoking is dangerous on so many levels."

Leonid sneered. "What do you mean?"

"The cigarette stubs you left at the crime scenes led us straight to you."

From his mouth came a string of Russian profanities. Nonplused, Fiona smiled. "Now you'll never get a chance to win back your poker losses."

As Leonid squirmed on the floor, she stepped over him, nodded to the officer, and left the house. Outside, she approached the cops securing the tape.

"Any word on the van?"

"We brought it to the police yard."

"Where's Mancini?"

"He took off with my partner and the guy you nailed. They're taking the suspect to the hospital."

Back in the patrol car, Fiona checked her phone. Two missed calls from Julia—both marked urgent.

Chapter 64

Earlier that evening, Julia sat at her desk at One Federal Street, in the heart of Boston's financial district. A deafening clap of thunder startled her. She looked out her eighth-floor window just as a jagged bolt of lightning split the dark sky. She reached over the arm of her chair for her briefcase and looked inside. Just as she feared—no umbrella.

Large drops of rain splattered against the windows. She decided to clear her desk and head home. Hesitantly, she placed her hands on the computer keyboard. Should she check her emails? What if there was another message from her stalker? She wavered, then shut down the computer. She would wait until morning. The disturbing emails seemed less daunting when read in daylight.

She grabbed her briefcase, then stopped at the restroom. Assessing her image in the bathroom mirror, she pulled a tube of lipstick from her purse and applied it. You never knew who you might run into on the subway.

When the elevator doors opened on the eighth floor, it was packed. Julia squeezed in. Outside the building, she scanned the street for the usual umbrella vendors. None. "Oh well," she muttered, lifting her briefcase over her head as she hurried toward the South Street subway entrance. "It's only water." By the time she reached the steps, she was soaked.

On the subway, droplets slid from the tips of her crimson hair. Julia shivered, regretting her choice of a light jacket over a raincoat. She promised herself a hot bath the moment she got home.

Five stops later, the train pulled into Central Square Station. Julia rode the escalator up to the exit. The storm still raged.

Commuters entering the subway station shook water from their umbrellas. Galoshes squished against the slick floor as they stepped onto the escalator.

Since the threatening emails began, Julia had made a habit of walking the six blocks to her apartment along well-lit and busy streets. But tonight, given the downpour, she opted for a more direct route. She was confident the unmarked police car trailing her—the one she saw outside her apartment building that morning—would follow her down the dark side streets.

Two blocks from her apartment, Julia passed a park shrouded in darkness. On pleasant days, she'd sit on one of the park benches with a newspaper, watching young mothers and nannies monitoring toddlers on seesaws, jungle gyms, and slides. She could envision the day when one of those children might be hers.

Her thoughts drifted to Fiona's good-looking partner. There had been something between them the other night—something in the way he looked at her, the quiet concern in his dark eyes. She'd ask Fiona to set them up.

Halfway past the park, Julia glanced over her shoulder. Her eyes widened; her heart raced. A dark figure had emerged from the shadows, matching her stride. She quickened her pace, checking his progress. He sped up, closing the gap between them. Frantic, she scanned the street for the unmarked police car. Nothing. The road was deserted.

Clutching her pocketbook, hands clammy, she fumbled for her phone and dialed Fiona. No answer. She crossed the street, away from the park, and tried again. Voice mail. She turned her head and gasped. There was no time to leave a message. Her pursuer had crossed the street, too. The distance between them was shrinking fast.

Julia quickened her pace. She wanted to scream, but no one would hear her on the deserted street. The footsteps behind her grew louder. Panicked, Julia ran toward a house with lights shining in the front windows. She bolted up the porch steps and rang the doorbell. No one answered. Frantic, she pounded on the front door. Her stalker was almost to the house.

Julia closed her eyes and prayed to God for a miracle. The door opened a crack. Behind it, she saw the squinty eyes and bushy white brows of an elderly man.

"Help me," she said. "I'm being followed."

He hesitated, then began to close the door.

Tears streamed down her cheeks. She put her palms together, pleading. "He's going to kill me. For the love of God, let me in."

The old man paused, then unlatched the door and opened it. Julia turned back just in time to see her pursuer retreat, vanishing into the night.

Chapter 65

Early the following morning, Fiona sat at her desk writing up a report on the captured felons. She had intended to do it the night before but spent most of the night at Julia's trying to calm her. It was unfortunate that Mahoney had to send the detail trailing her to Lewis Street.

"Ahem," said a voice in front of her desk. She looked up to see Vinnie holding a copy of the *Boston Globe* in front of her. Pictures of the two detectives, provided by the police department, and one of the crime scene appeared on the first page.

"Wow," Fiona said. "Front page coverage."

Vinnie winked at her. "We did all right—partner."

She felt her neck and face flush. Staring at the newspaper photos, she had to admit that she and Vinnie looked good together.

"Hey, by the way, how's your friend doing?"

"Julia?"

"Yeah."

"I went to see her last night. Someone followed her from the subway to her home after work. She managed to elude him, but she was distraught."

"Weird that the perp shows up when the tail isn't there. Do you think he knew, or was it an unfortunate coincidence?"

"Don't know," Fiona said, picking up the phone. Let me see how she's doing."

She dialed Julia's number. Vinnie left the paper on her desk and walked back toward his. "Say hello to her from me."

"Hi," Fiona said when Julia picked up the phone. "Feeling better?"

"A bit, but I had a hard time sleeping. Kept waking up and thinking the man who followed me was standing by my bed, ready to strangle me."

"That's normal after what happened last night."

"Are the cops going to tail me?"

"Yes. They're outside your building." Fiona paused. "Are you up for some questions today? You were too upset for me to ask you last night."

"Okay."

"Did you see anyone who resembled the guy who followed you in the subway or at the station?"

"No, I never saw his face. He could have been sitting next to me for all I know."

"Could you give me a physical description?" Fiona picked up her notepad and pen.

"Not really. It was pitch black. All I remember was that he was big and scary, wore boots, and what looked like a ski parka."

"Anything distinctive about his gait? Did he walk with a limp?"

"I really didn't stop and analyze his gait. I was too busy running away."

Disappointed, Fiona put down the pen. "Any new email messages?"

"I'll check."

She tapped her fingernails on the desk while Julia booted up her computer. "Oh my God. There's an email message from him."

"What does it say?"

Fiona heard a gasp on the other end of the line.

"Julia, what does it say?"

"You were lucky last night. You won't be the next time."

Chapter 66

Fiona parked the patrol car in front of the familiar green two-family home on Christian Way, right next door to Jim Foley's place. Angela Wysocki stood behind the storm door, watching as Fiona and Vinnie made their way up the sidewalk.

"I saw you comin'," she said to Vinnie, ignoring Fiona as she opened the door. They stepped inside.

"We have a subpoena to search the premises," Vinnie said, producing an official-looking document.

Angela pulled a pair of glasses from the pocket of her housedress and scanned the paper. "Just so you know, I had no idea what Denny and that Russian dingbat next door were mixed up in."

"You're not being charged with anything…yet," Fiona replied coolly.

Angela handed the document back to Vinnie and scowled at Fiona. "If you need me, I'll be watchin' TV with my mother-in-law."

Fiona glanced toward the living room and noticed the large screen TV had been replaced with a much smaller one. "What happened to the big TV that was here last time I visited?"

"It's in the garage. I don't want any ill-gotten goods in my house."

Fiona and Vinnie began their investigation in the basement, cataloging the items stuffed almost to the ceiling in the damp, musty cellar. After combing through closets and drawers upstairs, they found nothing of interest in the rest of the house. But the garage was another story. No wonder the van was parked in the driveway—

there was barely space to move among the TVs, video equipment, antique tables, and assorted goods crammed inside.

Once they wrapped up the search, Vinnie and Fiona returned to the house to speak with Angela. “We need to ask you about the van,” Vinnie said.

“When am I getting it back?” Angela asked.

“For now, it’s part of the crime scene,” Vinnie stated. “It was used to transport stolen property.”

“Well, I need it,” she said, arms crossed.

“When we’re finished with it, we’ll return it.”

Angela pouted, her half-closed eyes nearly vanishing in the folds of her lids. “The van’s not Denny’s. It’s mine. My father gave it to me when he passed.”

“Do you have the registration?” Vinnie asked. “It wasn’t in the vehicle.”

With a groan, Angela pushed herself off the couch. “Do you need anything else while I’m up?”

Vinnie smiled. “No, just that.”

Angela waddled out of the room, returning a few minutes later with the registration. Vinnie examined it. “Who’s Stanley Prehodka?”

“My dad.”

“When did he pass?”

“1992.”

Vinnie’s eyes opened wide. “Eighteen years and you haven’t changed the registration?”

"Didn't see the need," Angela said, her jaw clenched.

"Is the van insured?"

"Don't know, you have to ask Denny."

Vinnie shook his head and handed the registration back to Angela.

Fiona opened her notebook. "Do you know who's used the van recently?"

"All our neighbors have. Last week, Stupid next door—how the hell could he rent to someone from the Russian mafia?—borrowed it to move some of his son's stuff into his new apartment. The week before that, the Zalinski's across the street took it to haul some appliances from Home Depot. It was my dad's van. I don't use it much, so I let whoever needs it borrow it."

"Did you keep any records?"

"Nope. The only thing we asked was that whoever took it brought it back with a full tank."

Fiona scribbled a few notes, then tucked the pad back into her pocket. "We'll need a list of everyone who's borrowed the van. Approximate dates would be helpful."

Angela squinted at Fiona and shook her head. "A lot of people used it. It'll take me some time to remember who, let alone when."

"Just do the best you can," Vinnie said, flashing his most disarming smile.

Angela patted her hair and smoothed down her housedress, grinning at the detective in return. She turned to Fiona. "So, when do I get the van back?"

“Sorry,” Fiona replied. “Like Detective Mancini said, it’s still part of the crime scene. Ownership doesn’t change that.”

Angela sighed. “Since I don’t know when Denny’s coming back, I’m putting…”—she gestured to her mother-in-law, absorbed as usual in her soaps—her in a ...” She mouthed the words *nursing home*. “My brother’s coming this weekend to help. I need the van to move her stuff.”

Vinnie sighed. “You might want to consider renting a U-Haul.”

“Humph,” Angela muttered, folding her arms and plopping down on the couch.

“We’ll be leaving now, ma’am,” Vinnie said as he and Fiona headed for the door. Angela made no move to accompany them. “Don’t bother getting up. We’ll let ourselves out.”

Once outside the Wysocki’s home, they crossed the lawn and rang the bell next door. Joe answered, greeting Fiona with a warm hug.

She stepped back and smiled. “This is Vinnie Mancini, my new partner.”

The two shook hands.

“What can I do for you?” Joe asked.

Vinnie pulled an envelope from inside his jacket. “We have a subpoena to search your tenant’s apartment. Can you let us in?”

“Sure. Give me a minute.”

Joe returned with a key and unlocked the door to the unit. He followed Fiona and Vinnie into the living room. “You don’t need to stay, sir,” Vinnie said. “We’ll let you know when we’re done.”

Once Joe left, they slipped on gloves and methodically searched the unit. Inside the bedrooms, stolen goods were piled in disorganized heaps. The dresser drawers overflowed with jewelry and other valuables stolen during the burglaries.

Two hours later, the investigation was complete. As they descended the stairs to the ground floor, Fiona held the key. “I’ll return it to Joe,” she told Vinnie.

While Vinnie made his way to the car, she rang Joe’s doorbell. When he answered, Fiona handed him the key. “Here you go. Thanks for your help.”

To her surprise, Joe clasped her hand. “I need to talk to you. Do you have a moment?”

“Not right now.”

“This might be out of line, but could I stop by your place tonight? Around seven?”

Fiona hesitated, curious. “Sure. Seven would be fine.”

“Until this evening then,” Joe said, releasing her hand.

Vinnie glanced at Fiona when she got in the car. “What did Foley want?”

“Wants to talk about something. Said he’d come by tonight.”

“What do you think he wants?”

“No idea. Maybe he wants us to go easy on his wife-beating son.”

“I’m for putting the SOB away,” Vinnie said.

“For once, we agree.”

Fiona gave her partner a sideward glance as she pulled out of the parking space. “We need to send forensics in for Leonid’s fingerprints.”

She checked her watch. “It’s almost noon. Do you want to grab a bite at Smiley’s? It’s just a couple of blocks away.”

“Sure,” Vinnie said, cracking his knuckles.

The sound sent a chill down Fiona’s spine. “Could you not do that?”

Vinnie started to say something, thought better of it, and smiled. “Whatever the lady wants.”

Chapter 67

Seated in Smiley's, halfway through their burgers, Vinnie took a sip of soda and leaned back. "So, what's the deal with you and that Joe fellow?"

Fiona looked up. "What do you mean?"

"That hug when we arrived. I think he has a thing for you."

"Don't be ridiculous, I'm dating his son."

They ate in silence for a few minutes, the clatter of cutlery and the low hum of restaurant conversation filling the space. Then Vinnie spoke again. "How's Julia doing?"

"She got another threatening email," Fiona said, her voice tight.

Vinnie reached for the ketchup, dousing his fries. "I'm sorry. She's a nice kid. Is she seeing anyone?"

Having just taken a bite of her burger, Fiona took a moment to answer. "I don't think so."

"Think she'd go out with me?"

Fiona choked, nearly spitting out the burger. She grabbed her water and took a big gulp.

"You okay?"

Still drinking, she nodded. Vinnie's apparent interest in Julia had caught her off guard. She forced a smile. "Probably. She'd definitely feel safe dating a guy who carries a gun."

Vinnie grinned. "Maybe we could double date. You know, you and her brother, me and Julia."

Ignoring the queasy feeling in her stomach, she smiled. "I'll see what I can do."

Chapter 68

Fiona was lounging on the sofa watching TV when the doorbell rang. Jasmine's ears perked up. The dog sprang from her position near Fiona's feet and dashed toward the front door, barking furiously.

"Who is it?" Fiona asked into the intercom.

"Joe Foley."

She buzzed him in. As she moved to open the door, she grabbed Jasmine's collar. The dog growled and strained against her grip.

When Joe entered the apartment, Jasmine howled, her teeth bared. "I don't know what's gotten into Jasmine," Fiona said. "Let me put her in my bedroom."

While Fiona tended to the dog, Joe wandered around the apartment, glancing at the photos displayed on the end table and mantelpiece. Reentering the room, she saw Joe holding the picture of her and Ciara. "Is this your sister?"

"Yes. That's me and Ciara."

"You two look remarkably alike. She's very pretty."

"Thanks."

Fiona gestured toward the couch. "Please, have a seat. Would you care for anything to drink?"

"No thanks. I just finished dinner."

Fiona sat at the other end of the sofa. "What can I do for you?"

Joe leaned forward, his voice tense. “I’m frustrated. My daughter’s been getting threatening emails, and the police aren’t doing a damn thing.”

Fiona frowned. “That’s not entirely true. We’ve assigned someone to follow her.”

Joe scoffed. “A lot of good that did. The stalker nearly got her last night. If she hadn’t had the presence of mind to knock on a stranger’s door, I don’t even want to think of what could’ve happened.”

“We’re stretched thin,” Fiona said, her tone defensive. “We’re doing the best we can.”

Joe got up from the couch and began pacing. “Well, your best isn’t good enough.”

“I’ll speak to the Chief and see if we can beef up the surveillance.”

Joe paused, his expression softening. “I hate to put this on you, but my kids mean everything to me.”

“I know,” Fiona said softly. “I know.”

Chapter 69

The biting March wind did little to dampen the enthusiasm of the crowd gathered outside the roped-off entrance to the nightclub on Saturday night. Billed as one of the most exclusive clubs in Boston, it lived up to its hype. For every person that made it through its hallowed doors, three were turned away. Mickey pulled out his wallet as he approached the large, muscular doorman, checking IDs.

"He's got a VIP card," Julia whispered to Vinnie and Fiona as they edged closer to the attendant. "That, plus a twenty, should get us in."

The doorman's lips curled into a knowing smile as Mickey handed over his card and the cash. Unclipping the red velvet rope, he made a sweeping gesture for the four to enter.

Inside, they shed their coats and hats, handing them to the cloakroom attendant. Julia tossed back her hair. Silken strands cascaded over her bare back and shoulders. She wore a sleek black halter top over a short skirt that showcased her shapely legs. Stiletto heels added several inches to her height. Fiona, dressed more modestly in an emerald green sweater and knee-length black skirt, suddenly wished she'd chosen something a bit more daring.

Vinnie gave Julia an appreciative glance. "You sure you don't want to keep your jacket? Not that I want you to cover up your..." he cleared his throat, "lovely blouse. Just thinking you might get cold in that outfit."

Julia twirled a strand of hair around her finger and smiled. "I'll be fine. It heats up fast in here."

Fiona felt like gagging. What was with the suggestive remark? She'd never seen this flirtatious side of Julia before—and Vinnie was grinning like a Cheshire cat, clearly enjoying every second of it.

Mickey, familiar with the club's layout, took the lead, guiding the group up the wide, red-carpeted staircase. As they ascended, they passed clusters of young women in short skirts and towering platform heels, clinging to their sharply dressed dates. The scene resembled a movie premiere—minus Jennifer Lawrence and Brad Pitt. The steady thump of bass-heavy music pulsed through the building, blending with the hum of conversation and laughter.

"Pool or dancing, ladies?" Mickey asked over his shoulder.

"Pool," Fiona said quickly.

"Dancing," Julia countered.

Mickey pulled a quarter out of his pants pocket. "You call Fiona, what's pool?"

"Heads," she said.

Mickey flipped the coin. "Tails…looks like we're dancing."

Vinnie gave Julia a high-five and slid his arm around her waist, pulling her close. Fiona frowned. She had the feeling that she had just lost more than a coin toss.

Chapter 70

Trailing behind Mickey, the group climbed the stairs to the third floor. Fiona quickened her pace until she was beside Julia. "Please, tell your father not to worry," she said quietly. "The Chief assured me there'll be a police tail on you until the missing women case is resolved."

Julia gave her a puzzled look. "My father? He doesn't even know about that guy who's been following me."

Fiona blinked. "I don't understand. He came to my house last night, furious that the police weren't there the night you were nearly attacked."

"I never told him about the emails or that incident. He has enough on his mind without worrying about me."

"Then how did he find out?"

Julia shrugged. "No idea. Unless Owen said something. I did tell him all the gory details, but he swore he wouldn't say anything to dad."

Strange, Fiona thought as she caught up to Mickey. *Why would Owen tell Joe? Why stir up worry like that?*

***

A live band blasted music from a platform at the far end of the room. The crowd moved like a tide. Only arms and torsos were visible as dancers bobbed to the rhythm—a cluster of buoys in a restless sea.

A hostess led the group to a small table in a far corner of the room, well away from the dance floor. Dissatisfied with the location, Mickey requested another table.

"I'm sorry," the hostess said politely. "But this is the only empty one we have."

Mickey sighed and reached for his wallet, but she gently placed a hand over his. "It won't make any difference. We really don't have another table."

Before the drinks even arrived, Vinnie and Julia had disappeared onto the dance floor. Within seconds, they were swallowed up by the crowd. Occasionally, Fiona caught a glimpse of Julia's jet-black hair or Vinnie's purple shirt, his jacket long since discarded. The music was deafening, making conversation nearly impossible, even though Fiona was practically sitting on Mickey's lap.

When the band shifted to a slow song, Mickey stood and offered his hand. Fiona took it, and he guided her to the dance floor. As they swayed together, she peered over his shoulder and spotted Vinnie and Julia, wrapped in each other's arms, moving in sync with the music. The song ended, and the tempo surged again. The crowd erupted into motion, gyrating to the relentless beat.

Frowning, Fiona turned to Mickey. "I just can't get into this music."

"That's okay," Mickey said, taking her hand and leading her off the dance floor. "We'll wait for another slow one."

Back at the table, Fiona watched the dancers, feeling a sense of disconnection. The music didn't move her. It never had. She couldn't recall ever being excited about the latest rock star or trending band. Sure, there was that phase in high school and college when music seemed to define friendships. She remembered heated debates among her friends—Eminem versus 50 Cent, who was the better rapper. But she'd never really cared.

Mickey touched Fiona's arm and leaned in, his lips moving—but the pounding music swallowed his words. She pointed to her ear and moved closer, but his voice was still barely audible. "Do you want to go?" Sweeter words were never spoken. She nodded without hesitation.

Raising a finger to signal *just a minute*, Mickey turned and vanished into the sea of gyrating bodies. Fiona watched as he disappeared into the crowd, only to return moments later.

"Julia and Vinnie will grab a cab," he said. "We can head out."

Fiona closed her eyes, a wave of relief washing over her. Finally, this miserable night was coming to an end.

Chapter 71

The arraignment of Denny Wysocki and Leonid Soldatenkoff took place on Wednesday, March 24. At the bench, Judge Thomas took a sip from the mug of coffee beside him, rolled his shoulders, stifled a yawn, and watched the attorneys shuffle papers. With a nod to the bailiff, the proceedings began.

"United States of America versus Leonid Soldatenkoff and Denny Wysocki, case number 10 C 1854"

Jill Mathewson, the prosecuting attorney, removed a pencil from behind her ear and stepped up to the podium. She opened her file, unbuttoned the jacket of her slate-gray suit, and looked up at the judge. "The defendants are charged with armed burglary and attempted homicide. They were apprehended at the scene by detectives Vincent Mancini and Fiona Sullivan of the Belmont Police Department."

Each defendant had retained separate counsel. Gordon White, representing Soldatenkoff, ran his manicured fingers through his steel-gray hair. A senior partner at one of the city's most prestigious firms, he was considered a formidable adversary. Clearing his throat, he addressed the court, his basso profundo resonating through the chamber.

"My client," he began, gesturing toward the burly Russian in the dark suit seated beside him, "is a first-time offender. He has only limited proficiency in English and was unaware of Mr. Wysocki's intentions until they were already inside the residence. For this reason, he pleads not guilty."

Mathewson responded by holding up a plastic evidence bag containing two black cigarette butts with gold foil filters.

“These are Sobranie black Russians—the brand smoked by Mr. Soldatenkoff. They were recovered from two separate burglary scenes. A third, still undergoing analysis, was found at the crime scene. Lab results confirm Mr. Soldatenkoff’s DNA in the saliva on all three. We contend that this was not Mr. Soldenkoff’s first foray into burglary.”

The defense attorney raised an eyebrow and whispered something to Leonid. The accused shrugged his shoulders. “May I approach the bench, your Honor?” White asked. The judge nodded.

Both attorneys stepped forward. White spoke first. “We maintain that the original sample of the defendant’s DNA was obtained illegally. Therefore, we request that the cigarette butts not be admitted into evidence.”

Jill Mathewson stared at her opponent, eyes narrowed, face flushed. “The prosecution disagrees. The cigarette butts were recovered from two separate burglary scenes and are part of the physical evidence. Additionally, Mr. Soldatenkoff voluntarily submitted to a DNA saliva test, which confirmed he smoked the cigarettes in question.”

White’s tone turned sharp. “Your Honor, due to my client’s difficulties with English, he did not fully understand the ramifications of the saliva test. He was entitled to an interpreter—none was provided.”

Judge Thomas fixed his gaze on White. “Unless you can substantiate that claim, Counselor, the DNA evidence will be admitted.

“Yes, your honor,” White replied through clenched teeth, somehow managing to preserve his obsequious smile.

The judge turned to Wysocki's attorney, "Mr. Kenny, how does your client plead?"

"Guilty, your Honor."

Mathewson glanced at the defendants, "Due to the nature of the crime—home invasion robbery with a deadly weapon—the prosecution requests that both Mr. Wysocki and Mr. Soldatenkoff be denied bail."

White cleared his throat. "As we've stated, Mr. Soldatenkoff is a first-time offender. We ask that bail be set at $100,000."

"Mr. Kenny?" the judge asked.

"We request the same for Mr. Wysocki."

Jill Mathewson's eyes narrowed. "Judge, Mr. Soldatenkoff is a flight risk. He's a Russian national. In addition, he fired at a police officer. We strongly urge that he be remanded in custody."

Leonid, expressionless until now, scowled at the prosecuting attorney. White quickly stepped between him and the bench to shield his client's face—but the damage was done. Judge Thomas squinted at the defendant, his jaw tightening. "Mr. Soldatenkoff will be remanded in custody."

The judge turned to the prosecuting attorney. "Is Mr. Wysocki also a flight risk?"

"We suspect Russian money is involved, but we're still determining the extent."

Wysocki's lawyer shook his head emphatically. "My client is not a beneficiary of any Russian largesse. This is his first conviction. He's an American citizen and, unlike Mr. Soldatenkoff, lacks the resources to retain private counsel."

"Bail is set at $200,000," the judge announced.

Two officers stepped forward to escort Leonid away. Jill Mathewson cast a triumphant glance at White. Denny conferred briefly with his attorney before being led away to await bail. At the back of the courtroom, Vinnie and Fiona watched as the scene unfolded.

"Jill's a sharp attorney," Fiona remarked.

"And quite the looker," Vinnie added.

Fiona gave Vinnie a disgusted look. "Seriously, is that all you notice?"

A cocky smile on his face, Vinnie rose from his seat. "Lighten up, Sullivan. Let me buy you lunch."

Chapter 72

At a luncheonette just a few blocks from the courthouse, Fiona slid into the booth across from Vinnie. After they ordered, Vinnie asked her about the white van.

"I got a report from forensics just before the preliminary hearing. The fingerprints from both of the suspects were on the door handles and sides of the car."

Vinnie raised an eyebrow. "Why weren't they arraigned together?"

"Money," she said flatly. "Whoever bankrolled White didn't want Denny in the mix. Thought it would weaken the Russian's defense. My guess? Leonid's going to flip and throw Denny under the bus."

Vinnie drummed his fingers on the table. "Think he'll walk?"

"Hard to say. But we might have another angle."

"What?"

"Kidnapping. Forensics found blood on the inside of the driver's door. DNA analysis identified it as AB RH negative—rare—same type as Muriel, the missing hairdresser.

"Do you think he's our serial killer?"

Fiona shrugged. A crescendo of ringing bells sounded from the parka hanging over the back of her seat. "It's Mahoney," she said, reaching for the cell phone.

"How do you know?"

"Doorbell. That's the ringtone I gave him," Fiona said.

Vinnie smirked. “What’s mine?”

“A duck.”

He blinked. “You’re kidding.”

Fiona flipped open her phone. “Hi, Chief.” She listened intently for several minutes. “Yeah. They were both convicted.”

Vinnie watched as Fiona placed the phone back inside her jacket pocket. “What’s up?”

“Nothing major. The Chief just wanted to know the outcome of the trial. Ready to go?”

They paid the bill and stepped out into the afternoon chill. Once inside the patrol car, Vinnie pulled his phone out and dialed. From Fiona’s jacket pocket came sounds of quacking.

Vinnie shook his head. “Classy.”

Chapter 73

The ringing of the telephone woke Fiona. Half-asleep, she reached for the receiver on the nightstand beside her bed.

"Did you read this morning's paper?"

"Mom?' Fiona mumbled. "What time is it?"

"Nine thirty. Aren't you up yet?"

"It's Sunday."

"Are you going to mass?"

"I'm exhausted. I'll walk Jasmine, then crawl back under the covers."

"You haven't been to church in ages."

"Please, not this again."

"Anyway," her mother continued undeterred, check today's *Globe.* There's a front-page story on Henry Winfield. He was acquitted of four of the murders—including Ciara's."

Fiona sat up, suddenly alert. Her pulse quickened.

"The article says that he probably didn't commit any of the murders."

"I'll call you back later after I read it."

She hung up and threw on a pair of jeans and a sweatshirt. Sunlight streamed through the partially opened blinds. She rummaged through a dresser drawer for a clean pair of wool socks and slipped them on, followed by her orange-and-navy duck boots. Once dressed, she opened the bedroom door. Jasmine was waiting, tail wagging, ready to jump.

Fiona uttered her usual morning mantra. "Down, Jasmine. Be a good girl. I haven't even had my morning coffee yet."

In the kitchen, as Jasmine pranced excitedly back and forth, Fiona opened a can of dog food, spooned it into a bowl, and filled another with water. Jasmine dove in, devouring the meal while Fiona brewed a cup of coffee. After a few sips, she felt a wet muzzle nudge her arm.

"Okay, okay. We'll go for a walk."

They headed downstairs, Jasmine straining at the leash. Outside, Fiona scooped up the Sunday *Globe* and placed it inside the stairwell door. She'd read it later.

Jasmine did her usual territorial sniffing and peeing. She paid no heed to her impatient mistress. Suddenly, the sound of a doorbell rang out. Fiona reached into her jacket, recognizing the ringtone.

"Hi, Chief. What's up?"

"I need you and Mancini to come in today. Ever since Winfield was found innocent of those murders, the phones haven't stopped. People are panicked, especially with those other women still missing."

"You know today's Sunday, right?"

There was silence on the other end of the phone.

"Just kidding. Give me half an hour."

"OK. I'll call Mancini," Mahoney said.

Chapter 74

"This is not how I planned to spend my day off," Vinnie said as he sat down beside Fiona's desk. "I promised Julia we'd play tourist, hit the Gardner Museum, and all that crap."

"You like art?" she asked.

"If my companion is hot enough, I can tolerate it."

"So, Mahoney did you a favor."

Vinnie gave Fiona a half-smile, stood, and followed her to Mahoney's office. They found the Chief in front of his desk, the phone ringing nonstop.

"You gonna answer that?" Vinnie asked.

"No point. It's the same thing every time: 'When are you going to catch the serial killer?' 'Is he behind the missing women?' 'Do you even have a suspect?'" He paused, pulled a handkerchief from his pocket, and wiped his brow. The phone finally stopped ringing.

"I want you two to take another look at those files of the murdered and missing women. See if you can find anything that might be useful."

Vinnie shook his head. "But Chief, we've combed through those files a million times."

"So now it will be a million and one. Get to work."

As the phone rang again, the detectives stepped out of Mahoney's office and returned to theirs. They approached the murder board. Photos of the victims stared back at them—Ciara's among them. "What could be the tie between the four abductions and the earlier murders?" Vinnie asked.

"They all come from in or around the Boston area," Fiona said. "And, once again, they are all young, attractive, and of Irish descent."

"Think they were random? Like the perp just spotted them on the street?"

Fiona handed Vinnie half the files. "Here—take these and go through them again. I gave you Ciara's. I'm too close to her case—I might be missing something."

Vinnie nodded, and the two returned to their desks. An hour later, he slid into the chair beside her. "I found a common thread—at least between these two cases."

Fiona looked up expectantly.

"In both, a piece of jewelry was missing."

"That's right," she said slowly. "Ciara had a heart-shaped locket from her boyfriend. She wore it every day. It wasn't on her when she was found."

"Think the killer tried to fence it?"

"No. At the time, the police checked pawn shops and other likely places. We even got a photo of the locket from the manufacturer and ran it in the local newspapers, hoping someone would remember seeing it. It was never found. I think the perp kept the jewelry as a souvenir."

Fiona leaned back in her chair and continued. "Same pattern in the other cases where bodies were recovered. Each victim was missing a piece of jewelry. And not the most valuable stuff. One of the women was wearing an engagement ring worth approximately $1,000. The killer took her fake gold earrings, which may have cost fifty bucks. That's another reason," Fiona added, "That I don't think he's a thief. When the wallets were recovered, none of the money or credit cards was missing."

Vinnie rubbed his eyes wearily. "Mahoney's not going to be happy if this is all we've got."

Fiona sighed. "We can't fabricate evidence. There was no DNA on the victims. With the first group, all but one were raped—most likely post-mortem. No semen, though. He must have used a condom. Nothing under the fingernails either, even though the bruises and scratches show they fought back."

Vinnie leaned back in his chair. "What kind of killer takes jewelry as a souvenir?"

"A sentimental one. He took something that lasts. Something that won't decay with time."

Vinnie closed his files and threw them across Fiona's desk. "How about the owner of the white van?"

"Angela Wysocki?"

"Yeah. Did she give you the list of who borrowed it and when?"

"She tried. There were about fifteen friends, relatives, or neighbors who she thinks might have used the van. But she had only a vague notion as to who borrowed it and when."

Vinnie rose from his chair and stretched, joints cracking. "I think that's all we've got for today. Tomorrow, let's start working through the list—track down everyone who borrowed that van, one by one."

Fiona nodded, gathering the scattered papers. "That's probably the best way to go, although it's going to be a grind."

Vinnie gave a half-smile. "Who knows? Maybe we'll get lucky."

Chapter 75

Unable to speak, his mouth stretched wide, his eyes shut tight, he lay back in the chair as the young woman poked and prodded with metal tools. He felt exposed. Vulnerable. Sweat beaded on his forehead. Was it her closeness—or his nerves?

He opened his eyes and studied the hygienist's face. He liked the smattering of light freckles on her cheeks, visible above the white mask. Her nametag glistened beneath the dental lamp: *Heather O'Malley*. She was the reason he came in four times a year instead of the usual two.

Heather carefully set her tools on the tray and turned to the counter. She peeled off her mask and latex gloves, then scribbled notes onto his chart.

"Dr. Rafferty will be in shortly," she said, adjusting the chair so he could sit upright.

"How do they look?" he asked.

"Pretty good," she replied. There are just a couple of teeth that I want the doctor to take a closer look at."

He hesitated, then smiled. "So…how come someone as pretty as you isn't married?" Heather's cheeks reddened. "Sorry. Didn't mean to embarrass you."

Heather handed him a small plastic bag. "I put an extra dental floss in here. Make sure you use it."

She left the room, but the scent of her perfume lingered. It reminded him of the fragrance in the air after a spring rain. He closed his eyes and thought about kissing each scented part of her perfect body.

He'd been fortunate so far. One more, he told himself. Just one more, and he'd be done—retire the garrote, so to speak. The next target was already chosen. But Heather... she kept slipping into his thoughts, uninvited. He'd find a way to include her. She would be the second-to-last—his penultimate.

Chapter 76

That night, he waited in the shadowed doorway—the same one he'd used when Maureen Doyle became his first graveyard victim. Heather followed the same routine: the bus from the dentist's office in Watertown to her apartment off Trapelo Road. Conveniently, her route took her past the cemetery. A grave had been dug earlier that afternoon, ready for a funeral scheduled for the next day.

He had decided not to transport his "angels". Since the police had confiscated the van, moving the young women had become problematic. Renting a vehicle was risky. Even if he used an assumed name and the fake license his friend had made for him, there was the risk of leaving evidence behind. He prided himself on leaving no trace, but what if he'd missed something? A fingerprint on a door handle, a stray fiber?

It was early April, and there was a hint of springtime in the air—a time of rebirth and copulation. The sensuousness of the season aroused him. He reached down and rubbed his genitals just as a middle-aged matron passed by. She gave him a disgusted look. Averting her glance, he put his hands in his pockets. After she walked by, he looked up. The bus was approaching.

Several passengers got off. Heather O'Malley was the last to descend. Instead of trailing her the three blocks to the cemetery, he turned down a side street, circling the block at a brisk pace before jogging the final stretch to the graveyard. He slipped through the front gate, then crossed diagonally to the wall of bushes that shielded him from the eyes of the young woman making her way home.

He should've worn something lighter. The down-filled parka, gloves, wool cap, and heavy knapsack were suffocating. Sweat trickled down his back as he inhaled the cool night air and crept toward the hedge opening—the same one he'd used before.

Peering through the bushes, he flinched. She was only about fifty feet away, moving at a rapid pace. He'd misjudged the time it would take her to walk the three blocks. Unlike his first victim, Heather wore practical nurse's shoes, not stiletto boots.

Heart racing, he moved stealthily along the bushes to the next opening and peeked out. No one was there. Where had she gone? Then he spotted her on the other side of the street, walking at a faster clip. Why had she crossed the street? Had she seen him?

For a moment, he considered abandoning the plan. But his adrenaline was surging. He reached into his knapsack and pulled out the garrote. Just in case, he took the knife, too.

Shoving the backpack under the bushes, he glanced up and down the street. Empty. Adjusting his cap low over his forehead, he darted across the road. Heather turned at the sound of his footsteps and screamed. She bolted in the opposite direction, calling for help.

He gained steadily on his victim, closing the gap with every stride. When he was behind her, he wrapped his arm around her neck. She screamed in terror. No time to use the garrote. He whipped out his knife and held the blade against her throat. With one swipe of the weapon, she ceased yelling.

Blood gushed from her neck and covered his clothes. A car approached from Trapelo Road, its headlights illuminating the dark street. He turned the lifeless form toward him and kissed her, tasting the blood on her lips. The car slowed. For a brief moment, the killer contemplated dropping the body and running. However, it then picked up speed; the driver probably did not want to intrude upon the two lovers.

Waiting until the car was out of sight, he lifted Heather into his arms and carried her across the street and into the cemetery. A trail of red droplets marked his path. He'd come back later to get rid of them. Once behind the hedges, he grabbed a towel from his knapsack and wrapped it around her neck to stem the bleeding. With the bag slung over his shoulder, he hoisted her again, walking backward to ensure no blood was visible. Luckily, the distance was short.

At the edge of the open grave, he pulled back the tarp and lowered her body into the hole. He set up the ladder and climbed down. The adrenaline had drained, leaving only a dull ache and a thirst he couldn't quench. A beer would've helped. Or something stronger. The night had unraveled. The thrill was gone.

***

The chirping of birds awoke him. Disoriented, he shook his head. "Shit," he muttered, "it's almost morning."

Now fully awake, he pulled a shovel from the backpack. There was no time to pleasure himself. That would have to wait until his next and final victim. He dug with urgency. The softened earth, no longer frozen, made the task easier. Once the hole was deep enough, he placed the body inside, along with her purse, his blood-soaked jacket, and the towel. Usually, he would check the contents of the purse, but today, there was no time.

He hesitated. A souvenir? She wore little jewelry—just a watch and a friendship ring. The watch would do. He slipped it into his backpack, then covered the body with dirt, tamped down the mound, and climbed out.

Standing at the grave's edge, something caught his eye: a cell phone nestled in the corner. He checked his pocket. It wasn't his…it had to be Heather's. It must have fallen out of her purse. His pulse quickened. He couldn't leave it there; he had to retrieve it.

Preparing to climb back into the grave to recover it, he noticed a gravedigger driving a backhoe in the distance. *Damn, no time to get it,* he thought.

He hesitated, calculating. The phone would be buried soon enough, muffled beneath the casket and layers of earth. No one would hear it. No one would know. He quickly pulled the tarp back into place and slipped through the hedges before the gravedigger could spot him.

Chapter 77

The following afternoon, dressed in funeral attire, he hid in the grove of trees to await the arrival of the mourners. The casket was positioned above the open grave. It would be lowered following the service. In the distance, he spotted the slow procession of cars winding through the gates.

Awaiting burial was Mrs. Francis G. Peabody. The obit in the paper claimed she was ninety-two, mother of five, grandmother of twelve, and great-grandmother of three. She was also a proud member of the Daughters of the American Revolution. Heather, he thought, should feel honored to share a grave with such distinguished company.

The mourners—there must have been at least seventy—gathered around the casket. They reflected the pedigree of the deceased: tailored suits, designer coats, quiet elegance. A woman in a veiled black hat dabbed discreetly at her tears with a lace handkerchief. A toddler in patent-leather Mary Jane's, white anklets, and a dark coat and bonnet stared at the group from her father's arms. Voices were hushed, expressions appropriately grave. He drifted closer, blending into the crowd until he stood just feet from the open grave.

The minister arrived and opened his prayer book to signal the beginning of the service. The sound of voices trailed off.

"We are gathered together…" he began.

Then from the depths of the open grave came the unmistakable sound of a duck quacking.

Gasps rippled through the crowd. A woman near the front clutched her chest and collapsed. The quacking repeated, louder this time.

A teenager pulled out his phone. “Hey,” he said, “someone else has the same ringtone as me.”

Chapter 78

Mahoney leaned back in his chair and whispered a silent prayer. Finally—a break in the case. The mayor had called yesterday, furious. Another young woman, a dental hygienist, had been reported missing. Mahoney assured him the department was working double shifts, but the mayor wasn't satisfied. A group, including the parents of two of the victims, hounded him daily, demanding answers. There were complaints that the police department wasn't doing its job. Belmont citizens wanted results.

Mahony had dispatched Mancini and Sullivan to investigate the latest disappearance. They had traced the alleged victim's route home from the bus stop and found evidence of foul play, but nothing else. The incident replicated that of the first victim, Maureen Doyle, but still no bodies and no suspects. That is, until the call from the funeral home changed everything.

***

When Fiona and Vinnie arrived at the cemetery, the casket had been removed, and police had placed yellow tape around the open grave. Inside, an officer knelt beside the partially uncovered body of Heather O'Malley. He looked up as the detectives approached.

"Finally," he said, "our killer messed up."

"What happened, Bobby?" Fiona asked.

He held up a plastic evidence bag. Inside was a cell phone, smeared with dirt. "He left this behind. It was lying in the corner of the grave—completely exposed. Must've missed it. It rang during the funeral."

Fiona slipped on a pair of latex gloves and dropped down into the grave. She shook her head as she studied the sweet-faced victim.

"Forensics have already been here. I took pictures and called for a bus," Bobby said, standing up. "Mark's gone to get a rope ladder."

"Got it," Mark said, waving the ladder overhead. A few minutes later, after affixing it to the side of the grave, he and Vinnie climbed down into the hole.

They carefully brushed away more dirt from the corpse, bagging a bloodied jacket and a knife lying beside her. Fiona crouched beside the body, her eyes scanning the wounds. "Throat's been slit." She murmured. "Clothes are intact. Doesn't look like a sexual assault."

Vinnie examined the victim's hands. "Two broken nails. She didn't go quietly—definitely put up a fight."

"There's some matter under her fingernails," Fiona noted. "Could be from the killer."

At the sound of the ambulance, Vinnie stood up. "We'd better get out so they can remove the body."

They watched as medics carefully lifted the woman's body from the grave. "We've got our work cut out for us," Fiona said to Vinnie. "Everyone interred in or around the dates of the disappearances of the other missing women will have to be exhumed. We have to check if the victims' bodies are buried beneath the caskets."

Chapter 79

Fiona stood in front of the murder board, hands on her hips. Standing beside her, Vinnie studied the portraits of the missing women. It had been a week since Heather O'Malley's body had been found. Since then, the remains of three more victims had surfaced. Only Muriel, the hairdresser, was still unaccounted for.

The press was relentless. Each new body led to the exhumation of at least four graves, stirring public outcry. Families of the deceased were furious over the disruption of their loved ones' final resting places. Meanwhile, residents clung to the hope that the killer's capture was imminent.

Forensics revealed a disturbing pattern: all but the last victim had been sexually assaulted postmortem. This provided a possible link between these murders and those that had occurred earlier—the ones falsely attributed to Winfield. Although the last victim had been stabbed, the other three had been strangled. In each grave, police recovered a garotte buried beside the body.

"Something happened with Heather that made her murder different," Fiona said. "The killer seemed rushed. Sloppy. Not as meticulous as before."

"Forensics ran DNA tests on the material under Heather's nails," Vinnie said. "Whoever our killer is, he's had no prior arrests. There were no matches in the database."

"That rules out a few suspects," Fiona said. "At least among those who had access to Angela Wysocki's van—Denny Wysocki and Leonid Soldatenkoff. Both are in the system."

Vinnie's brow furrowed. "Any leads on the bloodied jacket found with Heather?"

"It was a black Eddie Bauer Skyliner down jacket—one of their best sellers," Fiona replied. "Mickey even has one."

"What's our next move?"

"The killer's likely lying low until the heat dies down. We need to revisit the graves where the bodies were found. There might be evidence we missed."

"Should we split up? Each takes two?"

"That's probably best. The relatives of those buried with the victims will want the coffins returned to the graves as soon as possible. We don't have much time."

By week's end, Fiona and Vinnie regrouped to compare notes. DNA uncovered from the other victims confirmed they'd all been killed by the same person. Interviews with friends and relatives revealed another detail—each woman was missing a piece of jewelry.

Despite the mounting evidence, there was still no suspect. Not even a person of interest. Mahoney remained optimistic, but the case was far from closed.

Chapter 80

Rain pelted the silver Corvette parked on the deserted residential street. Shrouded in thick fog, the streetlights cast an eerie, otherworldly glow. Inside the car, Ed Foley stared at the place that had been his home for fourteen years.

He'd been parked for some time. Though the heater was on, the rawness of the night seeped through his jacket. He blew on his hands and rubbed them together. Leaning over the seat, he grabbed a can of beer from the back, snapped it open, and drank deeply. A loud burp followed the final gulp. He tossed the empty can on the floor. It clanked against the half dozen other cans in front of the passenger seat.

Wiping his mouth and chin with his sleeve, he lit a cigarette. He squinted to see through the rain-streaked windshield, his bloodshot eyes focused on the familiar house. Cigarette dangling from his lips, he tapped his fingers on the steering wheel, his nails making a clicking sound on the metal frame.

He watched the familiar pattern of lights. At six o'clock, the only illumination came from the rear of the house, where Mary was preparing supper. The upstairs rooms remained dark. Emily and Sean were most likely in the kitchen as well, seated at the table, vying for their mother's attention. Their chatter would continue until Mary served them dinner.

After dinner, Mary would clean up with Emily's and Sean's help. Then, the kitchen would go dark, as lights appeared in the living room and upstairs in the kids' bedrooms. Emily and Sean would do their homework, then text and chat with friends until lights-out around ten. Downstairs, Mary would settle in—reading, knitting, or watching TV.

Sadness crept into Ed's eyes. He missed his family. He hated living alone. Most nights, he drifted from bar to bar, picking up some easy lay. But she'd leave the next morning—or sooner if she had a husband waiting. He had tried to reconnect with Sally, but she had threatened to file a restraining order if he ever came near her again. Fuck that cunt detective. Because of her, he was freezing his ass off in his car outside the house he still called home, instead of watching TV in a recliner by the fireplace.

Ed cracked open another beer. With each gulp, his anger increased. How the fuck could he be kept from living in his own home? He still paid the mortgage. He still paid all the utilities. This was America, for Christ's sake. What about his rights? Fuck that judge. Fuck that detective. And fuck his father for letting her into his house.

The clock on the dashboard read 10:15. The lights were still on in the kids' room. *C'mon, Mary, get them to bed. They've got school tomorrow*. If he were inside, they would have been in bed fifteen minutes ago.

Five more minutes passed. The lights remained on. Ed took another swig. *What the hell is Mary doing? Didn't she know it's almost ten-thirty?* Court order or no court order, he had to restore some stability in his fucking home.

Ed zipped up his jacket and pulled on his Red Sox cap. From the glove compartment, he retrieved his gun and checked the chamber. Outside the car, he blinked rapidly. Although the rain had subsided, the fog made it difficult to see. He tried to focus his eyes. His head felt funny, probably from all the beer. Plus, he had to pee.

Mud clung to his boots as he trudged behind the garage. He unzipped his fly and relieved himself, then staggered toward the back porch, tripping on the bottom step. Fearful of having been heard, he crouched down in the bushes. He waited, shivering in the cold. No one appeared. Holding the porch rail for support, he tiptoed up the steps.

He tried the storm door. It was unlocked. Relief flickered across his face as he pulled a key from his pocket and slipped it into the back door lock. Mary hadn't followed through on her threat to change the locks. He turned the knob and crept inside. The sounds emanating from the TV in the front room masked the squeak of the closing door.

Ed recognized the guy's voice on the television. What was his name again? Ray. Ray Romano. *Everybody Loves Raymond.* That show had been the source of countless arguments. He wanted to watch the sports channel; she wanted to watch Raymond. It was her favorite show, so she said. He watched it a few times but couldn't stand it—the men all came off as jerks. No wonder Mary liked it.

Out of habit, Ed removed his boots before entering the kitchen. He crept toward the hallway, just a few steps from the living room. He didn't want to startle Mary. She might scream and alarm the kids. But as he passed through the hall, his foot caught the leg of a small table. He stumbled. *Damn,* he thought. *That wasn't here before.*

Mary muted the TV. "Who's there?" she asked, her voice trembling.

She peered down the hallway. "Eddie? Is that you? What are you doing here?"

"I just wanted to see you and the kids," he said. "I've been sitting out front in the car for hours."

Fear crept across Mary's face. She made a movement toward him, hesitated, and then stepped back. "You're not supposed to be here. And you've been drinking. I can smell it from here."

"Just let me warm up and I'll leave," Ed said, his voice low. "I'm freezing my ass off out there."

"You need to go," Mary said firmly. "The kids will hear you."

"What are they still doing up?"

"Please, Ed. Just leave."

Ed moved closer to Mary. Mary instinctively backed away, her eyes darting to the phone on the end table beside the couch.

"Don't pick up that phone."

Her shaking hand lifted the receiver. Ed lunged toward her, yanking the phone from her grip, then pulling it out of the wall. His face twisted with anger. "I said, don't pick up the phone. Didn't you hear me, bitch?"

Mary shrank back, trembling. Ed grabbed her wrist and struck her across the face. She cried out, stumbling to the floor.

"Mom," Sean screamed from the top of the stairs. Looking up, Ed saw his children staring at him in horror, their eyes wide with fear.

"Stay away from her," Sean shouted.

Ed's rage surged. He turned back toward Mary, who lay curled on the floor, and began kicking her as she lay screaming.

"If you touch her again, you'll be sorry," Sean warned, his voice shaking with anger.

Ed responded with another kick to Mary's side.

Sean disappeared into his room and returned moments later, clutching his Swiss Army knife. He bounded down the stairs. Emily screamed. Sean leapt onto his father's back and drove the blade into his neck. Ed collapsed, clutching the wound, blood pouring through his fingers as he groaned in agony.

Mary scrambled to her feet and rushed to the kitchen. With trembling hands, she grabbed the wall phone and dialed 911. Within minutes, sirens wailed outside the house. A heavy knock rattled the front door. Emily hurried down the stairs and opened the door to two paramedics.

"Where's the victim?" one of them asked. She pointed to the living room. The paramedics rushed in and knelt beside Ed, assessing the wound.

"Get the stretcher," he said to his partner.

As the paramedic exited, two policemen stepped inside. Their eyes swept the room—Ed bleeding on the floor, Mary seated on the couch between her children, her son with his face buried in his hands. Emily watched the paramedics administering aid to her father, who continued to moan on the floor.

"I'm Officer Bobby Clark," one of the officers said. "Can someone tell me what happened here?"

Tears streamed down Mary's cheeks as she raised her face, mottled with bruises. "That's my husband," she said, voice trembling. "I have a restraining order against him. He broke in and started beating me. My son stopped him."

Bobby squinted and studied the victim. "I remember you. We were here a few months ago."

Mary nodded.

Bobby turned to Sean, gesturing toward the bloodied knife lying beside his father. "Is that yours?" Sean, eyes lowered, nodded silently.

Officer Clark motioned to his partner, who slipped on latex gloves, retrieved the knife, and placed it in a plastic evidence bag.

“How’s he doing?” Clark asked the paramedic.

“He’ll survive.”

A second paramedic entered with a stretcher. Assisted by his partner, they lifted Ed onto it and wheeled him out to the waiting ambulance. Outside, neighbors in hooded jackets, most carrying umbrellas, gathered on the street. They watched as the ambulance pulled away, its siren blaring.

Mary stared at the crimson stain on the carpet. Her next call would be to Fiona.

Chapter 81

Ed scowled at Fiona as she entered the interrogation room. "I ain't talking to you—even with my lawyer present."

"That's up to you," Fiona replied calmly. "But if you cooperate, the judge might be more lenient."

Ed turned his back to her.

"Suit yourself," she said and left the room.

A few minutes later. Vinnie entered with Ed's attorney. Gordon White shook his client's hand. "Your father hired me to represent you."

Watching behind the one-way mirror, Fiona turned to Mahoney. "How can Ed afford Gordon White? He's one of the most expensive lawyers around."

"I asked White the same question. Evidently, Joe Foley refinanced his house to cover the cost. Said no kid of his was going to jail. I can't decide if he's a good parent or just a fool."

Inside the interrogation room, Vinnie took a seat across from Ed. "We need to ask you a few questions."

"Only if that other detective isn't listening."

"I don't know who you mean, but I'm the only detective in the room," Vinnie replied evenly.

Ed shifted his large frame in the chair. His attorney sat next to him. "Do you want to tell us what happened last night? Vinnie asked.

Ed glanced at his lawyer, who gave him a subtle nod.

“I was sittin’ in front of *my* house drinkin’ a beer,” Ed began. “Mary was letting the kids stay up way too late.” He turned to his attorney. “Without me around, the kids do whatever they want; they run wild. Mary can’t control them for shit.”

Vinnie leaned forward. “And then what happened?”

“I went in through the back door. I was freezing. I asked Mary to let me warm up. She told me to leave or she’d call the cops.” His voice rose. “I got pissed. After all, that was *my* house, *my* living room, *my* damn fireplace. Who the hell does she think she is, telling me to leave? I pay all the bills; she doesn’t do a damn thing.”

Vinnie lowered his voice. “Did you hit your wife?”

“No. I moved toward her. I guess she got scared. She started to back up, slipped, and fell.”

“So, you never touched her.”

“No.”

“Did you kick her when she was down?”

Ed’s eyes narrowed. “Hell no. Who said that?”

“Your son. He claims you kicked her twice.”

“That ungrateful brat. He’s lying,” Ed snapped. “He came at me and sliced my neck.” He turned, revealing the bandaged side to Vinnie. “He could’ve killed me.”

“We spoke to your wife, son, and daughter—separately. They all told us the same story. You knocked Mary down, beat her, and kicked her. They say if your son hadn’t stepped in, she’d be dead.”

“That’s bullshit.” Ed turned to his attorney. “You see what’s happening? They’re ganging up on me. I swear to God, I never laid a hand on her.”

"So, you're sticking to your story?" Vinnie asked.

"Damn right I am. It's the truth."

Vinnie stood up. "Then I guess we're done here. See you in court."

Ed Foley was arraigned three days later. Since he was in violation of his restraining order, Judge Thomas denied bail. He would remain in custody until his trial.

Chapter 82

"Look, I found another one," Rebecca shouted.

Fiona clapped as the young girl ran across the backyard toward her, holding a blue Easter egg high above her head.

"That's great," Fiona said. "Your basket is almost full."

Even though Easter had come early this year, the day was unseasonably warm. Fiona sat on Joe Foley's back porch, basking in the late morning sun. Mickey had invited her to join the family for an Easter egg hunt and dinner. Her mother was not pleased that her daughter wouldn't be spending the holiday with her. Fiona had tried to compensate by inviting Mickey to meet her parents on Palm Sunday. They'd even sat through high mass at the local parish. Still, her mom had called Fiona yesterday to see if she had changed her mind about coming to North Andover for Easter.

After sitting beside Fiona on the porch steps to count her stash, Rebecca got up to search for more eggs. Fiona noticed the grass stains on the back of the seven-year-old's starched yellow dress and the mud on her white Mary Janes. Ann shook her head. "Guess I should have brought a change of clothes for the egg hunt.

The revving of a motorcycle made Fiona turn just in time to see Owen take off down the driveway with Sean seated behind him. Emily lounged nearby in a deck chair, soaking up some rays, her skirt hiked above her knees, and a half-filled basket of Easter eggs resting beside her.

"Aunt Ann, Sean doesn't have a helmet on," Emily said.

"They're just going around the block. They'll be right back," Ann replied.

"Well, Mom would be furious if she knew."

Ann glanced at her niece, a half-smile on her face. "You're not going to tell on him, are you?"

"No. I guess not," Emily replied, closing her eyes and leaning back to soak in the warmth of the sun. Glued to the portable radio, Mickey sat on the porch rail, sipping beer and listening to the Sox opener against the Yankees. Nearby, Haim relaxed in a chair, absorbed in his book.

After a few minutes, Rebecca returned, a dejected look on her face. "I can't find any more colored eggs."

"Let's go ask your grandfather if he hid any inside," Fiona suggested.

Taking Fiona's hand, the two went into the house. They found Joe in the living room, deep in conversation with Mary. Their serious expressions made Fiona pause. Probably about Ed, Fiona thought. Still in jail awaiting trial, Joe was most likely urging Mary not to press charges against his son.

"Grandpa, grandpa!" Rebecca called out, running to Joe. "Did you hide any eggs in the house?"

He smiled at his exuberant granddaughter. "Yes, I did." He peeked inside her basket. "Looks like you're going to be the big winner of this year's Easter egg hunt."

"I think so, too. No one else is even looking—Emily's tanning, and Sean went for a ride with Uncle Owen."

Mary made a move to get up. Joe stopped her. "That's okay. Your kids are getting a little old for Easter egg hunts."

Just then, Rebecca shrieked with delight. "I found another one." She reached over her grandfather's shoulder and plucked a purple egg from the windowsill. "C'mon, Fiona," she said, tugging on her arm. "Let's check out the rest of the house."

Fiona trailed after Rebecca as she charged into the kitchen. She added two more eggs to her basket. "Do you think there are any in the back rooms?" she asked.

"Maybe in your granddad's den."

Rebecca darted down the hallway. Inside the den, the sound of snoring came from a recliner in front of the TV. "Shh," Fiona whispered. "Granny's sleeping."

"We can still look and be very quiet, like this." Rebecca tiptoed into the room.

Fiona shook her head. "We'll look here later," she whispered.

Out in the hallway, Rebecca opened the door to the cellar. "How about here?"

"Okay. Let's see what's down there."

She flipped on the light and led the way down the steps—the same steps on which Rebecca's grandmother had fallen to her death. Fiona shuddered. The basement smelled damp and musty. A single light bulb hung in the center of the cellar. She turned it on. Stacked boxes filled the basement, except for a workbench and tools in one corner.

Rebecca moved closer to Fiona and grabbed her arm. "I'm scared." Fiona was about to suggest they go upstairs when something on the shelf above the workbench caught her eye.

"You go upstairs. I want to check something out."

As she moved toward the far corner of the basement, the sharp clap of Rebecca's shoes echoed on the steps behind her. Fiona turned on a second light over the workbench. On the shelf, she spotted several rolls of synthetic white cord—identical to the garrotes used by the killer. Beside them lay a handful of wooden dowels. She slipped one of the rolls of cord into the pocket of her slacks.

On the floor next to the table sat a small cabinet. She pulled on a drawer knob. Locked. She opened a drawer in the workbench and retrieved a key ring from the back. Kneeling in front of the cabinet, she inserted one of the keys into the lock. She tried to turn it.

Suddenly, a large hand clamped down on her shoulder. Fiona dropped the key chain and shoved the hand away. She sprang to her feet and grabbed her assailant.

"Whoa," Owen said, startled.

Flushed, Fiona pulled back. "Sorry. You shouldn't sneak up on people like that."

"Me? What are you doing snooping around down here?"

"Rebecca brought me down to look for Easter eggs."

"So, where is she?"

"She went upstairs."

"That's where you're going, too," he said, steering Fiona toward the steps. "Stay out of our business. You've done enough damage to this family already.

Chapter 83

Early the next morning at the police station, Fiona sat in the conference room with Vinnie, Jill Mathewson, and the district attorney, coffee cups by their side. Fiona produced a roll of white cord and placed it on the table. "I'm sending this over to forensics, but I'm sure it'll match the string used by our killer to make the garrotes."

Jill leaned forward. "Where did you find this?"

"In Joe Foley's basement."

"Does he know you took it?"

Fiona shook her head.

Jill sighed. "Then we can't use it. You obtained it illegally."

"But," Vinnie said, "we might still be able to trace it. Let's check which stores in town carry this brand and see if Joe—or someone in his household—bought it."

Fiona set down her coffee. "I don't think Joe's our guy. Owen, his son, found me snooping around the workbench and got aggressive. He's often at Joe's place, supposedly building furniture in the basement."

Vinnie sat back in his chair. "Then let's see if Owen turns out to be the cord buyer."

Jill tapped her pencil against the table. "If you can link the purchase to him, I might be able to get a warrant for the Foley house."

"Hopefully," Fiona said, "he hasn't gotten rid of the cord and dowels yet."

"Any prints on the garrotes uncovered in the graves?" Jill asked.

Fiona shook her head. "Our killer was meticulous. He must have used gloves. There were no prints anywhere. But we do have semen samples. He didn't use a condom, probably figured the bodies would never be discovered."

"I'll pull a photo of Owen Foley from the DMV," Vinnie said. "Fiona, see if you can get a list of local stores that carry that brand of synthetic cord."

"On it," Fiona replied.

As the three got up and made their way to the door, Vinnie pulled Fiona aside. "I'm going to talk to the Chief about putting a tail on Owen Foley."

"Smart move."

Before leaving the station, Fiona passed by Rick's office. The door was ajar. Peeking in, she saw her former partner, head tilted back and snoring like a freight train. She walked over and jabbed his arm. Rick bolted upright, blinking at his attacker.

"You sound like the horn of a ship lost in a fog," she said. "I hope you confine your noisy breathing to the office--otherwise Jeanne's going to kick you out of the bedroom."

"Not only do you wake me up, but you also insult me." Rick yawned. "So, how's it going? Your new partner working out?"

"He's okay, but I still prefer my old one."

Rick grinned. "So now I'm old."

"You know what I mean," Fiona said, smiling.

"Hear the serial killer case has taken a new turn," Rick said.

"You heard about the cell phone in the grave?"

Rick chuckled. "The perp finally slipped up. I would've loved to have seen the mourners' faces when it went off."

"Me too."

"Any suspects?"

"Yeah. Remember Mickey Foley's brother, Owen? The reclusive one?" Rick nodded. "He got really upset when he caught me in his father's basement on Easter."

"How does that make him guilty?"

"Well, I was snooping around the workbench—apparently, Owen uses it frequently to make furniture—and I noticed rolls of synthetic cord and dowels. We checked it out and found it was the same type of cord used to make the garrotes found in the graves with the missing women."

"Were his prints on them?"

"No. We couldn't get any prints off the garrotes—he probably wore gloves."

"I don't know Fiona. That's awfully flimsy evidence. Does anyone else use the workbench?"

"According to Mickey, no—just his brother." Fiona continued. "Plus, there's the white van, the one that belongs to Angela Wysocki. We found blood from one of the victims inside. We know Owen used the van--allegedly to transport his finished projects from his dad's place to his own."

"I thought a lot of people used that van."

"True. But we asked Angela to make a list of everyone who borrowed it and when. Turns out, one of the two dates that Owen had lines up with one of the disappearances."

"What does Mahoney think?"

"He says there's enough evidence to justify putting a tail on Owen."

Rick looked wistfully at Fiona. "Wish I could be with you when you nail the bastard."

"I do, too."

Chapter 84

That evening, after walking Jasmine, Fionna logged on to her computer. She checked her inbox—only one new message. Her pulse raced when she saw the familiar sender: *tsk10. He's contacting me*, she thought.

She opened the email. *Let's meet.*

Fiona typed quickly. *Where?*

Another message appeared almost instantly. *The cemetery on Elm. In the pine grove*

Her fingers flew across the keyboard. *When?*

She held her breath until the reply appeared. *Tomorrow night at midnight, alone or no meeting.*

Fiona smiled faintly as she typed her response. *I'll be there.*

A final message flashed across her screen. *Until tomorrow, then my angel.*

Fiona immediately forwarded the emails to the computer expert in Boston. But given how fruitless the search had been with the messages sent to Julia, she doubted they'd be able to trace the sender's location.

Jasmine padded over and nudged Fiona's leg. Fiona reached down and stroked her dark fur, her thoughts swirling. A chill ran through her. Tomorrow night, she would finally come face-to-face with Ciara's murderer.

***

He shut down his computer and went into the bedroom. A face-to-face meeting with Fiona Sullivan. It had been a long time coming. She was so naïve. They'd crossed paths countless times, and she'd never suspected a thing. He didn't doubt she'd come alone. She was desperate to meet him—desperate to confront her sister's murderer. He smiled to himself. She would be his final angel.

But just to be on the safe side, he thought, *I'd better take along a backup.* He opened the bottom drawer of the dresser and withdrew a long, locked mahogany box. Reaching into his pocket, he retrieved a small key and slid it into the lock. With a soft click, the lid lifted. Resting on the maroon velvet lining lay a Browning Buck Mark pistol, fitted with a silencer. He checked the chamber—loaded. Satisfied, he placed the weapon on the nightstand. A thrill coursed through him. That night, he drifted to sleep dreaming of angels.

Chapter 85

Mahoney sat at his desk the next morning, reading the emails sent to Fiona by *tsk10*. "I can't let you meet this guy without backup," he said firmly.

Fiona leaned forward. "But if you're trailing Owen Foley, you'll know when he heads to the cemetery. You won't be far behind."

Mahoney removed his glasses and rubbed his eyes, clearly unconvinced.

"What if I bring my dog with me?" Fiona asked.

Mahoney raised an eyebrow. "Does he carry a gun?"

"First of all, Jasmine's a she. And second, she's got something better than a gun—jaws strong enough to snap a leg."

He shook his head. "The perp wants you alone. Even if I buy that Jasmine could back you up—which I don't—he won't show if he sees the dog."

A knock on the door interrupted them. Mahoney waved for Vinnie to come in.

"Sorry, I'm late," he said, taking the chair next to Fiona. "I was checking if there would be any burials at the cemetery tomorrow."

"And?" Mahoney asked.

"There is. The grave will be dug pretty close to the pine grove."

Mahoney replaced his glasses and shook his head. "Your partner wants to meet the perp with no backup—unless you count her dog."

Fiona twisted in her chair to face Vinnie. "But I won't be in danger," she insisted. "You'll be staking out Owen. As soon as he leaves his apartment, you call me—I'll have my cell—and you follow him to the cemetery. He won't be more than a minute or two ahead of you."

"If the perp is Owen," the Chief interjected.

"He's our prime suspect," Vinnie replied.

"Then why the emails to Julia—his sister?"

Fiona turned to the Chief. "I think he was trying to throw us off. While our officers were tied up trailing Julia, he targeted and killed another victim."

Mahoney sat back in his chair and stared at the ceiling. Suddenly, he leaned forward. "Vinnie, you've been to the cemetery?"

Vinnie nodded.

"Is there any place near the pine grove where you can hide?"

"There's a mausoleum in the center of the grounds. With night vision goggles, I'll be able to see what's happening. But if I need to take a shot, it's out of range."

Mahoney tapped his fingers on his desk. "Let's go with that. Our team won't be far behind the perp." He looked at Vinnie. "You'll be there if there's a problem."

Fiona smiled. "And don't forget Jasmine."

Chapter 86

A sliver of moon hung low in the dark sky as Fiona and Jasmine stepped through the cemetery gates. She wrapped her scarf tightly around her neck to ward off a biting wind. Unhurried, she let Jasmine sniff every bush, shrub, and tombstone they passed. It was 11:45—fifteen minutes until her meeting with *tsk10.*

Out of the corner of her eye, she caught the hunched figure of Vinnie crouched behind the mausoleum. Jasmine let out a low growl and moved toward the crypt. Fiona yanked her forward, hoping the perp—if he were already there—hadn't noticed the detour and realized she wasn't alone.

Her iPhone buzzed in her pocket. With her back to the pine grove, she slipped it out and read the message: Suspect still in apartment. *Damn*, Fiona thought, *if he hasn't even left yet, he won't be here for at least another half hour.*

"No rush," she whispered to Jasmine. "The perp's taking his time.

Her phone sounded again. A text from Vinnie. *Saw some movement on the other side of the cemetery. Going to check it out. Will you be alright?*

Fiona texted back. *I'm good.*

She ambled toward the pine grove, Jasmine trotting beside her. It was 11:55. Another tritone from her phone. She checked the screen: *None of the local vendors ID'd Owen Foley as the purchaser of the confiscated cord. Suspect still in his apartment.*

Fiona grimaced. If Owen were coming, it wouldn't be until closer to 1 a.m. Was he stalling to make sure she'd be alone?

She walked over to a bench facing the pine grove. The evening mist had left it damp, but with nowhere else to wait, she sat anyway, ignoring the chill that seeped through her coat. The wind had died down. Fiona loosened her scarf and undid the top two buttons of her jacket. Her fingers drifted to the necklace she was wearing—the one given to her by Mickey.

Jasmine strained against her leash. "C'mere, girl." Fiona pulled the dog toward her. "Looks like we'll be here for a while." She unclipped the leash, letting Jasmine sniff around the clearing.

Suddenly, Jasmine froze, ears pressed against her head. A low growl rumbled from deep in her throat. Fiona jumped up. Too late. Jasmine bolted into the pine grove. Fiona raced after her. "Jasmine, come back! Come back!"

A figure stepped out from behind a tree. Jasmine leapt. A gun went off. Fiona gasped as Jasmine was struck midair and crumpled to the ground. She rushed to her side. The dog was whimpering, blood seeping from her shoulder.

"I told you to come alone," a voice said.

Fiona looked up. A man stood before her—tall, dressed in a dark parka and ski mask, a pistol with a silencer in his hand.

"Get up," he ordered.

Fiona continued to stroke Jasmine's bloodied fur, sneaking a glance at her attacker.

"Get up, or I'll shoot you right here."

Eyes on her blood-stained hands, Fiona took a deep breath and rose slowly.

"Turn around," he said. "Hands flat against that tree."

Fiona obeyed, leaning forward against the pine. She cringed as his hands swept over her body. He found her phone, silenced it, and hurled it into the trees. Then he lifted the bottom of her slacks and retrieved a weapon from its ankle holster. Jasmine whimpered behind them—soft, broken sounds. Fiona's muscles tensed. She needed to take control.

"Walk," he said.

She moved, casting anxious glances back at Jasmine. The dog hadn't moved. Once clear of the grove, Fiona's captor directed her to turn left. They followed a narrow path flanked by tombstones.

"Stop."

Fiona halted before a tarp-covered pit. Sweat trickled down her spine.

"Get in."

He stood two feet from her, pistol leveled at her chest. Through the ski mask, she could see his eyes—cold, unflinching. She glanced back to where Jasmine lay, overwhelmed by a feeling of nausea.

It couldn't be Owen. Not unless he'd slipped out unseen. The mask muffled his voice—familiar but distorted. She couldn't place it.

He nudged her forward. "I said, get in."

Fiona stooped down, lifted the edge of the tarp, and stared into the black void below.

"C'mon. Move. Jump in."

At the rim of the grave, the scent of freshly turned earth filled her lungs. Rather than jump into the dark hole, Fiona squatted down and eased her feet over the edge, sliding down the side to soften the fall. Stones and clumps of dirt tumbled with her. Her boots struck the bottom, and she pitched forward into the darkness. She pushed herself upright, surrounded by silence and shadow.

Anger and guilt threatened to overcome her: anger that Jasmine had been shot, guilt that she had brought her to the cemetery. But now wasn't the time to unravel. She had to stay sharp, wait for Vinnie… or for her moment to strike.

The quiet was shattered with the slap of a ladder against the grave wall. A figure descended, flashlight beam slicing through the dark.

"Don't get any ideas," he said, light in one hand, pistol in the other.

"Who are you?" Fiona demanded.

"You know me. Your sister knew me better." He chuckled.

Fiona's face burned with anger.

"It's hot down here," he muttered. "And what the hell—you won't be talking to anyone after tonight."

He peeled off the ski mask and wiped his face with it. Thick, dark hair streaked with gray. Fiona's breath caught. Her voice was barely a whisper. "Joe?"

Chapter 87

Joe Foley leaned against the dirt wall, arms crossed, watching Fiona dig the hole that would become her grave. Perspiration dripped from her brow as she worked just fast enough to satisfy her captor. By slowing down, she hoped her backup would arrive before it was too late.

And where the hell was her partner?

She continued to dig. The only sounds in the pit were the scrape of the shovel into the earth and the thump of the dirt landing on an ever-growing mound.

Fiona paused, wiping her brow.

“Keep digging,” Joe said.

She didn’t move. “Why did you do it?”

“What?”

“Kill my sister.”

Joe’s eyes darkened. “She was my first angel.”

Fiona leaned on the shovel, her breath shallow. “Why her?”

“She was perfect. Beautiful. Innocent.”

“How did you even know her?”

“She brought her watch to my shop. It took several days to fix. She kept coming back. She was so grateful…”

“Is that where you met the other girls?” Fiona asked.

Joe smiled smugly. “Always the detective. Always asking questions. Too bad,” he said, his voice suddenly harsh. “You’re not going to be able to tell anyone the answers.”

“And your wife?” she pressed. “Did you kill her, too?”

Joe’s eyes narrowed. His face became taut. “Why would you ask that?”

“I just wondered. She fell down the stairs, right? Or was she pushed?”

Joe hesitated. “She found your sister’s necklace on my desk and compared it to the photo in the newspaper—the article that said it was missing from the victim. She started asking me too many questions—just like you.” He stepped closer. “No more talking, just dig.”

Fiona resumed, her shovel slicing into the earth in a steady rhythm. The sound seemed to soothe him.

“Why did you send Julia those threatening emails?” she asked.

“To throw you off. I’d never harm my daughter.” He continued in a mocking tone of voice. “And my plan worked. It kept your team busy chasing false leads.”

Fiona continued to dig, furious with herself for ignoring the signs. She’d seen the cord and dowels in Joe’s basement, so why did she conclude the killer was Owen? Joe’s charm, his tenderness with his mother and the kids... it had blinded her. He had played the role perfectly—a true psychopath.

After several tense minutes, Joe assessed the hole Fiona dug. “You can stop, it’s deep enough.”

His gun trained on Fiona, Joe ordered her to fold the digging tool and place it back in his knapsack. “Give me the garrote,” he said.

Slowly, she pulled out the weapon with which he planned to kill her.

"Take off your clothes. Fold them and place them on the side of your grave."

Fiona started with her boots and socks, then removed her jacket. As she peeled off her sweater, she noticed the shift in Joe's expression—his eyes lit up, his mouth twitched. He was distracted, fixated. By the time she stepped out of her slacks and undergarments, his breathing had grown shallow and erratic.

In a low, sensual voice, she asked him, "Do you want my necklace as a keepsake of our meeting?"

Lulled by her voice, his eyes drifted from her breasts to her lips.

"It's the only piece of jewelry I have on."

"Okay," he murmured. "Let me have it."

Fiona unclasped the necklace slowly, letting the gold and diamond heart dangle like a pendulum in front of his face. "Catch," she said, tossing it into the air.

As Joe's eyes followed the trajectory of the necklace, Fiona lunged—knocking the pistol from his hand. He stumbled back against the dirt wall and collapsed, the gun skidding behind him.

Bits of dirt and stone pressed and cut into Fiona's skin as they struggled for the weapon. Pinning Joe's shoulders with her knees, Fiona reached over his head, her breasts almost in his face, and grasped the pistol. She cocked the barrel and pressed it into his chest. "Don't move or I'll shoot."

Joe lunged for her hand. She slammed the barrel against his face. His jawbone cracked; blood streamed from the side of his mouth.

Fiona sprang to her feet. Suddenly, a flashlight beam sliced through the darkness, illuminating Joe's crumpled body.

Above them, the tarp shifted. Vinnie peeled back the cover and descended the ladder into the hole.

"It's about time," Fiona snapped. "Where the hell were you?"

Vinnie smirked. "Nice to see you too. I was topside, waiting for the right moment. If I had jumped in earlier, he might've shot you. You okay?"

"I'm fine, but Jasmine…"

"I called a vet. They sent an ambulance—she's at the pet hospital now."

"Was she alive?"

Vinnie nodded. Joe stirred, trying to rise. Vinnie drove his boot into Joe's shoulder. "Stay down, you piece of shit."

Conscious of her naked state, Fiona began dressing. With her back turned, she caught a sudden flash. "Damn it, Mancini, did you just take a photo of me?"

"Don't flatter yourself," he said, adjusting the camera. "I'm documenting the crime scene."

Suddenly, Mahoney peered in from the top of the hole. "Just got here. Everything okay down there?"

Vinnie winked at Fiona. "It was, until Detective Sullivan decided to get dressed."

Chapter 88

The following morning, Vinnie and Fiona stood outside Joe Foley's home, search warrant in hand. When repeated knocks went unanswered, they unlocked the door using the key taken from their prisoner. Though they suspected the house was empty, they drew their weapons and methodically cleared each room on the first floor. Once satisfied, they descended into the basement.

While Fiona checked out the workbench area, Vinnie sifted through the pile of boxes and other miscellaneous items stacked in the cellar. The cord and dowels were no longer on the shelf, but the cabinet beneath the bench remained untouched. Fiona opened the center drawer and retrieved the key ring she'd discovered on Easter Sunday. The first key didn't fit. Nor did the second or third. But the fourth clicked.

"Mother lode," she murmured.

Curious, Vinnie joined her. Inside the cabinet were the pieces of jewelry Joe Foley had taken from each victim—including her sister's silver heart necklace.

They spent another hour searching the house before moving to the garage. There, they uncovered more damning evidence: a container filled with white cord and dowels, a blanket with several stains that appeared to be blood, boxes of surgical gloves, wool scarves, and black wool face coverings.

After combing every inch of the garage, they returned to the house and Joe's den. Vinnie paused in front of the computer. "We need to take this with us and have the forensic experts in Boston examine it."

"I'm sure we'll be able to retrieve the emails Joe sent to Julia and to me."

"She's leaving Boston."

"Who?" Fiona asked as the two dismantled the computer.

"Julia. She said she couldn't stay here, not with everyone knowing she's the daughter of a serial killer."

"Where's she going?"

"She's not sure. Just as far away as possible. Her firm is expanding into China, and she's asked to be transferred."

"That's a shame. None of this was her fault," Fiona said.

"That's just what I told her. But I don't think it made much difference."

Later, back in the patrol car, Fiona turned to Vinnie. "Would you mind stopping by the vet before we head to the station? I dropped Jasmine off this morning after picking her up from the pet hospital."

"Of course," he said. "How's she doing?"

"The vet wanted to keep her overnight for observation. It broke my heart to leave her," Fiona said.

"Is she okay?"

"She might walk with a limp, but she was pretty lucky. The bullet hit her shoulder—just above her right front leg."

"When can you take her home?" Vinnie asked.

"Hopefully this evening."

Fiona pulled into a parking spot in front of a red brick building on Main Street in Watertown.

“I’ll just be a minute if you want to wait in the car.”

Vinnie opened the passenger door. “I’ll come in.”

The minute they entered the facility, Fiona heard a familiar bark from the door behind the receptionist’s desk. She greeted the gray-haired woman seated at the desk. “Hi, Miriam. This is my partner, Vinnie. How’s our patient?”

“Jasmine’s doing really well,” Miriam replied warmly. “Dr. Winston’s with her now. Let me check if you can go back.”

Fiona paced back and forth in front of the desk until Miriam gave a nod and waved them through.

In the exam room, Jasmine lay on a metal table while the vet carefully changed her dressing. At the sight of Fiona, the dog tried to rise, tail thumping weakly. Fiona rushed to her side, gently stroking her fur as Dr. Winston steadied her.

“She’s doing fine,” he said. “I removed the bullet. She’s on pain medication, and unless anything changes, she can go home tonight.”

Fiona’s eyes welled with tears. She leaned down and buried her face in Jasmine’s fur, whispering as the dog nuzzled her in return.

Chapter 89

The doorbell rang. Jasmine limped to the front door, barking sharply. Fiona pressed the intercom. "Who is it?"

"Mickey."

She buzzed him in and went out to greet him. Mickey smiled as he climbed the stairs, holding a rawhide bone in his hand. At the landing, he offered it to Jasmine, who snatched it eagerly.

"Come in," Fiona said. "I can't talk too long—I have to leave in about fifteen minutes." She didn't mention the award ceremony at the Belmont Police Station, not when her award was for helping apprehend his father.

"Do you want anything to drink?"

"No. I'm okay." Mickey took off his jacket and sat on the couch. The smile faded from his face. Fiona took the chair opposite him.

He stared at the floor, hands clasping and unclasping. After a long pause, he looked up. "You probably hate me."

Fiona bit her lip. "No. You're not responsible for your father's actions. I'm sure you would have stopped him if you had known."

Mickey exhaled, shoulders softening as he leaned back. "Even my closest friends don't know what to say to me. What do you say to the son of a serial killer?"

Fiona hesitated. "Vinnie told me Julia's thinking about leaving Boston. Maybe you should consider it too. A fresh start, somewhere where no one knows you."

Mickey was silent, his face solemn. To Fiona, it looked like he was wrestling with something deep inside. "What's the matter?" she asked gently.

"I don't want to leave you."

Fiona shifted in her chair, her expression tightening. "I care about you, Mickey, and I don't blame you for what your father did. But I can't keep seeing you. It's too painful. I'm sorry."

Mickey nodded and slowly got up. "I get it. I just hoped you might see me as more than Joe Foley's son."

Fiona got out of the chair, walked over to Mickey, and hugged him. "I do. I always have. And I always will. Let's stay in touch."

A flicker of hope lit Mickey's face. "Do you think…maybe with time…"

She pulled back and looked at him, her voice soft but firm. "No."

Chapter 90

Fiona stood quietly among the uniformed officers at the back of the large, wood-paneled meeting room in the Belmont police station. The space buzzed with anticipation, its solemn atmosphere softened by the warm glow of afternoon sunlight filtering through a stained-glass window, casting colorful patterns across the walls.

In the front row, seated on folding chairs with the other guests, Fiona's mother turned and beamed at her. Her parents had driven down from North Andover for the ceremony, and their presence filled Fiona with pride. She caught Rick's eye—he sat beside her father—and gave him a small wave.

Armed with his notes, Chief Mahoney stepped up to the podium. The mayor and two councilmen stood nearby, ready to present awards and offer congratulations.

Mahoney took off his glasses, pulled a cloth from his pocket, and wiped the lenses. After putting them back on, he picked up his notes to signal the start of the ceremony. Fiona listened as Mahoney read the names of her colleagues who received a Life-Saving or Chief's Commendation award. She felt honored to be part of such a distinguished group of men and women, officers who risked their lives to save drowning children, abused spouses, and robbery victims.

"And now," Mahoney announced, "the Belmont Police would like to recognize Detective Fiona Sullivan..."

The room fell silent as Mahoney began recounting the harrowing investigation that led to the capture of the serial killer.

"For her courage, her outstanding police work performed under imminent risk of serious bodily harm, and her extraordinary heroism, we are proud to present Officer Fiona Sullivan with the highest honor awarded by this department—the Medal of Valor."

Her face radiant, Fiona walked to the front of the room to receive her award from the mayor. The audience rose to its feet, applauding loudly. After shaking hands with the mayor and councilmen, she received a hug from Mahoney. "I've got another surprise for you," he whispered. "I'll tell you later."

After posing for photos for the *Belmont Citizen-Herald*, Fiona joined the other award recipients at a reception in the adjoining room. Surrounded by her family, she greeted each guest with warmth and grace, accepting handshakes and hugs from those who came to congratulate her. In the hum of conversation, she caught fragments of praise: "Outstanding work," "An inspiration to young women," "A credit to the community."

Finally, after what seemed an eternity, Mahoney took her elbow. "I just want to talk to Fiona for a few minutes. I'll bring her right back."

In his office, Fiona took her familiar seat across from him. He smiled broadly; his brown eyes twinkled. This was a face she hadn't seen before. Mahoney almost seemed relaxed.

"I'm really proud of you," he said. You're one hell of a cop."

Fiona blushed, her heart swelling with pride.

"I know your family's waiting," he added, "so I'll keep this short."

Mahoney took a deep breath; Fiona looked up expectantly. "You've been promoted to Sergeant, effective the first of the month."

Fiona's mouth fell open, her eyes shining with disbelief and joy. "Seriously? Thank you!"

Mahoney smiled. "Don't thank me. You earned every bit of it."

Chapter 91

Later that evening, Fiona, Rick, and Vinnie sat around a table at Savino's Grill, lingering over after-dinner drinks. Her parents had treated both her current and former partner to the celebratory dinner but had left earlier to make the long drive back to North Andover.

Rick swirled the brandy in his glass. "So, I guess you two wrapped up all the cases we were working on."

"Pretty much," Fiona replied. "I spoke to the DA last week. Denny took a plea deal—he gave up Leonid. With no priors, the judge sentenced Denny to three years with time off for good behavior. Leonid's probably looking at deportation."

Rick nodded. "What about Ed Foley? The spousal abuse case?"

Fiona's expression darkened. "He violated the restraining order. Even his expensive lawyer couldn't do much. Didn't help that he called his wife a 'fucking cunt' in open court."

Rick winced. "What did he get?"

"Minimum of a year and a thousand-dollar fine."

"Didn't his son stab him?" Rick asked.

"Yes, but he was defending his mother. No charges were brought against him."

Rick leaned back, shaking his head. "He should probably be given a medal."

Fiona stared at her former partner. She understood the sad look in his eyes. "You miss the action, don't you?"

Rick smiled half-heartedly. "It's tough, just sitting behind a desk."

Vinnie leaned forward, his hands folded on the table. "Have you decided what you're going to do?"

"Probably stay with the desk job," Rick said. "It keeps the peace at home."

Fiona thought she caught a flicker of relief in Vinnie's expression.

Rick glanced at his watch. "Speaking of family, it's getting late. I'd better get going. Can I give you anything for the meal?"

"Thanks, but no. My parents took care of everything."

As Rick lumbered around to her side of the table, Fiona stood up and gave him a big hug. "I miss you," he said.

"Me too." Sitting back down, she watched her gentle giant walk out of the restaurant.

Vinnie glanced at her. "Are you disappointed he's not coming back, and you're stuck with me?"

Fiona shook her head. "No. Not at all."

Vinnie looked at her, head tilted to one side as if he wasn't sure that she was telling the truth.

"I mean it," Fiona said. "I know we didn't get off to the best of starts, but you've kind of grown on me."

"You make me sound like some sort of fungus."

"Don't be silly. I haven't experienced any itchiness, scaling, or redness when you're around."

He gave her a wry look. "So, what do you have?"

Instead of responding, she took a slow sip of her brandy and shrugged, feeling warmth rise from her neck to her cheeks.

"You're blushing," Vinnie said, watching her closely.

"It's the drink," she replied, a little too quickly.

Vinnie gave her an "I don't believe you " look.

"Are you still seeing Foley's son?" he asked.

"No."

"What's going to happen to his old man?"

"He confessed. Said he didn't want to drag his family through a trial."

"How considerate," Vinnie muttered.

"The good news is that Henry Winfield will be released soon. Foley admitted to those murders, too. Of course, he didn't have much of a choice since we found the piece of jewelry he took from each of the victims in his basement. It was game over."

Vinnie finished the last of his drink and set the glass on the table. "Want another?"

Fiona glanced at her watch. "No, I think I'd better be going while I'm still sober enough to drive."

They stood and walked together out of the restaurant into the cool night air. "See you Monday," Fiona said, pulling her keys from her pocket.

Vinnie watched as she made her way to her car and climbed in. Once she was out of sight, he pulled out his phone and tapped on a photo—one he'd taken in the graveyard, Fiona's back turned as she dressed.

"Nice ass," he murmured. "Maybe I'll get to see it again someday."

Author bio

Patricia Williams spent seventeen years as a professor of Accounting at Fordham University, during which she published more than twenty scholarly articles in peer-reviewed journals. After retiring from academia, she turned her attention to fiction, pursuing her long-held passion for storytelling. In 2013, she completed the Stanford University Certificate Program in Novel Writing, an experience that helped launch her second career as a novelist. Since then, she has published four works of fiction. *Buried Beneath* marks her fourth novel and her second foray into the mystery/thriller genre.

www.ingramcontent.com/pod-product-compliance
Lightning Source LLC
Chambersburg PA
CBHW070637310726
48982CB00001B/315